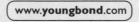
IAN FLEMING PUBLICATIONS LIMITED

www.youngbond.com

Also available in the **YOUNG BOND** series

Written by Steve Cole:
Shoot to Kill
Heads You Die
Strike Lightning

Written by Charlie Higson:
SilverFin
Blood Fever
Double or Die
Hurricane Gold
By Royal Command
Danger Society: Young Bond Dossier

www.youngbond.com
www.ianfleming.com

Also available by Steve Cole:
The Z. Rex Trilogy
Tripwire

RED NEMESIS

STEVE COLE

RED FOX

RED FOX

UK | USA | Canada | Ireland | Australia
India | New Zealand | South Africa

Red Fox is part of the Penguin Random House group of companies
whose addresses can be found at global.penguinrandomhouse.com.

www.penguin.co.uk
www.puffin.co.uk
www.ladybird.co.uk

Penguin
Random House
UK

First published 2017

001

Set in Bembo Schoolbook by Jouve (UK), Milton Keynes
Printed and bound in Great Britain by Clays Ltd, Elcograf S.p.A.

A CIP catalogue record for this book is available from the British Library

ISBN: 978–1–782–95243–5

All correspondence to:
Red Fox
Penguin Random House Children's
80 Strand, London WC2R ORL

MIX
Paper from
responsible sources
FSC® C018179

Penguin Random House is committed to a
sustainable future for our business, our readers
and our planet. This book is made from Forest
Stewardship Council® certified paper.

For Anthony Cole
My father, my friend

So we keep asking, over and over,
Until a handful of earth
Stops our mouths—
But is that an answer?

Heinrich Heine, Appendix to *Lazarus*, I (1854)

Prologue
Impacts

The motor car careered out of the wintry night and mounted the pavement, heading straight for the doors of a crumbling warehouse overlooking the Thames. For Anya Kalashnikova – her long nails snapping as she gripped the leather rear seat – time seemed to slow. The spilled glare of the rusting London streetlamp was like a spotlight through the window, the engine's roar swelling like a crowd's applause.

Just forty minutes ago Anya had been playing Giselle on stage with the youth troupe of the Ballet Russe de Monte Carlo. How the other girls envied her dancing such a difficult part, and at only thirteen years of age. '*Your grace is outstanding, your musicality flawless,*' Madame Radek had said proudly, back in Paris. '*One day you shall be prima ballerina for the finest companies and dance all across the world ... Prima Ballerina Assoluta!*'

The warehouse doors exploded as the Streamline powered through them into darkness. Anya was thrown sideways against hard, cold leather. 'Papa!' she shrieked.

There was no reply; her father was hunched silently over the wheel like an old woman spinning thread. He'd looked pale upon leaving the theatre – sweating, almost feverish. She knew he worked so hard, such long hours, and yet he'd insisted on waiting behind and driving her home.

'Things will be different next year,' he'd assured her. 'In 1933, life will change for us.'

It was good to hear Papa sound so positive. They'd moved to London for the sake of Anya's ballet career, and although he'd soon found work at an architectural firm, he didn't seem to enjoy it. Papa had grown thin and forlorn – a winter branch whose leaves had dropped. Oh, he put on a good front for his bosses, she'd seen that for herself, but his unhappiness at home had grown and grown. Sometimes Anya felt guilty. He insisted on driving her everywhere himself, but tonight he'd seemed so distracted. He'd taken so many wrong turns, and now—

Darkness swallowed the Streamline as it ploughed inside the warehouse, a single glowing headlight the only dim resistance. With a lurch, the car lifted into the air as it mounted some unseen obstacle. It hit the ground, and the cocktail cabinet inside the rear passenger door crashed open. Bottles, glasses and decanters flew out, and something heavy struck Anya's temple. She screamed, a discordant counterpoint to the screeching brakes as the car spun in a wide, protesting arc.

A cobwebbed concrete pillar loomed suddenly from tangled shadows.

Anya screwed up her eyes, and then the side-on collision punched all sense from her world. The door beside her buckled inwards and windows exploded into shards. She was thrown forward through the hail of glass, striking her head on the seat in front. The car was still in motion, gears grinding as it slewed on through the warehouse. Anya screamed again. In the cavernous space, every noise was amplified and flung back through the darkness. She clutched her ears, stomach turning.

Finally the automobile rolled to a stop that was almost tender, a short distance from a whitewashed wall. The single headlamp's light pooled over the cracked concrete, the unearthly glow reflected back inside the Streamline. The two-litre engine chuntered and muttered as if pleased with itself. Then the noise choked and died away.

Slowly Anya opened her eyes. The way she used to as a young child in the night, afraid of the Nordmann fir's needles tapping at her window in the wind, willing the darkness to make way for morning and the kindly smile of her governess. There was wetness on her face. *Tears?* she thought, touching gingerly. *Or something from the decanter?*

She wiped at her mouth and her hand came away sticky and dark. *Blood.*

Shock held back the pain, but not her fear. *What do I look like? Don't let it scar. Don't let me be ugly.* 'Papa?' She was afraid to speak too loudly in the sudden hush, as if she might somehow start the car moving again. The only sound was the ticking of the cooling engine and the slow shake of her breathing. 'Papa ... please ... ?'

Anya jumped at the clunk and creak of the door as it opened. The headlight went out; she couldn't see anything now, but smelled Papa's dry sandalwood cologne, and something else. A sweet, chemical scent.

'Papa?'

A handkerchief pressed down over her nose and mouth. *Papa's wiping the blood away.* Anya suddenly felt safer. This was better than waking to her governess. Papa was here. He would make things better.

Her skin grew cold and stung. An antiseptic, of course. She was feeling so sleepy. She felt like Giselle at the end of the ballet, placed on a bed of flowers and lowered slowly into the earth. Each night she descended breathless into the warm paraffin light of the under-stage, to the smell of Parma violets and wood shavings, waiting for the wave of applause to break in the auditorium above. But now she felt herself floating into a stronger, deeper darkness, beyond the audience; beyond anything.

Ivan Kalashnikov took the chloroform pad from his daughter's bloody face and wiped tears from his eyes. The cut on Anya's temple looked deep, but it would heal. Otherwise she seemed unhurt.

They had survived the crash, but the real ordeal was yet to begin.

Kalashnikov turned in the pitch-stinking darkness, pulled his fish-eye torch out of his pocket and played the beam around the warehouse. He'd failed to stop the car in the position he'd rehearsed. Well, small surprise: he was an architect, not a racing driver.

Outside he could hear the distant chug of a tug on the Thames, and the quarrelling of drunks. Sweating, panting for breath, he set his shoulder to the driver's doorframe and pushed the Streamline slowly forwards, leaving it to rest beside a towering stack of scaffolding poles. He felt sick; the poles were leaning precariously against a mouldering concrete pillar, just as he'd left them.

Everything was prepared.

Kalashnikov opened the rear door and shone his torch on Anya, lying curled up on the back seat. Poor child, she looked so peaceful. Carefully he manoeuvred her sleeping body until her right foot was almost brushing the filthy floor, as if she were about to rise and step out of the car and embrace him, bubbling as usual with the excitement and glamour of her night.

'It is as Grandfather liked to tell us,' Kalashnikov murmured. 'We are born under a clear blue sky ... but die in a dark forest.'

Slowly, deliberately, he pushed the car door half-closed against his daughter's protruding leg. Then he walked towards the heavy scaffolding poles. He stood, frozen still in the darkness for many minutes. His breathing grew huskier. He shook his head, hopeless. Helpless.

Finally, shaking and sobbing, he slammed his palms into the stack of scaffolding poles. With a torturous twist and the scrape of metal on concrete they toppled slowly, then smashed against the automobile with an unholy clamour. The door was thrown closed onto Anya's calf. The noise, thick and hard, scared the gulls from the ruins of the rafters, sent them laughing into the night high above the charcoal shadow of the Thames.

1
Which Way Now?

James Bond hid in the shadow of the war memorial, aware that his time was running out. He had to locate the target before it was too late.

'Twenty-one steps north . . . thirty-two west.' He looked up from the list of directions in his hand, glancing quickly around in case he was being watched.

No one in sight – yet.

James moved on from the war memorial, its looming figure of a fallen officer like a warning as he carefully counted his strides. Twenty-one steps north would take him into the parade ground, overlooked by windowed walls of ornate, castellated sandstone. The thirty-two paces west would lead him straight past a stretch of leaded-glass windows like a tin duck in a shooting gallery – unless he crouched down and waddled like the real thing. He wasn't meant to be skulking about here by himself, and if he was spotted . . .

Sinking to his knees, James grinned and cursed his friend Perry for steering him here. Which Way Now? was a game James had devised as a young boy. It was essentially a treasure hunt using points of the compass. Whether away in some wilderness or passing the last day of 1935's summer term here at Fettes College, the setter of the task would choose a start point and an end point and then take a haphazard walk between the two, changing bearing as often as he saw fit, recording the number of steps taken in each direction to reach the goal – where, ideally, a prize worth having would be concealed. The players had to follow the instructions precisely in order to find the treasure.

The young James had first played it with his father on an early holiday to Littlehampton, but the game had ended badly when he'd miscounted his steps, making it impossible for his father to find the end point, and the toy cavalry captain he'd hidden beneath a tree was never recovered. To commemorate that unknown soldier's sacrifice, he and his parents had played Which Way Now? together many times in its honour.

As he counted thirty-two, hunched over beneath the window, James shrugged off the memories; they were starting to sting. His parents were both dead now, killed in a climbing accident in the Aiguilles Rouges. *Will I ever be able to think about them without the hurt?* he wondered.

He glanced back at the war memorial: CARRY ON was inscribed there, and James accepted the command. He and Perry had played Which Way Now? on occasion to brighten their long, slow schooldays. Just last week, James had sent his friend on a risky route through the servants' hall for the reward of April's edition of *Spicy Detective Stories* hidden in the fireplace – said magazine purloined from a particularly hateful

8

prefect. Now, what had Perry left for him in turn? He looked down at the last instruction. *Nine steps north.*

The final paces took him to a wrought-iron grille set into the ground beside the building; it allowed light to pass through a dusty window on the lower-ground floor into the coal cellars. James smiled when he spied a package wrapped in butcher's paper and tied beneath the grille. The prize was his! With some difficulty he worked his fingers into the pattern of the metal and heaved the grille up and out of its housing in the stone. He then quickly freed the bundle. It looked like a bottle.

A message was scrawled across the paper:

J – Something for the long journey back to Pett Bottom. Here's to summer months of idleness before we're trooped back in September! PM

James smiled as he replaced the grating. Perry had departed Fettes last night on the sleeper train to London, but James had stayed on at his Aunt Charmian's request. She'd been visiting friends in Newcastle and wished for company on the journey home. He'd offered to meet her in England, but for some reason she'd insisted on coming up to Fettes. She was meant to be arriving any time now. James wished Perry hadn't concealed his instructions in James's study-bedroom quite so well; he'd only discovered them half an hour ago ...

'Ah, James, *there* you are!'

James jumped at the sound of Charmian's voice behind him and sprang up from the grille. She stood there smiling, wearing green woollen trousers, knee-length leather boots, a brown leather jacket over a cream blouse, and a silk scarf.

Beside her was Dr Cooper, James's housemaster. He was a handsome man, with a broad brow, strong features and hair as dark as the expression on his face.

'Bond, what on earth are you up to?' Cooper was bristling. 'Your aunt came directly to Glencorse House to collect you. I didn't know you'd slipped out. We spotted you disappearing round the back of the school from down the hill . . . what's that you're holding?'

James thought fast. 'I . . . remembered I'd ordered a gift for Aunt Charmian to thank her for coming to get me, and had it delivered to the school reception. I ran up here to collect it and was on my way back when I heard someone shouting out.' He shrugged. 'I thought it was coming from the coal store, so I came to see if anyone needed help.'

Aunt Charmian's eyes twinkled. 'I don't hear anyone.'

'I suppose they must have recovered,' James concluded.

'I see,' said Dr Cooper in a way that suggested he didn't. 'Well, Bond. It's a shame you don't show such admirable attention to duty in your study of the classics. But I commend you for buying your aunt a gift.'

Charmian smiled and took the wrapped package. 'Whatever did you get me . . . ?' She pulled away the paper to reveal a half-pint bottle of Younger's No. 3 Scotch Ale.

'Beer?' Dr Cooper looked askance.

'My favourite,' said Charmian quickly. 'What a thoughtful boy you are.'

'Dr Cooper teaches us to live by the Glencorse motto, *Nunquam onus.*' James gave a small bow to his housemaster. '*Nothing is too much trouble.*'

★ ★ ★

James and Charmian were still laughing over their performance as the 12.34 to Euston wheezed away from Edinburgh. Aunt Charmian had bought them seats in first class, and they had a compartment to themselves, with seats upholstered in deep red against the mahogany walls.

Charmian poured the brown beer into teacups and her face grew wistful. 'I believe we'll *need* a drink on this journey.'

'What is it?' James was intrigued. 'You didn't come all this extra way just to ride with me, did you?'

'I did not. There's something I need to show to you.' She rose, took her battered trunk down from the luggage rack and opened it. 'Something unexpected came in the post to me last week, James ... retrieved from a crevasse in the Aiguilles Rouges.'

Instantly James felt his stomach tighten. 'What?'

'It's been buried in the ice for three years.' Charmian pulled a khaki canvas-and-leather backpack out of her trunk, rumpled and stained with rust from the metal fastenings. 'This belonged to your father, James. He must've dropped it as he fell, that last day. And ... there's something for you inside.'

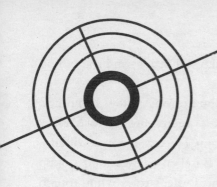

2

Voice from the Past

They sat together, James and Charmian, poring over the contents of the backpack as their carriage rattled over the tracks: two survivors who had lost so much too soon. Charmian explained that Andrew Bond's backpack had been uncovered by a summer thaw. Chanced upon by climbers and handed in to the police, it had been forwarded to the Bonds' old address; those who now lived there had redirected the pack to Charmian.

James felt a sense of reverence and quiet devastation as he reached into the pack. It felt almost as if by playing the old childhood game he had somehow summoned his father's memory in material form.

His fingers touched the relics inside. There was a thick woollen jumper; kid leather driving gloves (whose smell stirred in James precious memories of trips in his father's treasured 1926 AC 12 Royal drophead coupé); thick socks; a hip flask with the remains of a good whisky still inside; and something that brought tears to James's eyes.

Just prior to the holiday in Chamonix, Andrew Bond had visited Russia on business, as a sales representative for Vickers Armaments, the weapons company. He was away so often – and at their house just outside Basel in Switzerland young James used to love listening to his father's tales while toying with the latest memento bagged from a foreign land: a painted toy soldier, perhaps, or a book. James remembered getting chocolate when his father came back from this trip to the Soviet Union, but it seemed that Andrew Bond had been holding something back. In a thick brown envelope marked *James*, was a small statuette of St Basil's, the famous cathedral on Moscow's Red Square: it looked like a fairy-tale castle, an intricate work with onion-shaped domes, brightly striped like Christmas baubles, set atop the ornately patterned red-brick towers. There was a note included, that read simply, *Your uncle Max needs to see this!*

'He never did, though,' James murmured; the keepsake had stayed buried and Max Bond had died two years ago. 'Thing is, Father was back for at least a day before he and Mother put me on the train and left for Chamonix. Why didn't he give this to me then?'

'I couldn't say, James. It's strange that he didn't post this, either, since there's a stamp on it.' From a buttoned sidepocket Charmian had produced an envelope addressed to Max. 'Especially since I recall he sent a postcard to Max from Chamonix dated the day they got there ...'

'And within twenty-four hours he was dead.' Looking at the letter, James felt a stab of fire deep inside. Both sender and recipient were gone from the world. It wasn't fair. 'Can . . . can we read what he said?'

Charmian smiled. 'Of course. I just wanted to wait until you were here with me.'

Anticipation built quickly. James could hardly credit it: a chance to snatch a few moments of his father's company, lost across the years! But the message, written in a hurried hand, seemed to refer back to a past conversation and read strangely.

'*Max, what you'll find in Moscow will have great effect on London,*' Charmian read slowly. '*Talpid Henson speaks of rebuilding the mill. You must visit. All can be brought down with one blow.*'

'What does that mean?' James broke in. 'And who is Talpid Henson?'

'I'm sure I've come across that name before. A shared acquaintance, perhaps.' Charmian shook her head, the memory lost to her. 'I don't think Talpid's his proper first name though. Family *Talpidae* is the Latin classification for moles.' She smiled. 'A talpid is small, dark and furry with a tubular snout. Presumably your father's nickname for this unfortunate Henson fellow.'

'May I see what else he wrote?' James plucked the letter from her grasp. He glanced through some trivia about a fabled fishing trip back in '97 where the Bond men had apparently waited *years* for a bite, and then a thrill went through him to see his name mentioned in the last line: *Read to K, play with James to get more out of the French memory for a start. Sincerely, Andrew.* There was no other comment, and James was baffled. *Get more out of the French memory?*

'There'd be no end of those, given how many visits we all made to Chamonix.' Charmian shook her head. 'Strangely put, isn't it . . . ?'

James nodded, brooding. '*Read to K*: who is this "K", then?'

'I can't think who Max would be reading aloud to.' Charmian studied the letter and smiled. 'But, oh my, I remember that blessed fishing trip. Why he thought to write about it here, I don't know, particularly since it happened in 1901, not 1897. I remember, because Edward VII was to be crowned King. Andrew and Max were dispatched by your grandmother to fish the lochs at Auchindrain for brown trout, ready to feed the hordes at the street party. They came home dejected with half a dozen perch, having missed the whole thing!'

James nodded. Very much a Scottish memory, it seemed, rather than one from France.

The day dragged on, as did the train; the landscape stretched past the window. By the time they had reached London, changed trains and arrived in Pett Bottom, night had swallowed the world and Charmian suggested they turn in.

James complied, but couldn't sleep, thinking about his father and how little he'd really known him. He'd always imagined that one day he would travel the globe with Andrew Bond, become a part of his world. Now, of course, it was all too late, and the contents of the pack and the unsent letter kept scattering through his thoughts. *Talpid . . . ninety-seven . . . read to K . . . the mill . . .*

Then, in the very small hours, James remembered what Charmian had said about Max receiving a postcard from Chamonix.

He knew Charmian had kept her brothers' old correspondence ('It's the voice that brings people back to you, James, not their belongings'); it was all packed away neatly in the attic, and so, around five a.m., it was there that James made for, quietly padding about between the battered trunks full of weighty books and papers, and files with dated letters arranged by recipient. He began to sort through them as quietly as he could, but Charmian, a scarlet robe wrapped around her and her hair in disarray, soon appeared through the hatch in the floor.

'Inevitably, you're looking for this.' She held up a postcard. 'I remembered Max saying at the funeral how this must have been the last thing your father wrote, and how poor an epitaph it made. And I knew I'd seen "Talpid Henson" somewhere before. Shall we?'

They repaired to the kitchen for cocoa by the light of an oil lamp. It didn't take long to fully decipher the scrawled message on the postcard:

Max,

Returned from business. Talpid Henson speaks of rebuilding the bank for when you visit. Foundations dangerous? See also further correspondence and polish instrument in James's case to bring it all down.

Hope the broken note in the major key finds you well, or you it.

Andrew

'Polish *what*?' James muttered. 'I've never played an instrument.'

'Cryptic and confounding, isn't it?' Charmian smiled faintly. 'You know, to me this whiffs of a kind of overgrown-schoolboy code.'

'And to crack that code, you'd need a different kind of "major key".' James frowned. '*See also further correspondence* – does that mean the letter in the rucksack that Uncle Max never got?'

'Perhaps the two are meant to be taken together,' Charmian agreed. 'Our talpid friend sounds very busy, doesn't he? Rebuilding the mill in one letter and rebuilding the bank in the other.' She paused. 'Rebuilding *Millbank*, perhaps?'

'Millbank in London, you mean?'

'I don't know. But your father says that his work in Moscow will affect London.'

James remembered why the name rang a bell. 'Millbank was mostly pulled down after the great Thames flood of 1928, wasn't it? By 1932 rebuilding would have been well underway …' He frowned, a quiet thrill travelling down his spine. 'Uncle Max was still working for the Secret Intelligence Service back then – could this code be linked to his work?'

'Your father was a salesman for Vickers, not a spy.'

'He travelled the world selling weapons,' James argued. 'He must've come into contact with the sorts of people Uncle Max was spying on.'

'Perhaps. But whatever the mystery here, we're three years too late to do anything about it.' Charmian put the postcard picture-side up on the table; the monochrome mountains glimmered in the oil lamp's glow until she lowered the wick and blew hard to put out the light. 'I declare night to be restored. Let's go back to our beds and salvage what sleep we can.'

James dutifully trailed off to his room, but his mind was turning too fast for him to contemplate sleep. Any mystery he found tantalizing, but this — unfinished business between his father and his uncle? It couldn't be more personal!

To meekly accept that the mystery was done with was unthinkable.

If the truth can be found, James thought, *I'll find it.*

3

Tall Buildings and Their Secrets

He'd planned to pass the summer making his own diving equipment, ready to test it at St Margaret's Bay, but now James had a new purpose: to learn what it was his father had been trying to tell his brother, the spy.

If the postcard and the letter were two parts of a cryptic puzzle, what was the solution? *Play with James*, Andrew Bond had told his brother. *Polish instrument in James's case*. And yet James had never owned or kept a musical instrument, so he couldn't see how that might fit — not yet, at least. If Aunt Charmian was right — if the mole-like Henson's actions with a mill and a bank were linked to the rebuilding of Millbank — perhaps the fishing trip with the wrong year ascribed was another clue. Max would surely know the correct date, after all! And he'd said they'd waited *years* for a fish to bite, drawing attention to that number: '97' . . .

Could that be part of an address – number 97, Millbank?

It sounded fanciful to James, but with no other leads, the itch of possibility needed scratching.

Charmian had decided to pass on the cryptic messages to a friend of Uncle Max's at the Secret Intelligence Service, in case they were of any interest, so James offered to act as courier. It would give him time and opportunity to conduct his own investigations.

The SIS headquarters were situated near St James's Park station on Broadway. It was a nondescript office building, of which SIS occupied the third and fourth floors – in secret, of course. The sign on the front door was in the name of a fire-extinguisher company. The general public weren't supposed to know of the office's real purpose. James had been instructed to bring his passport for inspection before he'd be allowed in.

He rang the bell, and before long the door was opened by a young man with slicked-back hair and skin the same shade of grey as his suit. James produced his identity papers, the man checked them, then showed James into a drab and dowdy hallway with not an iota of glamour about it.

'You have something for us,' the man said, without enthusiasm.

Reluctantly James handed over the envelope with the correspondence inside. He'd carefully transcribed the words for his own reference, but to surrender the originals was difficult.

The young man took the envelope in silence.

'Is ... Adam Elmhirst here?' James asked. When he'd got caught up in danger in Los Angeles last year, Elmhirst, an SIS officer, had saved his life. James had hoped to ask him for help now. 'I met him once—'

'You're out of luck today,' the young man broke in. 'I'll tell him you asked after him. Goodbye.'

Before James could argue he was shown brusquely back outside. The door clicked shut and he stood smarting in the sunlight, dismissed.

So much for my errand for the day, he thought. *Now it's time to take care of my own business.*

Consulting Charmian's battered *A.B.C. Pocket Atlas-Guide to London*, James walked along Broadway, down Strutton Ground and Horseferry Road before turning right onto Regency Street. Ninety-seven Millbank was less than a twenty-minute walk away.

James saw that a new building now stood on the site, just beside the Thames's north bank: an international school, the Mechta Academy for the Performing Arts.

Since the catastrophic flood that had left Millbank in dank destruction, the whole area had been razed so that smarter, safer modern buildings could be built. The Mechta Academy stood out: a kind of white concrete cascade of enormous blocks arranged around an oval central tower. *Foundations dangerous*, his father had written four years ago. Well, the buttressing around the base of this building looked hefty enough to protect it from further flooding.

The building stood behind black wrought-iron gates, and James could see children in red and yellow uniforms exercising with teachers in the landscaped grounds.

So school hasn't broken up for summer? James frowned. *What are they doing in there?*

Perhaps international schools had different rules.

As one proficient in breaking rules of any sort, James resolved to learn more.

The next week saw James back in London, keeping a newly made appointment at the grand Public Record Office off Chancery Lane, to try and learn more about the Academy. He was asked for identification and was relieved he'd not removed his passport from his jacket since his last visit to the capital.

Dangerous foundations ... did it refer to the basics of the children's learning at the Academy?

It was possible, James supposed, although his father would have had no direct knowledge of it. Construction of number 97, Millbank had begun in 1931, and was still underway when Andrew Bond had died in '32. The name on the architect's plans was one Ivan Kalashnikov – a Russian national perhaps. James knew that diplomatic relations between Britain and the Soviet Union had been tense and difficult for years, each side accusing the other of spying and sabotage and worse. High-profile work by a Russian architect in the heart of Westminster must have raised some eyebrows in high places.

Max, Andrew Bond had written, *my work in Moscow will have great effect on London* ...

Records showed that Kalashnikov had been the architect of three other buildings near the River Thames – office blocks with a kind of brutal, functional grace that stood out in their environs. James studied the plans carefully, noting a few key features, but they failed to show the foundations.

What did you expect to find? James wondered sullenly. And yet an instinct, some gut feeling, told him to continue the search, to learn more. James had learned to trust that inner voice.

If the plans couldn't help him, he'd have to gain some first-hand intelligence. The Academy was clearly still open for its pupils, regardless of the summer break. *Let's see if it will open its doors to me,* James thought.

Having caught a bus to Millbank from Chancery Lane, James decided that the best way to gain entrance to the Academy was to make a damned nuisance of himself. With his father's old, rust-stained backpack over one shoulder, he marched up to the gates and repeatedly rang the bell.

Eventually a large man in his twenties, with high cheekbones and a dark demeanour, strode intimidatingly from the main building. Despite his sombre grey suit he looked more like a soldier than a teacher, and said nothing as he approached, interrogating with his eyes alone.

'I am here for the tour I arranged with your head of admissions,' James said boldly and, true to the spirit of his covert mission, decided to assume a false identity. 'The name is … Grande. Hugo Grande. My father believes I should board here. If I like what I see, I could be your latest and greatest pupil.'

The man glared and pointed past James, indicating he should leave.

James shook his head and checked his watch, which showed the time to be almost half past three. 'The tour was booked for three thirty. I'd show you the letter I received, but Father has it, and he's not collecting me till six. Perhaps you could check with whoever's in charge?'

Turning on his heel, the man stalked away.

'I'm not leaving!' James called after him. 'Not until I've been seen!' *Why wait for trouble for find me*, he thought, *when I can go looking?* So he stayed put, ringing the bell continuously for ten minutes. Finally the Slavic soldier returned and unlocked the gate, escorting James in the same stolid silence.

I'm in! James felt a familiar frisson of excitement. *What next?*

He was led into the cool of the school reception, where floorboards of sprung oak met pale wallpaper in tasteful neutrality. Another man was there, and this one could talk as well as glower. Towering and paunchy, he spoke with the air of one who mistrusts all things on principle. 'You say your name is Grande?'

'Hugo Grande, yes.' James was actually borrowing the name of his old schoolfriend, a dwarf; he thought Hugo would enjoy the irony of inspiring a tall tale. 'And you are . . . ?'

'I am Andrei Karachan.' His Russian accent was as heavy as he looked. 'The Director of Operations.'

So – the Soviet link ran further! James surveyed this 'Director': a wild crown of thick black hair danced around the bald spot in the middle of the big man's head, mirrored by a greying beard below. In the heavily pockmarked face, penetrating eyes shifted in suspicion.

'There is no record of a tour for a prospective pupil named Grande scheduled for this or any other day.' Karachan nodded to the escort then looked back at James. 'Having come here in error, you will now leave the premises.'

'Wait!' James took a step closer to Karachan, keeping poker-faced as he began his bluff. 'Do you really want to throw me out? My father is extremely high up in the Diplomatic Service, and a personal friend of the Head.'

The escort moved towards James, but Karachan barked something in Russian, held up a hand, and the man refrained from propelling James out through the door.

'Perhaps I could just watch the other pupils at work ... or is it play?' James smiled as openly as he could. 'Are there lessons right through the summer?'

'No. They practise – for the big show.' Karachan eyed the battered backpack on James's shoulder with disapproval. 'Wait here. I will find someone willing to speak to you.' He muttered some more Russian to his colleague; the Slav nodded, folded his arms and fixed James with a baleful gaze. Karachan headed for an inner doorway. As the door swung open, James saw a slender, dark-skinned boy in a loose cotton-drill suit with a shaved head and large brown eyes, looking in curiously. Remembering it was an international school, James supposed he was one of the older pupils. Karachan shooed the boy away as he swept through and the door clicked shut behind him. James was left alone in reception with his minder.

As the minutes passed, James began to sweat. What if Karachan was talking to the Headmaster right now and realizing James's deception?

He looked up as the inner door swung open again. This time a woman entered – lean and aristocratic. With her poise and graceful step she might once have danced professionally. The way she wore her hair, like a young 1920s flapper despite her age – her dark blunt bob cut just below her ears was now flecked with silver – suggested she found those days hard to leave behind.

'Well, well, what have we here?' Her *pince-nez* edged down the sharp slope of her nose as her grey eyes fixed on James with fascination. 'Hugo Grande, is this so?'

'That's right,' James began.

'A fine French name. I am Madame Gaiana Radek, the Assistant Principal here.' Her careful English was spoken a little eccentrically, the French undertones turning the *th* sounds into *z*s. 'I regret most strongly that there is no record of your application.'

James cleared his throat. 'Couldn't you spare anybody to give me a short tour? My father can't collect me until much later—'

'Without the letter of invitation you must have received, we sadly cannot help you.' Madame Radek shrugged helplessly. 'Rules and regulations – without them, where would a school be, eh? Especially one with such gifted pupils ... and such important parents.'

'Important?' James enquired.

'As you can see from the presence of Demir, here' – Madame Radek gestured to James's escort – 'we attend to the safety and security of our pupils at all times. Do please request that your father telephones again at his earliest convenience, yes? Now, forgive me, young Monsieur Grande, but I have an important show to rehearse with my most gifted pupils.' As she swept away towards the door, she threw a proud smile back at him. 'At the Royal Opera House, you know!'

'Very impressive,' James said politely, but she had gone and the door was already closing behind her.

'Move,' Demir growled.

'Yes, of course. One moment.' James dropped and pretended to tie his shoelaces. He knew he had to decide quickly – whether to leave obediently with the taciturn Demir, or seize the day and press on.

The choice was clear.

James dodged Demir and burst forward. Heart pitching wildly, he threw the door open and charged through into a tiled corridor that turned sharply twenty yards ahead, just as it had on the building plans. James pelted round the corner so that he was out of sight.

Demir, of course, came following – and fast. James ran no more, laid in wait; as Demir slewed round the corner, he kicked the Slav's ankle out from under him. Demir fell, but his hand caught James's sleeve and he dragged James to the floor with him. As they struck the polished tiles of the school corridor, Demir lashed out with a horizontal knife hand strike at James's neck.

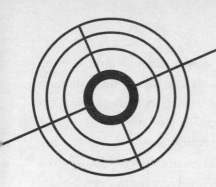

4
Dangerous Foundations

With a gasp, James twisted aside and the blow struck him across the back of his skull. Pain whiplashed through his senses. Demir scrambled back to his feet, making for a fire-alarm plunger switch on the wall.

No, you don't, James thought. He jumped up and charged at Demir, propelling the man's face into the wall. There was a smack of bone on masonry and the man's nose burst open like an overripe fruit. Demir's face painted a thick crimson snail-trail on the wall as he sank to his knees and then pitched backwards, unconscious.

James breathed deeply, feeling sick as he rubbed gingerly at the base of his skull. Demir had struck like an expert with the bottom of the handbone, near the wrist. If the blow had hit James's carotid artery, or the vertically flowing nerves in his neck, it might have killed him. This man might be employed by the Mechta Academy of Performing Arts for the protection of

VIPs' children, but he fought like a professional. James reached into Demir's jacket and pulled out his wallet; he found no identification inside. He replaced it and, searching instead in the man's trouser pocket, found a bunch of keys.

That such a capable fighter would rush straight for the main alarm when confronted with an unruly schoolboy jarred with James's expectations. What was happening here, besides rehearsals for some big show?

There was a storeroom across the corridor. James opened the door and manhandled Demir inside, building a wall of cardboard boxes in front of him to obscure the body. 'Stay sleeping,' James told the supine body, and sorted quickly through the keys until he found the one that locked the door. He only hoped that Karachan wouldn't come looking too soon.

James pressed on along the corridor, but self-doubt began to bite. *I've just assaulted a man trying to stop me trespassing in a school.* Sweat prickled on his palms. *Look at me, the dutiful, loss-torn son, out to finish whatever the hell his father started, no matter what. What the hell am I trying to prove?*

But he knew the answer. *I'm trying to prove myself, Father.*
To you.

James willed himself to stay focused. If he was caught now, he'd be in serious trouble, most likely with the police. He decided to finish his reconnaissance and, if he found nothing of note, well, let that be an end to it. *I'll get the hell out of here and never come back.*

He remembered from Kalashnikov's plans that there were several doors that accessed the basement area. By keeping to the main perimeter corridor he came to a door marked BASEMENT — NO ENTRY WITHOUT AUTHORIZATION, and tried it. It was locked. Before he could go through the set of keys, he heard the clean squeak of another door opening, back along the corridor, the way he'd come.

Demir? James held still and heard light footsteps coming his way. Spotting a door ajar on the other side of the corridor, he quickly crossed over and stepped into the disinfectant dark of a cleaning cupboard. Footsteps on the linoleum drew alongside his hiding place and James crouched to peer through the keyhole.

It was the black boy with a shaved head he'd seen looking in through the door earlier. Presumably this was one of the VIPs – Very Important Pupils.

With a sharp jangle of keys, the boy opened up the basement door and stepped through. The door started to swing closed behind him.

Great minds think alike. James darted out from his hiding place and pressed his toe to the door to stop it closing fully. He waited, breath held, for what felt like an hour, straining to catch sounds of movement from below. He heard a low, heavy creak. Another door? James slipped through the doorway and stood at the top of a staircase lit by the feverish glare of a bright-red bulb hanging from the ceiling. Cautiously he tiptoed down the concrete steps, peering into the shadowy space beyond the banister rail – then held still at the sound of scuffles coming from the floor.

Not just a door, James thought. *A trap*door.

Like a mole, digging underground . . .

The black boy was scaling a ladder, rising back up into the basement like a phantom from the floor below. After closing the trapdoor and bolting it shut, he crossed to a telephone mounted on the far wall. With his back to James, he picked up the receiver and quickly dialled.

'Demir is not in the basement, Karachan.' The boy spoke slowly, his voice, almost feminine, with no trace of an accent. 'The cargo is undisturbed.'

Cargo? In the crimson shadows James moved soundlessly down the stairs, back to the wall, and crouched down behind a dusty crate on the basement floor. Here was vindication: *I was right to come here.* The torch of investigation had passed from father to son – but just what had Andrew Bond discovered in Moscow, among the buyers and sellers of national security? For all the cautious code, to involve his brother the British spy – even his son – he must've believed it to be something important. Some Soviet plot that, fully three years later, had still not come to fruition. But why not? What was it?

By God, James swore, on his next trip to the 'fire extinguisher company' on Broadway, he would light a proper blaze under the SIS over this: let them try to put it out!

The black boy replaced the telephone receiver and then crossed to the steps, bare feet slapping against the concrete as he passed right by James. He climbed the stairs, switched off the red bulb and opened the door. Bright light from the corridor yawned and was swallowed as the door swung back shut. It locked behind him but James wasn't concerned; he'd noticed the knob that turned the deadlock from the inside.

Since this place has just been searched, it should be safe to stay here a while, James reasoned as he climbed back up the stairs, switched the light back on and then hurried down to the trapdoor. He unbolted the wooden hatch and lifted it. The space beneath was shadowy; it gave off a strong stink of almonds mingled with greasier notes of tar and plastic.

James swiftly climbed down into the large underground area beneath the trapdoor. The floor was concrete, and though he was almost six feet tall, he could still only brush the ceiling with his fingertips. He felt around for a light switch, flicked the metal nub, and a dim glow snapped on above him.

Looking around, James found himself in a kind of concrete bunker, built beneath the basement room to the same dimensions. *There was no sign of this on the architect's plans*, he thought. The sweet, oily smell was overpowering – *what the hell was stored down here?* He saw that the walls were stacked with wooden crates: full ones, neatly arranged, to his right, and a chaotic landscape of empties to his left.

James peered at the dark writing stencilled on the side of one of the full crates:

BLADE-RISE INDUSTRIES
DANGER
HIGH EXPLOSIVES
HEXOGEN 50LBS 1¼ x 8

James swore: there was enough explosive here to leave craters all over London, and manufactured by a British weapons firm too; he'd encountered Blade-Rise before, and their operations could only be described as shadowy. *All can be brought down with one blow*, Andrew Bond had written. But how had he known . . . ?

I suppose the military-level security makes sense now, at least, James thought grimly. Well, he'd pushed his nose into this outlandish business; now it was time to get the hell out and warn the authorities.

Warily James climbed up the bunker ladder and emerged from the trapdoor, back into the crimson shadows of the basement. He stood up, dusted himself down, and then—

From nowhere, hands grabbed him by his shirtfront and threw him to the ground. Down in the bunker, he hadn't heard the door open and someone come in. James rolled with the impact, used his momentum to right himself and scrambled up to grab his attacker in a neck lock.

It was the black boy with the shaved head; he must've seen James hiding, pretended to leave and then doubled back. James tried to tighten his grip on the boy, but then gasped as a hard elbow drove into his stomach. The boy spun round and propelled his left fist into James's jaw. The blow brought black specks to James's vision, but he stayed upright, feinted back and then darted forward to punch the boy in the chest.

The boy neatly sidestepped James's attack and then mirrored its movement, as if to show James how it ought to be done – swiftly and without mercy. James couldn't feint back in time and knuckles cracked, hard, into his ribs. Angry and hurting, James slammed the boy back against the wall. Hands reached for his throat, but he brought both arms up to break the stranglehold and then turned for just a second, ready to elbow his attacker in the stomach and throw him over his shoulder. But James was too slow. Something hard struck the back of his neck – a fist like steel that sent stars shooting behind his eyes – and he knew nothing else.

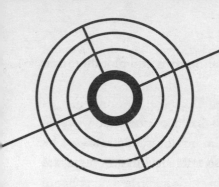

5

In the Cell

It was the steady pounding of his head that stirred James back to life. He awoke in a large, bare room that could've been anywhere. Daylight came in through a barred window high in a whitewashed wall. The reek of disinfectant burned the back of his dry throat. He was lying on a hard, narrow bunk and there was a bucket beside a door with a small grille in it – an iron door he knew must be locked.

This is a cell, thought James, with growing certainty and a sinking heart. He'd been shut away inside enough of them to know at a glance. Where was he, and how long had he been out? Gingerly he felt the back of his head and, with a wince, introduced his fingers to a large and impudent bump there.

Well, what of it? He was still alive, wasn't he? Determination gathered in his sinews. The felling blow hadn't broken the skin, and certainly not his spirit. He closed his eyes, the crates of explosives hard and bright in his memory. What was it to be used for? How much had his father known of a plot that must stretch back so many years?

And whose lair am I caught in now?

James got up slowly, waiting for the expected wave of nausea to catch up with him. It did not disappoint. *Passport*, he remembered. *I was carrying my passport.* He felt for it in his jacket pocket and found it intact.

Slowly, clearing his parched throat, he crossed to the door and banged his palm on it, wincing as the metal echoes thundered about him. He held the tremor from his voice as he called, 'Hello? What's going on?'

Almost at once he heard footsteps, and the shutter on the door grille jumped open. A dour-faced man peered in at him; with a rush of relief James noted his dark-navy police uniform. 'Awake now, are you, son?'

'Where . . . where am I, please?'

'Lambeth police station,' the officer replied in his broad south London accent. 'James Bond, if that passport's really yours' – James nodded, and winced at the pain that caused – 'you've been arrested for criminal trespass, and for inflicting grievous bodily harm upon one Demir Brachacki at the Mechta Academy, Millbank. In addition, you assaulted a pupil . . .'

'That pupil attacked me first.' As defences went, James knew that his own sounded feeble. 'Officer, you have to listen to me: there are explosives in the basement – beneath it, in a bunker, I mean. Have you searched the school? There's a trapdoor—'

'Slow down, son. You'll be interviewed in due course.' The policeman's craggy face softened. 'Take it slow, eh? You look like you could use a cuppa. And some aspirin, maybe?'

James nodded gratefully. 'How long was I out?'

'Four hours or so.'

'Shouldn't I be in hospital? This lump on my head—'

'The police surgeon checked you over. You're fine.'

'Well, can I at least make a telephone call?'

But the policeman had already gone. James paced about, his heart beginning to pound again. He was surprised that the powers at Mechta had released him into police custody, knowing what he'd discovered, but the obvious answer didn't elude him for long: *They'll have cleared away the evidence by now. Even if I convince the police I'm telling the truth, there'll be nothing to find.* Still, at least he was safe. In time, Charmian would get hold of the family solicitor, and he would surely smooth things over and persuade the authorities to release—

The key rattled noisily in the lock. James looked over, surprised, as the door was pushed open and another policeman entered – a sergeant – escorting a slim, wiry woman with a bob of greying hair.

'Madame Radek,' he breathed.

'We meet again, Monsieur Grande.' The woman's voice was almost musical, but her gaze was hard and fierce. 'Only, now I know you are a spy, hmm? A spy named James Bond! Someone employed you to sabotage rehearsals for my gala production. I insist that you tell me who.'

James snorted at the ludicrous accusation. 'What?'

'Was it those Notting Hill harpies at the Mercury Theatre? The London Academy—?'

'I don't care about some stupid dance show!' James retorted, turning to the policeman. 'I'm waiting to make a statement about what happened to me – how can she charge in and interrogate me?'

'We have our instructions.' The policeman cleared his throat. 'A lot of important people send their nippers to this lady's school ...'

'And if you wish to take down a statement, Officer, then know that this boy gained unlawful access to the Academy and seriously assaulted staff and pupils.' Madame Radek was growing agitated. 'We present a gala performance at the Royal Opera House next week, with the King himself in attendance! And Master Bond here tries to bring down a scandal upon us.' She bustled over, chin thrust out like an offensive weapon. 'You are sent by the press, perhaps? An *agent provocateur*. A thug!'

'The boy took a proper wallop to his head, miss,' the policeman pointed out.

'He brought it upon himself, Officer,' Madame Radek affirmed. 'Mr Karachan, our Director of Operations, found him in the corridor with an injured pupil shortly before I arrived on the scene.' She glanced quickly at James. 'I could see that they were both in quite a state, and that he had lied about his identity – so I called the police myself.'

And probably saved my life, James reflected. 'Madame, please, don't you realize what's going on in your own school – what must have been going on for years?' He lowered his voice, keeping calm, hoping to mollify the woman. With the ear of people in power, she could be a powerful ally – *if* he could convince her. He launched into a brief explanation of what his father had hinted at, and of all he'd found there.

Madame Radek heard him out, but her eyebrows were like threads tugging her forehead into a pinched frown. Finally she turned to the sergeant. 'I trust you will promptly get to the truth behind this ludicrous story, Officer?' She shook her head firmly as she turned back to James. 'Whoever you are, whoever you're working for and whatever mischief you are hoping to achieve, nothing – nothing at all – is going to interfere with my grand production.'

'I told you what I saw,' James protested. 'You have to believe me!' But Madame Radek was already walking away. 'You're making it easy for them!' She cast one more look at him, eyes dark in her pale, powdered face. Then she slipped through the doorway and the sergeant followed her.

As the door swung shut and the key groaned again in the lock, James kicked the wall. He'd brushed the fringes of his father's unfinished business, but the heart of the mystery seemed only to be growing darker.

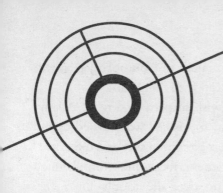

6

Breakout

James finally received a mug of tea and a biscuit from the first policeman. 'I've been here for hours,' he said. 'When is someone coming to take my statement?'

'Inspector's busy,' the officer said, walking away, but James couldn't hear much sound of business in the station, only the rumble of traffic and trains outside through the high window.

'I want to call my aunt,' he shouted. 'Can't someone take me to the telephone?'

No reply was forthcoming. James slumped heavily down on the bed. His tea had long since gone cold, and he was starting to eye the bucket in the corner without enthusiasm, when a commotion outside broke the station's sepulchral atmosphere. A familiar voice with an edge of the East End shouted down a protesting sergeant. 'I'm sure the old girl does have some powerful friends, mate. But James Bond's got one or two himself. I've shown you my authority – now, no one and nothing's going to stop me seeing him.'

James recognized the accent with surprise and relief. A key scraped in the lock, and the door to his cell was barged open by a familiar stocky man in a rumpled grey suit and a fedora, with an air of hard-boiled alertness about him. Small blue eyes twinkled and a grin spread over the tough-guy face. 'Well, well. We meet again, Mr Bond!'

'I don't believe it.' James stood and took his hand in a firm shake. 'Elmhirst! What are you doing here?'

'I heard you called for me last week at the office. When I heard this police report, I thought I should come and call for you.' Elmhirst turned to the sergeant. 'He's leaving with me, so you'd better get busy with the paperwork. Chop, chop, eh?' As the officer moved reluctantly out of the cell and closed and locked the door behind him, Elmhirst's face grew more serious. 'Those postcards from your father you dropped off – they confirmed a few professional opinions. Including *my* opinion that you would wind up in bother if you drew attention to yourself. Which, of course, you did. Worked out Mechta's address from your old man's clues, right?'

'I needed to know what he was trying to say,' James said. 'I tried to ask your office for help, but I was just about thrown out. Thought that, without any evidence, SIS would call it a cold case.'

Elmhirst looked at James and shook his head. 'It's an *old* case that's building up to boiling point. I've had Mechta under surveillance for some time.'

'SIS know about the Mechta Academy?'

'We've got a man called Karachan under observation. Served with the Latvian Riflemen in the Great War, until the

44

Russian revolution – then he threw his lot in with the Bolsheviks so he could shoot the nobility for pleasure and profit.' Elmhirst smiled grimly. 'Currently runs a violent subset of the British Communist Party.'

'Then you must know about the high explosives I found in the basement.'

'What?'

'You need to get a team down to Mechta right now!'

'Oh, sure, all tooled up with tommy guns to rat-a-tat the bad guys, right?' Elmhirst held up his hands. 'Just slow down, eh?'

James stared. 'You don't believe me either? Think I'm making it up like Madame Radek?'

'Don't mention that old bat to me.' Elmhirst shook his head. 'She's bent so many earholes about security for her royal gala show, *so* many times. VIP bigwigs galore are going, see, the head of SIS included, so we've been assisting the Met, running background checks on those involved. I s'pose I should thank her, really – that's how we found out about Karachan. He came over from Moscow three years ago, but he's just one cog in a very big wheel.' Elmhirst took off his hat and wiped his bald head with his sleeve. 'If I take a team into Mechta to search it from top to bottom, Karachan's bosses get the tip-off that we're on to their little plot – and who knows how they'll respond. They could go to ground, or else *use* that explosive rather than let it be captured.'

'*Use* it . . .' James looked up at him. 'Then you do believe me?'

'It would fit.' Elmhirst fixed his hat back on his head. 'And after your little visit today, some very loud alarm bells will have gone off. They got your real name, didn't they?'

45

James nodded, cheeks prickling. 'They must've searched me while I was knocked out. I have my passport with me.'

'Yes, well, I expect questions about you are being asked right now.' Elmhirst began to pace up and down. 'Staying locked up in here is probably the safest bet for you. But we don't have that option.'

'What are you saying?'

'Officially, nothing at all. But you have to know you're mixed up in the end moves of a long, long game – a Soviet plot that must be nearing completion by now.'

'Did my uncle Max know about it?' James asked.

'Not as much as your old man.' Elmhirst looked all around the room as if afraid he'd be overheard. 'You're involved. Have been since your dad named you in that letter: *Play with James . . . a major key.* That doesn't mean play a game, it means the game's afoot, and somehow you're vital to it all.'

James was lost. 'I don't understand.'

'You know your dad's message to your uncle was in code. You cracked some of it, which is how you ended up at the Academy. But there's more, and we need your help in order to understand it.'

James looked doubtful. 'I've read those words so many times, and I'm none the wiser.'

'Well, at SIS we've got a little more to go on,' Elmhirst said. 'And that leaves me convinced that you *can* help. In fact, you're going to have to.' He smiled. 'Still, first things first: getting you out of here. I've had a word with the duty sergeant – he understands—'

As if on cue, the bolts on the door slid back and the heavy key turned in the lock. The officer who'd brought in Madame Radek opened the door and came in, looking grave.

'I've talked to my superiors,' he announced.

'Good.' Elmhirst winked at James. 'Then we'll be on our way.'

'As you were, sir.' The sergeant retreated through the door and it slowly closed behind him. Elmhirst started towards it.

Then the door swung back open and smashed into Elmhirst's face. He reeled backwards with a gruff cry, falling on his side as the sergeant pushed back into the room and kicked him in the guts.

James flew to Elmhirst's aid, hooked an arm around the sergeant's throat to drag him away. An elbow thudded into his solar plexus, but James had been expecting the blow and tensed his stomach muscles.

The burning powder that the sergeant threw into James's eyes was a different matter.

Recoiling, James shouted out in pain, his eyes streaming, nose and throat burning. *What the hell was that?* He staggered back and tripped over the bucket, fell against the wall, banged the lump on his head again – but his eyes were stinging so badly now that he hardly noticed. He heard the sounds of violence close by, a gasp from Elmhirst and the sound of a blow. Someone stamped on James's leg and he winced and rolled out of the way, falling against his father's backpack. He grabbed it and clutched it to his chest. The pain in his eyes was almost unbearable . . .

An almighty thump reverberated through the wall James was leaning against. A moment later, strong hands grabbed hold of his arms and hauled him to his feet. James began to struggle, lashing out blindly.

'Oi! Hold up, Bond, it's me.' Elmhirst's breath brushed James's cheek. 'You all right?'

'I'm blind.' James's eyelids felt swollen with fire and he fought to stay calm. 'Some sort of powder . . .'

''S all right.' Elmhirst smacked his lips, then spat. 'Yeah, it's just ground cayenne pepper mixed with flour – old fighting trick from the Orient. They carry it wrapped in rice paper. Won't do any permanent damage. Maybe our friendly bobby here served with the Chinese Labour Corps in the war.'

'But why blind me?'

'Same reason he tried to stop me taking you away. Like I said, your trip to Mechta will have set off alarm bells in high places – and raised some pressing questions. Obviously Karachan's not their only agent.'

'But this man is a British policeman—!'

'You sure about that?' Elmhirst patted James on the shoulder. 'Look, let's save the whodunnits for later, eh? Chances are he's not the only one in this nick who wants you to stay put. We need to go.'

'Go?' James held on tightly to his father's pack. 'I can't see a damned thing.'

'I'll guide you. Just look down at the ground and keep quiet.'

James was jerked away by the arm, out of his cell and into the cool corridor beyond. The idea of depending on someone else, of surrendering control, made him feel sick; all his life he'd watched out for himself and his friends. But what choice did he have – left blind with eyes and nose streaming?

The station was quiet apart from the ring of their footsteps on the floor. With Elmhirst keeping him close, guiding his flight, James could hear the steady thump of the man's heartbeat. He was keeping calm. He was a professional. They would make it out of here.

James heard the duty officer call, puzzled: ''Ere, hold up! You can't just take him out of here?'

'All arranged,' said Elmhirst, quickening his step.

'Wait—'

But Elmhirst was waiting for no one! He practically pushed James through a doorway into the unexpected heat of the evening, along a path, heading for the growl of traffic on the road ahead; the station must be set back from the main street. He heard the bass hoot of a tugboat on the Thames, and blinked and rubbed his watering eyes furiously. Finally, through the tears, he saw the dark-blue blur of an Austin 12 taxicab looming up ahead.

'Who says you never find one when you need one?' Elmhirst tugged open the rear door, bundled James up over the High-Lot's running board and into the back, then slid onto the black leather seat beside him and slammed shut the door.

'Everything all right, guv?' the driver chirped through the glass partition.

'It's been a long day. Get going,' Elmhirst snapped. 'Mark Lane underground station. Quick as you can.'

'It's rush hour,' said the driver, 'and there's a lot of traffic round the bridge . . .'

'Here you go,' Elmhirst said calmly, and James heard the rustle of paper drawn from a billfold. 'There's a few bob extra if you get us there *tout de suite.*'

'*Naturellement, monsieur.*' The cabbie slaughtered the French pronunciation and proceeded to do the same to the Austin's gearbox as he took the car out into the traffic.

'You think we're being followed?' James murmured.

'Odds on,' Elmhirst agreed. 'Someone could've been posted outside the station to check that the bent copper did his dirty work. I didn't hang around to find out.'

'I can't believe he attacked you too,' said James. 'I mean, how on earth could he explain that away to the real police?'

'Put the blame on you?' Elmhirst pushed a handkerchief into James's hands. 'Make you seem unstable, get you locked up for longer as a danger to others ...'

'But when you came to, you'd tell people what really happened.'

'Who says I was supposed to come to?' Elmhirst shifted on the seat. 'I told you, James, you've poked your nose into something really big this time.'

'Never mind my nose, it's my eyes ...' James muttered, dabbing furiously at his swollen lids. To his relief, his sight was growing clearer. The looming hulks of bulky red buses, trundling alongside in a steady stream, slowly revealed their details: rows of faces stared blankly through dusty windows while advertisement slogans smeared across the length of the vehicles in horizontal strips – Wrigley's after a meal helped digestion and whitened your teeth! Maples had a sale on, today and every day! The busy grey blur on the pavements resolved into crowds of bowler-hatted commuters, pipes jammed between their lips as they scurried like rats from their workplaces. The freedom of the pale-blue sky stretched beyond the tall stone facades of the teeming streets. James saw a van from Meredith & Drew, a pack of their cheese sandwich biscuits painted on the back, promising *A meal for 2d!* His stomach growled.

'Where are we going?' James wondered. 'Why Mark Lane station?'

'Plenty of places we could go from there. West to Kensington, north to Liverpool Street, east to Dagenham . . .'

'So which is it?'

Elmhirst cast a wary glance at the cabbie and lowered his voice, speaking in James's ear. 'None of them. We'll get out at Mark Lane, go inside the station and then double back across the river on foot.'

'And give the slip to whoever might be following.' James considered for a moment. 'But where are we *really* going?'

'I reckon that the best thing to do is retrace your old daddy's footsteps . . .' Elmhirst put an arm around James's shoulder. 'I hear Moscow's lovely this time of year.'

7

On His Majesty's Secret Service

Moscow! James could hardly believe he might be flying there himself, helping personally on official SIS business. Excitement buzzed in his heart now that he had fresh hope of reaching the truth at the bottom of this mystery.

The taxi dropped James and Elmhirst at Mark Lane station. Elmhirst led the way through the entrance, pretended to scrutinize the map, then turned and walked straight out again onto Lower Thames Street. James's eyes still stung and watered, but he could see well enough to walk unassisted. In any case, he soon found it best to keep your head down when trying to barge through the busy pinstriped crowds. He held his father's backpack to his chest like armour.

'Rush hour works in our favour,' Elmhirst said. 'Chucking-out time for the suits will make us harder to spot.'

'You still think we're being followed?'

'In this game you get used to thinking, *What's the worst that could happen?* and then doubling it.'

Given his day, James could relate to that, but it was impossible not to feel excited as well as apprehensive with things moving so quickly. 'Are you serious about travelling to Moscow?'

'You're a popular boy, James. Wanted by both sides. But I think you'll prefer my protective custody to theirs.' He held up a hand to James's rush of questions. 'Not now, eh? Not in the open.'

James and Elmhirst were buffeted by the crowd as they made their way onto London Bridge. The roar of passing traffic filled James's ears; exhaust fumes caught in his nose and throat. He felt distanced from the crowds around him; they were heading home from work, another ordinary day marked off in their humdrum lives, while he ... where was *he* going? Suddenly he was a fugitive. The evening sun glittered on the gun-metal sweep of the Thames, and smoke belched from a steamboat chugging under the bridge, hazing his view of Southwark Cathedral. Perhaps, he thought, some of these humdrum lives held great secrets. Andrew Bond had been just another businessman racing home to see his family ... but what else had he been doing? Spying for his brother, and his country? Hunting out intrigue?

Once they'd crossed the bridge, Elmhirst guided James to the white steps on his right that led down to Green Dragon Court, a quiet cobbled street lined with shabby shopfronts and black-leaded bollards, and onto Middle Road. The smell of rotting fruit and vegetables carried through the warm air, and James turned up his nose as he and Elmhirst neared

Borough Market. Elmhirst strode confidently through the tussle of traders, customers and staff shutting up shop for the evening, making for a large, bald man with an egg-shaped head and a striped apron, who was loading wooden crates into the back of a Bedford delivery van.

'All right, Harry?' Elmhirst nodded his head. 'I'm taking you up on that offer of storage. Is it still available?'

'Way's clear, Mr Elmhirst,' Harry said, nodding past a sheet of cloth hanging down from the shop front behind his stall.

Elmhirst glanced about as if testing Harry's claim, and then ushered James inside the shop. It was an ill-lit tobacconist's, the air hazy with cigar smoke and cherry tobacco. James followed Elmhirst through a beaded doorway, down a flight of stairs and along a dark passageway that ended in a door with no handle, just a keyhole. Elmhirst produced a key, turned it and pulled the door open.

'SIS safe house,' he explained. 'A place to stay, always available at the drop of a hat.' As if to demonstrate, he took off his fedora and flipped it onto a hatstand. 'Storage for *you*.'

James went through the door and stared around the basement flat. The oak furniture looked new, the curtains clean, the tables and countertops spotless, but there were no possessions on display, no pictures on the walls; it was a neutral space, a place of passing through. The evening sunlight was turned away by a row of small, grimy windows level with the street beyond; all that was visible was a shifting vista of legs, shoes and bicycle wheels – a world going on outside from which James felt isolated. Everything had happened so fast.

James put down his father's backpack and turned to Elmhirst who, having locked the door, was looking through the cupboards in the small kitchenette. 'I need to telephone my aunt Charmian and let her know that I'm safe.'

'If you go out again, you may not be,' Elmhirst warned him. 'I'll let her know you're all right later tonight when I go to arrange our visas and the flights to Moscow. Don't want Intourist giving us a hard time.' He gave a grunt of satisfaction as he located the kettle, filled it, lit the gas ring with a match and put the water on to boil. Then he pulled out a tin of Ferndell coffee. 'No milk. We'll have to take it black.'

James couldn't believe how casual Elmhirst was acting. 'Who or what is Intourist?'

'Soviet state travel agency.' Elmhirst poured coffee grounds into two white mugs. 'They manage foreigners' access to Russia, make sure they don't see anything they shouldn't. Basically they are to tourism what indigestion is to a decent meal. Still, we should be able to give them the slip when we have to.'

James felt as if he were being dragged headlong into a penny dreadful. 'You say I'm a key, but to *what*? How did my father get mixed up in this?'

'Your old man's work for Vickers took him all over the world.' Slowly the blue flames from the gas ring made the kettle start to bleat. 'That would leave him well placed to meet with foreign agents. Including "talpid" types.'

'That's Latin for *mole*, isn't it?'

'And *mole* is an old word for spies. Although the Russian secret police – the NKVD, you know – use it more to mean informants within an organization. Your dad must have come into contact with one, somehow.' Elmhirst waited as the kettle was stirred to a steady whistle. 'What else can you tell me about those explosives you found?'

'They were manufactured by Blade-Rise.'

'Aha! I heard you had a run-in with Maximillian Blade himself at Christmas?'

'You could say so.' James shuddered at the memory. He turned his mind back to the present. 'Fifty pounds in each box. It said *Hexogen* on the side, I think.'

'Hexogen, yes. Also known as cyclonite.' Elmhirst lifted the kettle and joined in with its whistle. 'It's a new military explosive, more powerful and stable than TNT, and still on the secret list. A Blade-Rise lorry transporting the stuff to an ammo dump was hijacked last year . . . We found the driver's corpse but not the explosives.'

'Until today,' James said with a frown; clearly Karachan's group were as ruthless as they were well organized. He watched Elmhirst pour hot water over the grounds in the mugs, and breathed in the treacly coffee aroma. 'What do you think they're planning to do with it?'

'And why do you suppose they've been waiting for so long?' Elmhirst said. 'This plot's been years in the making. Until we found Karachan had smuggled himself into the country, everyone assumed that this big Soviet plot was hot air; ancient history – which you can bet is exactly what Karachan and his comrades wanted.' A few grounds were floating in the coffee; Elmhirst carefully sank them with drops of tap water trickled over a teaspoon, and then pushed a mug across the counter to James. When he spoke again, he shuffled awkwardly. 'I said I had intelligence that you didn't . . . Look, I won't coat it in chocolate, Bond. Back in '32, when your parents died, the high-ups at SIS were asking: was Andrew Bond in Moscow trying to blow the whistle on a Red plot . . . or was he helping to get one started?'

James felt a spike jam through his ribs. 'What?'

'I'm sorry.' Elmhirst's face was heavy as he blew on his coffee. 'After their deaths, evidence was collected from your parents' chalet in Chamonix. Evidence that was ... inconclusive.'

'But you saw what my father wrote!'

'*All can be brought down with one blow,*' Elmhirst reminded him, 'and: *a great effect on London.*'

'He was trying to warn Uncle Max!' James said hotly.

'Max was under suspicion himself. There's a theory that he got your father involved as a scapegoat.' Elmhirst put down his coffee, looking grave. 'Some thought that your mum and dad's climbing accident was a suicide pact – Andrew Bond knew he was going to be found out, and he couldn't bear the disgrace—'

'*Shut up!*' James stormed over to the door. 'I don't have to listen to this.'

Elmhirst tossed the key down on the counter. 'I know you're angry. But here's Rule One, Bond – you don't act without thinking. And you can't think straight till you know all the facts.' He gestured to the mug on the counter. 'Or till you've had a slug of good coffee.'

Shoulders slumped, James turned back to face Elmhirst. 'My father and Uncle Max would never betray their country.'

'I told you it was a theory – not that I believed it. Hear me out, all right?' Elmhirst picked up his mug. 'Max was kept under surveillance for a time, but there was no hard proof. Then he got sick, he died, and that was that. Or so we thought.'

'Did anyone ever see the postcard Father sent him?'

'Max showed me. Said it had him stumped.' Elmhirst shrugged. 'He insisted that he'd only used your father now and then to liaise with his informants abroad on routine matters. As a salesman for a well-known firm travelling around the world, he had a good cover. Apparently they'd agreed a simple substitution cipher for communications, and the fact that your dad didn't use that code in his postcard suggests two possibilities – one, the information he had was highly sensitive, or two ... he reckoned that someone was on to them.'

James felt a dismal feeling building in his chest. 'Perhaps that's why he took Mother straight to Chamonix when he got back from Russia.'

'Red agents were looking for him,' Elmhirst agreed. 'For him and perhaps for something important he'd left hidden in Moscow.'

'*What you'll find in Moscow will have a great effect,*' James quoted slowly.

'And when he wrote: *All can be brought down with a single blow,* perhaps he was talking about this Red plot – you know?' Elmhirst pulled a folded manila envelope from inside his jacket and passed it to James. 'Something that could bring the whole long-game crashing down, even after years of preparation, and clear the Bond family name into the bargain.'

James stared down at the envelope. 'And I can help find it?'

'Which must be why Karachan wanted you out of the way. Bet he was spitting when old Madame Radek swanned along and called the coppers on you.' Elmhirst smiled. 'When I ran into you last year, and saw how well you could handle yourself, even in the big leagues – well, I telephoned a few of the SIS boys who worked on the case to see how they'd feel about bringing you out to Moscow for some answers.'

'Truly?' James felt his cheeks prickle with pride. 'You didn't say anything.'

'They reckoned you were too young. I didn't want to push it.' He shrugged. 'Now, a year later, and after all that's happened today, I reckon pushing it's the only option left.'

'Pushing it all the way to Moscow,' James breathed, his heart skittering in his chest. Trouble had a knack for finding him, but here it felt as if the invitation to danger was official: partnering one of His Majesty's Secret Service officers to the austere capital of the Soviet Union! He looked over at Elmhirst. 'Chasing the answers to dangerous questions has become a bit of a habit.'

'I saw the way you were back in LA, Bond. Some habits aren't meant to be broken.' Elmhirst leaned forward, suddenly fervent. 'When you find something that stirs your soul the way danger stirs yours … something out of the ordinary that gives you purpose … keep hold, 'cos life's a long old stretch without it. Sure, you'll chase after gold and you'll chase after love – but when you get them, and keep them, the thrill goes, Bond. It rots into comfort. Danger, on the other hand … Danger won't let you catch it. You can chase it your whole life, but it'll never be done with you.'

Lost for words, James nodded slowly. He felt overwhelmed, like he was standing on a precipice. 'This is all so sudden.'

'You're damned right it is. There's a flight at nine thirty

tomorrow morning from Croydon Airport – provided I get the travel documents we'll need.'

'But Aunt Charmian's bound to hit the roof if I tell her I'm going to Moscow.'

'Without even a change of underwear!' Elmhirst chuckled. 'I'll square things with her tonight from Broadway if you like.'

'Yes, please.'

'I reckon she'll be all right. I'll be giving you my personal protection. I've been assigned to protect the King of England himself at the Opera House next week; if that doesn't impress her, what will? If it's good enough for His Majesty ... And you can telephone her yourself from the airport tomorrow.' Elmhirst grabbed the keys from the counter and unlocked the door. 'I'd best be off. Stay here, nice and quiet, and see if you can make sense of any of those documents I gave you, eh? Be sure to lock the door behind me.'

James heard the click of the door and stood in the anonymous room, lost in thought. His father had told so many tales of his travels around the world, but it was the murky intrigues of Russia that had most fired James's imagination: a land where free enterprise was frowned upon, a socialist state where the government decided what you earned, controlled what you watched and read and heard, and decreed what was good for you. Where the rich were detested and the secret police could take a man away simply on the spiteful say-so of a neighbour, never to be seen again ... Now it seemed that James was to be thrown into the frightening wellspring of these stories, and the thought of it left him thrilled – as if fate was pulling him forward, while his father's ghost, and Max's too, pushed at his back.

'I'll clear your names,' James whispered, 'for good.'

He locked the door as Elmhirst had instructed, then sat down at the counter and swigged from the mug of coffee. He slid his finger under the manila flap of the envelope and got to work.

8

Code Above the Clouds

The flight to Moscow from Croydon Airport would take two days and cost almost fifty pounds for them both – a small fortune. James sat in a comfortable leather seat aboard the sleek, gleaming all-metal Douglas DC-2. Her two 875-horsepower Wright Cyclone engines enabled her to fly at speeds of 200 miles per hour. James loved the sensation of speed and the way the DC-2 roared through the sky at 10,000 feet, riding the frequent turbulence like a wayward bronco, did not disappoint.

He hadn't slept well in the safe-house bed, replaying events in his mind, and he was doing it still. Last night Elmhirst had telephoned Charmian and reassured her that the trip was a necessary one and that James would be well looked after. He'd also advised her to stay out of town for a few days, in case anyone came seeking her nephew. James had called her from the airport on the number she'd given Elmhirst – that of an archaeologist friend in Maidstone.

Charmian sounded stoic and a little husky. 'Running headlong into danger again, then, James?'

'This time, I hope I'm running *from* it.'

'Well, this is one mystery the family needs to have solved,' she said. 'I wish you luck.'

'Is . . . that it?' James was glad in a way but also surprised. 'I was afraid you'd be cross.'

'Just come back safe. Goodbye, James.'

James had put down the receiver. 'I think she's more upset than she's letting on.'

'Course she is.' As he'd led the way over to passport control, Elmhirst had clicked his fingers. 'I forgot to say – Charmian told me she'd worked out who Henson is – you know, the fella your dad mentions. Apparently he and Max, they both had the same Latin master, Nathaniel Henson. The scourge of Eton, they used to call him . . .'

The plane jumped suddenly with fresh turbulence, and James was jogged back to the moment. *Why would Father throw in his old Latin tutor's name?* he wondered. *To draw attention to 'talpid' being Latin for* mole, *I suppose . . .*

He stared down at his father's old backpack, which he'd taken into the cabin as carry-on luggage. All last night he'd puzzled over the subtle paradoxes of the words and phrasing of both the letter and the postcard – and the extra materials Elmhirst had secured.

One was a typewritten sheet of paper, headed:

Left for collection. <u>Nash marsh!</u>
James and Cardinal Henson

Beneath the title were scattered gibberish groups of letters and numbers:

Sep 42 Ori 33 Sep 31 Occ 57 Mer 21
Ori 18 PLAMIA 47 Occ 62
Sep 59 IUNOSHEI 45 . . .

On the list went, its entries baffling and impenetrable.

What to make of it? *Nash marsh* meant 'our march' in Russian, so Elmhirst said, while *plamia* meant 'flame' and *iunoshei* meant 'youths'. There was the mysterious Henson again, apparently a cardinal this time; a cardinal was someone high up in the Roman Catholic Church ... As for what the rest of the words and numbers meant, James had no idea. But he figured that what had been left 'for collection' could mean only one thing: the evidence that could supposedly *bring down the plot with one blow* ...

Or bring down London.

Last night, in the quiet of the safe house, James had stared at his father's documents until Elmhirst came back, four hours later, under cover of the dark, with a small trunk full of fresh clothes for James ('If they don't fit, how quickly can you lose some weight?'), and entry visas and documents to give them diplomatic immunity. James could tell the agent was disappointed that Andrew Bond's papers hadn't made perfect sense at a glance, but he reassured James that the answers would surely come in the end if he could only think ... *think* ...

Jolted by fresh turbulence, James realized he'd been starting to drift off to sleep, and shook his head crossly. This experience was too exciting to doze through! He loved the engine's hard-pounding buzz through his bones, the sensation of being tossed in the air. Cheerful blue curtains framed the incredible vista through the windows: endless sea below, and a sky that could outstretch heaven. Last October KLM had entered a DC-2 just like this one in the London-to-Melbourne air race, and it had nearly won. James imagined himself a pilot, making some record-breaking flight from one glamorous, far-flung location to another, racing all comers, forcing himself and his machine to the limit as they blurred as one through the sky.

Blurred is right, James thought dourly. His eyes were still sore and stinging, and he looked around for the flight attendant. The DC-2's cabin was built to house fourteen passengers, seated in single rows of seven on either side of the wide black stripe of the aisle, but only eleven were flying today. James had no one sitting behind him while Elmhirst was seated to his left, smoking a cigarette. The stewardess, a tanned platinum blonde with eyes wider than her bee-stung mouth, walked past and he asked her to fetch him a wet flannel.

Elmhirst stubbed out his cigarette and smiled at James, but James sensed a tension behind the look. He pulled out the other two pieces of paper and placed them on his lap. The first seemed total gibberish:

READ T O K Amat victoria curam
14 − 4/376 − 11/5232 − 7/353 − 21/1 . . .

The combinations of numbers scurried over the paper on legs of black, handwritten ink; to James they meant precisely nothing. *Read to K, play with James* − the long-lost letter had instructed Max to do as much. *Polish instrument in James's case to bring it all down.*

'Your uncle never asked about this instrument case of yours?' Elmhirst enquired. James shook his head. 'Suppose he felt you'd suffered enough after . . . what happened.'

'Suppose,' James agreed. But the suffering went on. *Think!* he told himself.

You've got to find whatever Father hid so you can clear his name — and learn what Karachan and his friends are really up to . . .

The Latin James recognized, at least, even without a Henson to drum it in: it meant, *Victory favours those who take pains.*

In the early hours of the morning, over bread, cheese and beer, Elmhirst had explained that the message bearing that expression used an old intelligence trick called a book cipher. The words in the message to be sent were substituted with the location of those same words in a particular book: so '14 – 4/3' should refer to the third word of the fourth line on page 14. If a particular word could not be found in the book, then the first letters of different words could be used to spell it out. The important thing was that both the sender and the receiver of the code needed not only the same book, but the same edition, to be sure that the precise position of the words tallied.

'At SIS we spent an age trying to work out which book your old man was using,' Elmhirst went on. 'When Max was in the field, he always used the King James Bible: widely available, with chapters and verses clearly marked. But the Bible doesn't work as the key here. That's obviously not what *James's case* refers to. Whatever that message is, he must've thought it too important to trust to a regular cipher.' He smiled suddenly. 'It's a shame I've never read the Bible properly in my life. I could try praying.'

James sighed. '*Polish instrument in James's case* . . . That seems to tie in with the instruction to *play with James* in the postcard.'

'Play an instrument,' Elmhirst agreed. 'Or polish it, like the old genie lamp in the stories . . .'

'Perhaps the French memory is a song?' James said with sudden inspiration. 'A song I loved when I was little?'

Elmhirst stared at him. 'Where did you keep your gramophone records?'

'With my books, on a—' He stopped dead. '*James's case*. What if it's a *book*case!'

'And the key is something you kept there – the liner notes on a record sleeve maybe? Or a book about music?' Elmhirst shifted forward in his seat. 'It would have to be something he could get hold of easily, either in Moscow or Chamonix – if it was a different copy, the position of the words wouldn't match and the code couldn't be cracked.'

'My old bookcase was crammed with books and 78s. But they sold our flat back in 1932, and Aunt Charmian got me different furniture.'

'Think, James.' Elmhirst leaned closer. 'Try to list the ones you remember. The ones your dad would remember. One your uncle Max could've read to someone called K, or Kay, or whose name started with K . . .'

'*Kidnapped* by Robert Louis Stevenson?' James suggested. 'That starts with a K. I had a record of someone reading bits from *The Water Babies* . . . there was an adaptation of *Dr Jekyll and Mr Hyde* that was much more exciting than the original . . .' Then inspiration sparked and James sat up straight. 'Hold on. What if it's not *Read to K*? What if . . . what if it's, *Read T.O.K.*!'

'I'll bite. T.O.K.?'

'*The Trumpeter of Krakow!* It's an American novel set in Poland. Father brought it back from New York in 1930; it had won some big book prize, the Newbery Medal, so he thought I'd like it.'

'*T.O.K. – Trumpeter. Of. Krakow.*' Elmhirst nodded slowly. 'That's your musical instrument, James. A *Polish* one!'

'And that line in the postcard about the broken note!' James felt gooseflesh prickle his arms. 'The trumpeter never finishes his warning fanfare; he's killed suddenly in the middle of playing the note.'

'It fits.' Elmhirst's smile spread slowly. 'A big prize-winning book would have a good shelf life – and a good chance of getting into travel bookshops.' He took a deep puff on his cigarette and stubbed it out, as the stewardess returned with the wet towel for James. 'Good work, Bond. When we stop in Sweden, I'll speak to SIS and see if we can track down a copy.'

The aeroplane stopped at Amsterdam and Copenhagen before landing at Stockholm at three fifty p.m. The journey would not resume until nine a.m. the next morning, when they'd catch a flight with Aeroflot, the Russian state airline.

Elmhirst had booked them rooms at the Hotel Hellstens Malmgard at Södermalm, in the heart of the Swedish capital. It was a converted eighteenth-century mansion, with sash windows bright white against walls of olive and ochre. It had been built around a quiet cobbled courtyard with an old, gnarled chestnut tree that sent branches looming over the windows of James's small but comfortable room.

Elmhirst had gone out to contact his superiors with James's new intelligence. Restless, James left his room and, taking his father's backpack, walked down the road to the sprawling green oasis of the park at Zinkensdamm. The sun felt warm on his skin. A wide blue channel of water stretched out before him, serene and beautiful, and a breeze riffled his dark hair. It was all a lot more calm and attractive than the bank of the Thames, but James decided he much preferred the grime, grit and thrust of London.

But both here and there are a far cry from old Krakow. James cast his mind back to the book, in case he remembered any more clues. It was a historical novel, as he recalled, about a family fleeing from the Ukraine to settle in the old Polish capital. The story explored the folk tale of a trumpeter in a high tower who was sworn to play a salute every hour on the hour, day or night. When an army of Tartars invaded Krakow, the trumpeter raised the alarm with his playing, and continued through the chaos until cut down by a Tartar arrow through the heart, the fanfare dying on his lips.

Like the trumpeter and his fanfare, James had never reached the end of the story. He'd left it on the shelf, despite his parents' encouragement, and now felt a deep pang of guilt and melancholy. *I must've disappointed them.* The thought of the old trumpeter, raising his desperate alarm, but ignored by an ungrateful child, sat heavily in his head.

Even so, after so many years of feeling emptiness and loss without his parents, at this moment James felt closer to his father than perhaps he ever had. It was a feeling that brought a balm to his soul that made some of the horrors he'd lived through seem just a little easier.

'You're not a traitor, Father,' James said out loud. He was damn well going to prove it.

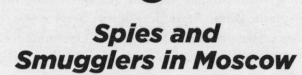

9
Spies and Smugglers in Moscow

The odyssey into Red territory continued early the next morning as James and Elmhirst were hefted through the iron-grey skies in a Junkers Ju 52. They arrived in Riga just after noon for a fuelling stop and for some passengers to disembark, then flew on into Russian airspace, landing at Velikiye Luki mid-afternoon before reaching Moscow's Khodynka Aerodrome just after six in the evening.

'Take these,' Elmhirst told James, palming him something as he undid his seatbelt. 'Stick them down your sock.'

James looked down at a roll of banknotes – roubles and US dollars – then back at Elmhirst. 'Spending money?'

'Sorry to turn you into a smuggler on top of everything else.' Elmhirst made to scratch his ankle, and pushed a similar wad of notes down into his shoe. 'There are strict limits on how much currency you can take into Russia,' he explained.

'The rouble can't be exchanged for foreign money – the state made it illegal, to protect the economy: they're investing billions in industry, and can't afford the value of the rouble to go down on the foreign markets—' Perhaps he saw James's eyes starting to glaze over because he grinned and broke off. 'All you need to know is that in Russia, money talks like nowhere else. There's pretty much no one we can't bribe with hard currency . . .'

James nodded and felt a warm rush of adrenalin. 'What happens if we're caught?' he said quietly. 'If they find out you're with the British Secret Intelligence Service—'

'I'm on a fake passport,' Elmhirst said. 'Operating secretly.'

'Are there other British agents here in Moscow who can help us?'

Elmhirst gave a humourless laugh. 'You really have no idea how underfunded our section is. Spies cost money, and most of our focus is in Germany right now. Out here, a junior at the British Embassy in Smolenskaya bribes clerks on the Congress of Soviets for information and pays local villains to report on what the secret police are up to. But he knows we're coming; we'll see what help he can scare up for us.'

Nerves jangling as he neared the customs desk, James tried to adopt the same stooped shoulders and weary expression as most of the travellers in the airport. As it turned out, customs went through his luggage and made him turn out his pockets, but nothing more. The visas Elmhirst had procured passed muster, both with the customs officers and the state representative from Intourist, who not only looked like a bad-tempered boar, but also sweated and stank like one. Heaven forbid that foreign tourists might make their own way through

Moscow! The state controlled all, including the impressions that foreigners would take back to their own countries . . . and, according to Elmhirst, the most important impression was that the Bolshevik revolution had turned Russia into a socialist paradise.

The man from Intourist had their luggage transferred into a shining black GAZ-A motor car, which he proceeded to drive for them. To James the car looked much like a Ford Model A, with only the marque badge standing out as different, but the female guide accompanying them to the hotel (as thin as a rake, with long dark hair and a sour expression) assured them that this car was far superior, having been built in the fine Russian city of Gorky. 'The smoke of chimneys is the breath of Soviet Russia,' she declaimed.

Smiling awkwardly, James turned to Elmhirst, who was slumped beside him in the back seat, his fedora pulled down over his eyes, and lowered his voice. 'Why are they taking us to the hotel in person?'

'To make sure we check in, and that our stories check *out*.'

'And will they?' James knew Elmhirst's cover story – '*I'm an international businessman who regularly visits, you're my nephew and possible apprentice*' – but it sounded thin to him. 'I know you didn't have much time to set it up—'

'I've filed corroborating papers in the usual places they search. Just relax.' Elmhirst tipped his head back to look at James from under the brim, spoke more loudly. 'Intourist makes sure that foreign visitors receive free transport to their accommodation, the services of guides and interpreters, escorted visits to museums and tourist attractions . . .'

'Keeping us on a lead,' James realized.

'I am not certain of what you speak,' the female guide said coldly. 'With foreign espionage committed daily, for your own safety as well as that of our citizens, precautions must be taken.'

'You take all the precautions you like,' Elmhirst told her. 'We're glad of the care you take of us.'

Of course we are, thought James.

It took almost an hour and a half to reach the centre of Moscow. James stared out of the car window, marvelling at the sheer size of the crowded city. They drove along highways like great grey arteries, pumping cars and motor buses and trams, each thickly covered in dust, all over the city, to squares and canals, across new bridges lined with grand buildings, past wide open parks and fine embankments ornamenting the river; all of them symbols of the city's greatness and strength. And yet to James, much of Moscow seemed to be a giant building site. He saw crumbling townhouses, fenced off in mid-demolition, standing cheek-by-jowl with modern apartment blocks still in the awkward embrace of scaffolding and tarpaulins.

Their guide in the back seemed mindful of what they saw. 'We rebuild Moscow now,' she announced, 'as the model for proletarians and communists throughout the world, who will be inspired to follow it. Our capital's glory will reflect the regime that erected it.'

'I see,' James said politely. But everywhere he turned he saw people queuing on the busy pavements for newspapers, for food from market stalls, out through the doors of shops and stores.

Their sweating driver called from the front: 'They wait in line for the latest Soviet goods. They are proud of what their country produces.'

'Most of them won't even know what they're queuing for,' Elmhirst muttered. 'They see others lining up and worry they'll miss out.'

The car turned onto Moscow's steep main drag. 'This is the *ulitsa Gorkogo*, or Gorky Street,' the guide intoned, 'named for the great revolutionary writer, Maxim Gorky.'

'Last time I was here they called it Tverskaia,' said Elmhirst.

The guide smiled thinly. 'With the past swept away we build a strong future in its place.'

Shouldn't the future grow out of the past? James wondered.

Their destination finally came into sight: the opulent, over-ornamented sprawl of the National Hotel, which towered over its single- or two-storeyed neighbours like a mother hen over her chicks. It looked more like a museum than a hotel, James decided, decorated with natural stone and stucco, marble and stained glass. The frivolous frontage was topped by a dynamic socialist mural showing cranes, pylons and a woman in a tractor: a tribute to the Soviet economy's might.

'Can I telephone Aunt Charmian?' James wondered. 'Tell her we made it?'

'Of course!' Elmhirst smiled, but then lowered his voice to a whisper. 'Don't even think of using the telephone out here. Hopeless service and the censor's always listening in. They'll cut off your conversation if they sense any funny business.' He must've noticed James's disappointed look, for his tone softened. 'You can call from the British Embassy when we visit tomorrow. Though even that's not guaranteed clean.'

The guide regarded them coldly as they conducted their muttered conversation. 'Do you require any further information?' she broke in.

75

'I don't think so,' Elmhirst said. 'But if anything occurs, we can ask you tomorrow on our tour of Red Square, can't we?'

'Red Square?' James queried.

'The centre of Moscow,' Elmhirst explained. 'Where you'll find the Kremlin, Lenin's tomb—'

'Yes, but why are we going there?'

'Since you may be working out here, nephew,' Elmhirst said heavily, 'I thought you'd like to get a feel for the place.'

'Oh, I would.' James nodded eagerly. 'Thank you.'

'You will enjoy it,' the guide said firmly.

James and Elmhirst followed her inside the ostentatious hotel and across the mosaic floor of the lobby. The man at the desk spent many minutes carefully checking the visitors from England into adjoining rooms, and the Intourist guide went away, apparently satisfied that her charges were staying put.

'Telegram for you, Mr Elmhirst,' the man at the desk announced, passing over a white envelope.

Elmhirst stuffed the telegram into his jacket pocket and winked at James. 'That'll be from my *SIS*-ter.'

James's heart jumped. *A translation of the ciphertext?*

Elmhirst glanced around the lobby then back to the man at the desk. 'Er, the lift . . . ?'

'The elevator does not work, sir.' The man signalled to a young man at the concierge's desk. 'Allow my colleague here to assist you.'

The porter was scrawny, with a moustache like a sick caterpillar, but insisted on taking all three of their bags before leading them up the marble staircase. Fine furniture and large vases littered the landings, and James wondered if the decorations had been seized from Russian aristocrats and left here to encourage decadent foreigners to consider the follies of their ways. There was a chemical stink of insecticide that grew stronger the further they went along the carpeted corridor. James took in the dull pastoral paintings on the wall, in their tarnished frames; he felt they were present less to entice the eye than to hold up the wallpaper.

The porter stopped outside a white oak door and put down the bags. Suddenly a man burst out of the doorway opposite and smashed the porter face-first into the door. He was paunchy, dark and bearded; James recognized him at once, and swore.

It was Karachan from the Mechta Academy.

Karachan grabbed the young man by the shoulders and threw him at James. James glimpsed the porter's terrified bloody face flying into his own, then he was down in a tumble of limbs, dropping his backpack as he fell. He heard a terrific thump of impact close by, struggled out from beneath the groaning porter and saw that Karachan had Elmhirst by the throat, up against the wall. Elmhirst's eyes were rolling back in his head and his breath sounded thick in his throat.

Before James could even blurt out a warning, Karachan produced a flick-knife and, catching the sharp point in the lining of Elmhirst's jacket, jerked the blade upwards, ripping the fabric so that the contents of his pocket spilled onto the floor.

He's found out about the telegram, James realized. *About Father's clues to what the Russians are doing.*

James grabbed for the envelope, but Karachan stamped a heavy boot down on his wrist. James shouted and snatched his hand away. But as Karachan stooped to grab the telegram, Elmhirst slumped over on top of it, apparently out cold. At the same time James kicked out with his foot and knocked the knife from Karachan's grip.

The porter was crawling away, screaming for help. A door opened and a man in a dressing gown peered out, frowning.

Karachan didn't hesitate. He scooped up James's backpack, then turned and raced away along the corridor.

'No! Give that back!' James scrambled up as the man in the dressing gown came out to help. James pointed him towards Elmhirst and the porter, then sprinted after Karachan. *The lifts are out of order*, James recalled. *Perhaps I can knock him down the stairs and grab the backpack—*

But Karachan clearly had other ideas. He stood in front of the open doors to the lift shaft, pulling on black leather gloves. With the gloves in place, he hurled the backpack into the abyss.

'No!' James shouted. He had precious few things to remember his father by as it was; no one was taking that from him!

With unexpected agility, Karachan jumped into the shaft, grabbed hold of the lift's winching cable with his gauntleted hands and started to slide down like a fireman on his pole. With a muttered curse and no hesitation, James leaped after him. He gasped as the cable's thick metal twine bit into his bare palms. Vibrations whipped through it as Karachan descended the wire, hand over hand into the blackness.

James knew he had no choice. Blood roaring in his temples, he wrapped his forearms around the cable and dropped, gritting his teeth as friction seared his flesh. His heart seemed to jump into his throat; he was as good as falling.

Then his feet crashed down onto Karachan's broad shoulders, jarring the big man loose. Triumph and fear flared through James's senses as he lost his grip too and plummeted through space. He heard a metallic crash echo around the lift shaft, and a moment later he'd landed hard on something that rang like steel under the impact. *The top of the lift car*, he realized in a daze. The backpack must have landed here, ready for Karachan to collect. With fresh desperation, James groped for it blindly with stinging fingers.

But what he found was Karachan. Pain screamed through his head as a boot connected with his cheekbone, sent him rolling over the lift's roof. Something long and hard-edged dug into his side. *The cover to the inspection hatch*, James thought dimly. *The way inside the lift through the roof.*

He kicked out blindly, hoping to land a lucky blow. Yellow light bled up into the shaft from the lift car as Karachan yanked up the inspection cover. Lit from below, his coronet of hair and dark beard gave him the look of the devil, wild shadows dancing about him as he threw the backpack down inside the lift car.

James scissored his legs around Karachan's left leg and then twisted hard. The big man lost his balance, tumbled against the wall. James slithered down into the lift car, landing awkwardly on the metal floor. He looked up, panting for breath, and saw Karachan jump through the hatch, ready to use James's ribs for a soft landing.

Desperately James flung himself to one side and the huge, heavy boots slammed into the floor, missing him by inches. Without hesitation, Karachan stooped for the backpack – but James kicked it away. The big man raised the back of his hand and tried to swat him as he would a fly.

Instead of recoiling, James fought instinct and, leaping to his feet, lunged past Karachan, ducking under the blow. From behind, James closed his forearm around Karachan's neck. Karachan made a thick, choking, spluttering sound, but James clung on, supporting his chokehold by grabbing his right fist with his left and squeezing it towards him, intensifying the pressure on his assailant's neck.

Gasping, Karachan pushed hard against the lift doors, trying to crush James against the metal wall. But James would not let go, shouting in anger to give himself strength.

Suddenly the doors were wrenched open with a protesting screech. Two porters flanked a startled concierge, who broke into angry Russian. Thrown off balance by the opening doors, Karachan managed to shake James free and made a final grab for the backpack, but one of the straps had caught around James's ankle. With a groan of frustration, Karachan gave up on it and charged through the three hotel workers like a wing-forward making for the goal line, demolishing his opposition.

The concierge ordered his porters after Karachan in pursuit, then loomed angrily over James, who lay exhausted on the floor, desperate for breath.

'Get away from me,' James snarled, clutching the backpack to his chest. The concierge was gesticulating in outrage, harsh-sounding words bursting from his lips, when another figure ran up.

James closed his eyes, fearing the worst and trying to summon strength enough to face it, when he heard a familiar voice: 'Hold up, Bond. You're all right now.'

'Elmhirst?' James's eyes snapped open. 'Thank God . . .' He watched as the agent put an arm around the concierge's shoulders and steered him to one side, speaking Russian in a low voice and tucking a small roll of banknotes into the man's top pocket. The concierge looked doubtful, but only for a moment – he turned, clapped his hands, and ushered the gawping onlookers away.

As Elmhirst turned back to him, James got wearily to his knees and then to his feet.

'You all right, son? What the hell were you thinking, taking the plunge like that?'

'I just couldn't lose this backpack,' James clutched it close as Elmhirst guided him away across the lobby. 'Are you OK?'

'Karachan cracked my skull against the wall and out I sparked.' Elmhirst grimaced. 'Reckon I'm getting old.'

'I can't believe he's come all this way after us,' James said.

'He was after that translation of your old man's code. Question is, how did he know about it?'

James nodded slowly. 'And how did he know where we were staying, right down to the floor?'

'SIS sent the telegram with the translation via the British Embassy here in Moscow.' Elmhirst's eyes were flint. 'Someone there must have passed on the information. It's the only answer.'

'The Russians have an agent in our embassy?' James felt his eyes widen. 'So if we do need assistance over here—'

'We can't risk it. Can't have the enemy knowing what we're up to. The Embassy is off-limits – as of now.'

'Then ... we're on our own.' James felt an uneasy excitement. 'Let's look at the telegram, see what it says?'

'Not out here, conspicuous as hell.' Elmhirst nodded towards an oak door. 'Casually, together with a couple of large drinks at the American Bar.'

'I suppose it's safer to stay in public sight,' James said grudgingly.

'Well, yes. But why d'you think we're staying at the National, Bond?' Elmhirst brushed down his ruined jacket. 'It's one of only two places in the whole of Moscow where you can get French vermouth, Scotch whisky and Gordon's gin, even if you have to pay through the nose. And the old girl from Odessa who runs the bar knows the night manager pretty well, if you know what I mean. She'll be able to get us into a new room without going through official channels.' He looked at James again, and his demeanour softened a touch. 'It's all about who you know, Bond. Who you know, what they can do for you, and how you can get them on your side.'

James raised an eyebrow and almost smiled despite himself. 'And the large drink?'

'Oh, yes.' Elmhirst clapped him on the back. 'Yes, Bond, it's definitely all about the large drink.'

10
Riddles Within Riddles

James sat impatiently on a couch in the National's American Bar while Elmhirst worked his charms on Elizaveta, the lady from Odessa: a buxom woman in late middle-age squeezed into a cocktail dress of silks and chiffon in midnight blue. The same colour had been daubed about her eyes, which peeped out with forced gaiety through a straggle of blonde curls. Elmhirst reached into his inside jacket pocket and handed her a neat stack of banknotes, which she counted with the casual skill of a croupier.

The bar, half filled with hard-bitten men in suits, was just how James pictured an old-fashioned gentlemen's club. There were lots of high-backed leather armchairs, ornamental tables with crystal ashtrays, an enormous marble fireplace gaping from scarlet wallpaper. But the opulence was faded, there was a smell of cabbage behind the expensive cigar smoke, the ashtrays were chipped, the chairs had buttons missing from the upholstery.

'Come on, Elmhirst,' James muttered. He had wound the straps of his father's backpack around his forearm, glancing about to make sure no one was taking undue notice, wary of anyone walking through the door. He was itching to know what the telegram had said before anything else could happen.

Finally Elmhirst joined him with two drinks: a Scotch on the rocks for himself, and a brandy for James. 'There. You've had a shock. Get some of that down you.'

James sipped, wincing at the fiery taste but grateful for the steadying warmth in his chest.

'It's cost me enough, but I've sorted out accommodation,' Elmhirst said quietly. 'Our room won't be on the public record.'

'Can't we just find a different hotel?' James asked.

'If we check out of the National, Intourist will get to hear and we'll have the NKVD taking an interest.'

'The secret police ...' James trailed off as Elmhirst pulled the torn and crumpled envelope out of his pocket. 'My father's coded message.'

'Part of that "further correspondence" he mentioned in his postcard back in 1932,' said Elmhirst, pulling the telegram from the envelope and scanning its contents. 'Only Max never got the message because, with the letter buried in the backpack in the Aiguilles Rouges, he had no clue which book to use to transcribe it.' Elmhirst drained his Scotch and slid the paper across to James. He signalled to a waiter for another drink. 'Seems that for every riddle we solve, we get another.'

A slow shiver prickled along James's spine as he read:

LADY WITH VEIL RISING THROUGH RANKS. KNOWS
WAY TO SMUGGLE LIVE BODIES AND MATERIALS

TO ENGLAND IN TIMBER CARGO. SLEEPERS.
WORKFORCE. FOUR POINTS AROUND LONDON.
SUSPICIOUS SIS I LEFT CHAPTER AND VERSE
MOSCOW BURIED IN JAMES. YOUR EYES ONLY.

James read it over and over. 'The lady with the veil. No prizes for guessing who that is.'

'I've read the Corps of Intelligence Police files.' Elmhirst welcomed his second Scotch with an appreciative sip. 'This case really is personal for you, eh?'

James nodded absently, dwelling now on dark memories of the Russian agent he'd come up against last summer: La Velada, the woman working to bring Great Britain to her knees, and who'd come closer to killing him than anyone alive. He'd last seen her disappearing across the ocean off Cuba in a motor yacht, but to think that his father had known her too, years before . . . Had she realized the connection in Cuba? James pictured the bony, gloating figure, her face in darkness behind her veil, watching him like a cat watches prey: *The NKVD have agents all over the world. I thought you'd be aware of that, Bond . . .*

'I don't know about live bodies and materials,' James managed finally, 'but she had the means to send weapons to England hidden in shipments of timber.'

Elmhirst drank some more of his Scotch. '*Suspicious SIS.* Sounds like La Velada realized your dad had made contact with a mole in their organization, and was feeding the intelligence to Max.'

'Four points – could that be a reference to the four buildings around Millbank that Kalashnikov designed: Mechta Academy and the others?'

'It could.' Elmhirst nodded slowly. 'Yes, it definitely could.'

James tapped a finger on the telegram. 'What does *Sleepers* mean here?'

'Agents in long-term deep cover. *Moles*. Men and women given false identities so they can live ordinary lives in another country, securing useful positions of power, ready to act for the motherland when the call comes.' Elmhirst leaned forward suddenly. 'Know what I reckon, Bond? I reckon your father left some very sensitive info in Russia because he believed it would be found if he tried to take it out with him.' He took a large slug of his drink and smacked his lips. 'He wasn't a pro in the spying game – Lord knows, a pro wouldn't use three or four different codes in one report – so he needed a real agent, Max, to come and pick up the stuff and smuggle it out.'

'So now all we have to do is find it,' James agreed. 'You must be right about Karachan: if he's come after us in person, he must really be worried about what we'll find. A way to *bring it all down* . . .'

'So, if chapter and verse really are *buried in James*, James needs to unearth 'em, and fast.'

'He does.' James decided he needed another nip of brandy, though he grimaced at the taste. 'Why does Russia want to attack Britain, anyway? I thought they were trying to arrange peace treaties.'

'All governments try to arrange peace treaties – gives them longer to get ready for war, doesn't it?' Elmhirst signalled to Elizaveta for a third drink, and she smiled and nodded. 'Right then, "nephew", here's a quick introduction to Anglo-Soviet relations. You know that communism is the opposite of capitalism? Well, in the late 1920s we caught the Soviets trying to foment a communist revolution in Britain. We broke off diplomatic relations before they could overthrow our decadent way of life.' As if to illustrate, he drained the last of his second glass. 'Thing is, now, in the '30s, the biggest threats to the Soviet Union are Nazi Germany and Japan — both powerful, both aggressive and both eyeing up her territory. Russia needs allies if she's going to stand a chance of keeping her enemies' paws off — only most of the British cabinet would sooner see the Soviet Union taken down than help her stand. Stalin's convinced we'll sign a treaty with France and Germany that'll let Hitler expand the Nazi empire to the east without objection.'

James shuddered at the idea; he'd seen at first hand the kind of atrocities the Nazis were capable of. 'So the way to be sure that Britain won't sign that treaty is to weaken her, attack her capital city ... ?'

'And invade her,' Elmhirst agreed. 'Establishing a Soviet satellite state in the west of Europe, so that Russia has power enough to stand up to anyone.'

'And the key to stopping this ... comes down to ... me?' James stared at his half-empty glass, and wondered if it might ever seem half full again. 'I don't even know where to start.'

'With good, hard, positive thinking, James.' Elmhirst smiled as the waiter brought his third glass of whisky. 'Or good, hard, positive drinking, for a start. We'll get some dinner down our necks, a bottle of something strong, and snore the night away till it's time for our trip to Red Square — or until someone else comes after us, whichever's first.' He snatched up the telegram and stuffed it in his pocket, then clapped James on the shoulder. 'Welcome to the job, Bond.'

★   ★   ★

Half an hour later, James found that an air of weary resignation hung over the National's dining room, despite the apparent grandeur of the buffet on offer. Upon entering, he was confronted with an ornate arrangement of fancy dishes: sturgeon on a silver platter, omelette served between lobster tails with fresh caviar, little ramekins holding *oeufs en cocotte* with a chanterelle mushroom purée. Ranged behind them James noted quail, grouse and woodcock on serving plates dressed with neat salad garnishes. And yet behind the extravagant concoctions the room held an odour of disinfectant, and dead cockroaches made indents in the thick pile carpet like black bulletholes. A parade of wines in red, white and palest rose queued across the long table, but after his chest-warming brandy, James satisfied himself with a glass of Narzhan mineral water.

Just past midnight, after a dinner eaten largely in silence, Elmhirst led the way to their unofficial room on the fifth floor. Whatever leverage he'd used on the lady from Odessa, it had worked: the room held a view to brag about, straight down the street to Red Square – the heart of Moscow, of the whole country. And just beyond, the neighbouring Kremlin, the 'fortress within a city' that was the seat of Soviet power, its defensive towers crowned with great red metal stars that dwarfed the golden pinpricks in the sky above.

James pulled out his father's little statuette of St Basil's Cathedral, which, after its rough ride in the stolen backpack, now had a crack zigzagging up its middle. James traced the faultline with a finger, and found that in any case his souvenir did the true structure no justice. There it stood, unearthly and majestic, with the smoke cloud from a power plant blooming through the moonlight behind it, an outrageous, truly beautiful building.

'Built by Ivan the Terrible,' Elmhirst remarked. 'Legend has it that he ordered the architect to be blinded afterwards, so he could never build another like it.'

James snorted softly. 'I suppose Ivan didn't get his nickname from pressing wild flowers.'

'Not unless he was really bad at it.'

Elmhirst decreed that an oil lamp in the bathroom should be their only source of light at night, so that to any watching eyes outside, the room would appear uninhabited. While Elmhirst prepared for bed, James lit the lamp with matches from a half-empty book he found by the ashtray. He lay down on the chaise longue and, by the light of the summer night sky, peered at the fragments of his father's past, trying to imagine the intent behind the words. He wished he had some way of getting hold of Pritpal, an old friend from Eton who was a genius when it came to complex word puzzles like this. But who knew where Pritpal was now? And besides, his father was stating clearly that James himself held the key to the mystery.

So why don't I know what the hell it is?

Henson, the old Latin master ... a mole ... 'French memory' ... He shuddered as he thought of La Velada, turned his thoughts from her to the souvenir of St Basil's Cathedral. Why that landmark in particular? Had it simply been meant as a gift? In which case, why had it not been given to him? Then there was the Mechta Academy building, and the three others designed by Kalashnikov that could make up the *four points around London*. James remembered the high explosives stashed in the bunker beneath the school . . . where might they have been taken now?

Still turning over the tangle in his mind, James fell asleep, fully clothed.

Spears of sunlight pricked through the windows as the sputter of traffic on Gorky Street below rose to a steady drone. James parted his grit-filled eyes, wondering where the hell he was. When he remembered, he closed them again and offered a silent prayer to anyone listening that he might do what they'd come here to do as quickly as possible, and get back to England.

Agent Elmhirst was lying on the bed, also still fully dressed, right down to his boots. His breathing was hoarse, just edging on a snore. James got up from the couch slowly, quietly, to use the bathroom. In one smooth movement, Elmhirst rolled over, snatched a handgun from the bedside table and brought it to bear on James.

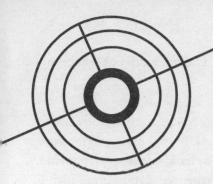

11

A Short Tour of Carnage

With a jolt of fear James threw his hands in the air. 'It's me! It's me!'

'Holy hell, Bond.' Elmhirst lowered his Colt New Service Revolver and took a shaky breath. 'Don't sneak around like that. After the attack last night, I might've blown your head off.'

James put down his hands, trembling with relief. 'Where'd you find the gun? You never smuggled it past customs?'

'Nah. Came with the room, didn't it?' Elmhirst sat down, replaced the revolver on the table and rubbed his eyes. 'Our lady from Odessa downstairs. Generous with her favours.'

'I'm glad you weren't as generous with your trigger finger.'

'Me?' With trembling hands Elmhirst took a small flask from under his pillow and swigged whatever was inside. 'I'll only murder someone if they really deserve it.'

James looked away, a little disquieted by Elmhirst's drinking; it could hardly be healthy, but then, neither was the man's profession. 'Does that include me if I can't work out where my father hid his information?'

'Don't try me.'

Turning to his trunk, James picked out fresh clothes: dark-blue DAKS trousers with pleated fronts, and a light-blue Oxford shirt with short sleeves. 'I'm looking forward to seeing St Basil's Cathedral for real this morning.'

Elmhirst yawned and stretched. 'The Intourist car will probably be late, or break down, or take us to Leningrad instead, but still . . .'

'A ride's a ride.' James joined in the forced joviality, but ached with the scars of the struggle last night, especially his raw palms. 'When is it coming?'

'Seven thirty, according to the itinerary. We've got time for breakfast first.'

After last night's late dinner James didn't feel hungry, but as he got dressed he reflected that this could be a long day. The DAKS that Elmhirst had picked up for him were a new and expensive design with an adjustable waistband; no need for belt or braces, and small rubber pads sewn inside held his shirt comfortably in place. He looked himself over in a mirror on the wall; the tailored fit and fine material made James feel older and more confident.

After slipping on his leather brogues and stowing his passport and visa in the backpack – in Soviet Russia it was a serious offence not to carry these at all times – James joined Elmhirst at the door, ready to leave. Elmhirst drew his gun and covered James surreptitiously as he moved slowly, alertly, outside. The corridor was quiet and gloomy, as well it might be at this hour of the morning. With no assassins in the laundry cupboard and no thieves set to pounce from the stairwell,

James and his unorthodox guardian left their room and proceeded down to breakfast.

The spread in the dining room had been replaced, but the dead cockroaches had not. James and Elmhirst were among the first to peruse the offerings: black bread; huge, stodgy bowls of porridge; open sandwiches thick with butter and cheese or sausage; a tray of small cottage-cheese dumplings called *syrniki* and, James's eventual choice, scrambled eggs with Bologna sausage and dill. Accompanying the food was thick treacly coffee or black tea taken with lemon and sugar. James stuck to the former.

'Almost seven thirty.' Elmhirst rose to his feet. 'Suppose we should wait in the lobby for our driver to show.' He led the way through to the cavernous marble space. 'Whatever you do, don't mention our little troubles last night. Act like nothing's happened—' He stopped, gripped James's arm and pulled him back behind a floral display on a marble pedestal. 'Uh-oh. Looks like trouble.'

Two men had entered the hotel. One had a long rodent-like face and a pronounced overbite, while his companion was hard-faced with a broken nose and short black hair, pulling smoke from a cheroot. They were gazing around, as if looking for someone.

James felt a shiver of dread anticipation. 'Who are they?'

'No one you want to meet.' Elmhirst stuffed the telegram into his hand. 'I'll distract them – you slip past and get outside. Lose yourself.'

'But I can help you—'

'Take an order for once in your life, Bond.' Elmhirst was calm, stony-faced. 'No heroics, all right? If the things we've found out fall into their hands . . .'

'I understand.' James held himself ready for flight as Elmhirst broke cover and strolled airily across the lobby towards the men. At the same time, gripping his father's pack, James circled round behind them, back to the wall. Elmhirst greeted both men in Russian, shaking their hands. What was he up to?

Perhaps Karachan sent these men here for me, James thought.

Heart starting to hammer, he slipped quickly out through the National's doors and into the bright morning sunshine. A black Ford Model A – or rather, NAZ-A, given the stand-in Russian marque – was parked just outside, its engine idling. *Is that the Intourist car?*

A scream from the entrance made James turn round. The rat-faced man that Elmhirst had greeted was reeling back through the doors, hands flailing at his blood-soaked throat. A gunshot followed, loud as a bell peal; James couldn't see what had happened for the terrified people swarming through the doors. Automatically he started through the throng to get to Elmhirst in the lobby.

But then someone gripped him by the shoulders and pulled him back. Caught off-guard, he started to struggle but found himself swept into the back seat of the black car, his face forced down against the cracked leather.

'Hey!' James shouted as, with a screech of tyres on cobblestones, the car reversed sharply away into the thin traffic on Gorky Street. 'What are you—?'

A man's voice, accent thick and English stilted, rasped into his ear. 'You come with us . . . You not hurt.'

James's thoughts were racing. Elmhirst's warning, then the man with the slit throat, the gunshot, now abduction . . . These could only be Karachan's thugs – or agents who answered to a higher authority. For all the bravado, James had recognized real fear on Elmhirst's face as he'd gone to meet the sinister men, to try to keep James from them. Why? He knew that James could handle himself, but what had happened in there? Who'd taken the gunshot?

These questions buzzed above the roar of the engine as the car thundered along the main road. Where was he being taken? It didn't matter, James decided. He would never arrive. Slowly, carefully, he twisted round and tried to sit up straight. The man who'd bundled him inside, with a face like a carbuncle that had formed around a bushy moustache, didn't hinder him; he had a cigarette to his mouth and his thumb to a lighter. It didn't produce a flame first time, but for a split-second the man glanced down to check.

That was all the time James needed. He swung his fist upwards. The man took the blow to the jaw, jerked back and bashed his head against the window. James punched him again in the face. A red split opened over his right cheekbone and his eyes flickered shut.

The man driving started shouting in angry Russian, swerving hard right onto another street. James got on all fours in the foot well, facing the rear passenger door. The car had slowed a little for the bend, but as he pulled down on the handle and pushed open the door, the road below was still a terrifying blur of grey and black.

James didn't hesitate. With his father's pack on his back, he brought his elbows together, kept his chin tucked into his chest to protect his head and then launched himself out with his right shoulder closest to the ground. There was a terrifying moment of flight, then the screaming pain of impact. The air was punched from his lungs as he rolled over and over, his senses assaulted by the spin and screech of traffic, the cries of onlookers, by the thumps and scrapes of his own body as he rocketed over the asphalt – and then smashed into a newspaper stand. An old man and his chair were sent sprawling across the pavement, the papers flapping madly through the air like birds with broken wings.

James was too winded even to shout out; he looked down at his trembling hands, knuckles oil-black and bloody, badly grazed. His shoulders felt raw beneath the backpack, his knees throbbed as he tried to get to his feet and recover his wits. A crowd was gathering to help the old man, pointing and staring. James saw that the black car had screeched to a halt and was reversing back towards him.

Staggering, his legs barely supporting him, James managed to flee. Where the hell was he? How far away was the National? If the police caught him now, who knew how long he'd be detained. James tried to force his body onward, but his legs sent only shooting pains in response. Even at this hour of the morning the street was busy with queues and commuters. James barged his way through, knocking aside anyone in his path, calling apologies until he realized his foreign words and English accent were arousing too much interest – and anger. He cut through a quieter alleyway, too narrow for the black car to come down, and then ran as fast as he could, dog-legging through the grimy streets and passages.

Lungs tight, breaths scrubbing at his throat, James eventually stopped running, leaned against a wall and stared about wildly. He couldn't make head or tail of the street names or signs in the Cyrillic alphabet, didn't know where he was or which way to go.

Then his frantic gaze fell and fixed on a dark, bearded figure watching him from the window of a burgundy saloon: Andrei Karachan. The car door swung open and Karachan got out, stalking swiftly through the crowds towards him.

James swore, turned and forced himself to run again. Up ahead he could hear the iron song of a tram. The red-and-yellow cars came into view, hauling themselves along between cobbles and cables ... Surely this was his best chance for escape? The tram trundled over a junction into another street, accelerating onto the straight with a thickening whine, and James sprinted after it, this fresh focus lending him strength and purpose.

No use. The tram was moving too fast, pulling away.

A young man in a cap rode a three-wheeled delivery bicycle out of a side street, right into James's path. For a moment James feared an attack and skidded to a stop, panting wildly. Then he realized that the bike carried a large wooden trunk full of *Izvestiya* newspapers. The youth stopped now to unload a bundle of the morning edition to a store on James's left.

There was no time to debate: as the delivery man marched into the store, James swung himself into the saddle and grabbed the handlebars, forcing his aching, trembling legs to pedal. By God, it was a stiff ride! How much did Russian newspapers weigh?

The young man emerged to find his bike pulling out into the traffic. He shouted after James. Glancing back, James saw Karachan still running after him.

I've just stolen a delivery bike in broad daylight in one of the world's biggest police states! James shook his head, sending the thoughts to hell: all that mattered right now was escape. He pedalled faster, stood up in the saddle to put more force into each thrust, swerving unsteadily past a motor car that was slowing to park at the kerb. As he turned the corner, James saw the tram up ahead slowing to pick up passengers, and made like an arrow for the stand. A snake of people waited at a turnstile for the tram to pull up alongside, ready to board. James gritted his teeth – clothes wet with sweat, cuts and scrapes stinging and chafing – and kept on pedalling.

The tram's doors hissed open and men and women began to shuffle inside. James coasted the final stretch along the asphalt, tugged on the brakes and leaped from the bicycle. He grabbed several copies of *Izvestiya* and worked his way along the queue, shoving them into people's hands. A few gave him kopecks in return, and by the time he'd bestowed his free newspapers on those people at the front, he was well placed to push in, pour the kopecks into the tram driver's collection plate, then stagger down the aisle to collapse into a wooden seat, gasping for breath, his heart striking his ribs like a percussion drill.

The last man boarded, but for a long moment the tram remained still. *Maybe the driver knows I stole the bicycle*, James thought fearfully. *Or she knows Karachan and she's waiting for him. The tram won't move until they come to get me. I've got to get off, got to keep running—*

Finally, with a jolt and a hum, the tram car started moving again. James licked his dry lips and muttered a prayer of thanks. He was still alive, still at large, and still had his father's old backpack and the clues it contained; the chance to help finish whatever his father had started.

He looked at the wall above the window for information on the tram route, hoping to recognize a name like Gorky or Red Square, but of course to his eyes the words were just a jumble of unfamiliar characters. Where was Elmhirst now? Was he even alive? The guides from Intourist would come to know what had happened: the violence, James's disappearance . . . How soon would word reach the authorities, the secret police?

And I can't even go to the British Embassy for help, James realized, his heart thumping. *Not if the Reds have a man there too.*

The old tram rattled and scraped along as if seething at its own inefficiency and, as the adrenalin ebbed, James had an inkling of how it felt. But brooding was useless. With nothing more constructive to do, James decided to sort through his set of clues again, and opened up the backpack.

Almost at once, his sore fingers closed on the pottery shards that had once made up St Basil's Cathedral. James felt a pang of regret; his father's final gift to him, never given, had now been pulverized in his jump from the car. After long years preserved in the Swiss ice, it had finally met a violent death on home soil.

James pulled out as many pieces of the shattered cathedral as he could find: the blue-and-white swirl of an onion dome . . . a minaret laced with gold . . . And the largest, tallest tower still intact. It was hollow, James saw.

A thin edge of paper, like a little white tongue, stuck out from the hole at its base.

Something's been hidden inside.

James's heart no longer pounded; as he fumbled with the slip of paper it felt disconnected from the rest of his body. The tram's whine lowered as it approached its next stop, but to James, unrolling the tiny scroll his father had secreted inside the souvenir, electricity was everywhere.

Holding his breath, James read the neatly printed words:

ul. Bolshaya Ordynka, 67, Moskva

An address, he realized, *here in Moscow*. Father had not just been bringing home a souvenir, but a vital piece of information. Only the intended recipient would expect to find it hidden there. No wonder the accompanying note in the envelope had urged James to show the statuette to his uncle . . .

'Of course!' James almost groaned aloud as part of the cryptic letter became blindingly clear to him at last. *Get more out of the French memory for a start* – the 'souvenir', of course! The word was French and meant *remember*. He couldn't believe that, in the rush of leaving, his father would then forget to hand the little cathedral to James. Perhaps he feared he was being watched, and didn't want to risk putting his son in danger. He must have planned to send the keepsake clue at the same time as the letter that was never posted . . .

James shook his head, looked out of the window. *Well, I've got it now, Father*, he thought. *Three years late. I've got a start at last: 67, Bolshaya Ordynka Street.*

12
The Girl on the Landing

Moscow was such a vast city: it took twenty minutes just to go two blocks on foot, and even the secondary streets were eight to ten lanes wide. James didn't know where the tram was headed or how he would find his way to his destination. He didn't speak the language and had no roubles for a taxi – only the wad of US dollars. And, as Elmhirst had pointed out, he couldn't even change them at a bank without breaking the law.

Perhaps I could hire a taxicab and then run away when it's time to pay the fare? he thought. But he didn't want to draw any further attention to himself and, after his last exit from a motor car, his whole body felt like it was being held together with pins and string. James thought guiltily of the newspaper delivery man, and hoped he'd been safely reunited with his bicycle. Then an idea struck him: he'd seen an English language newspaper here, the *Moscow Times*. If there were enough

English-speaking people in the city to warrant their own paper, there must surely also be a market for maps of the city in English – and larger newsagents ought to stock them.

James stared out of the tram window, keeping his eyes open for a likely-looking stop. They passed along a street lined on one side with fine old classical buildings, while the other side was rubble, boarded off by barriers ... He saw workmen with cranes, derricks and joists mounting a large red star on top of a high, austere tower ... saw motor cars and trolleybuses alongside the trams and horse-drawn carriages. The new and the old in Moscow seemed in constant competition, with the downtrodden people navigating uncertain lines between the two under a blanket of fear, caught in endless queues, waiting wearily for their turn. These were like scenes from a jerky newsreel, remote and foreign, and yet here he was, in the midst of it all, thousands of miles from all he knew. The danger, the strangeness of his surroundings made life feel so vivid and immediate.

When the tram reached the junction of two imposing avenues, most of those on board stood up, ready to alight. James reasoned that to be so popular, the stop must be in a busy area, and therefore likely to have what he needed. He got off the tram and crossed through the turnstile onto a busy avenue; he looked around, trying to get his bearings. The chimes of an old clock tower filled the air with rich, ringing precision, and James looked up sharply to check its face: nine in the morning, and yet he felt as if he'd already been up for weeks—

At the base of the tower a sudden, furtive movement drew his eye: someone ducking behind the crumbling stonework.

The image of Karachan, with his wild hair and staring eyes, was imprinted on James's imagination, and he felt a slow tremor through his guts. 'Karachan can't have followed me,' he muttered under his breath. 'Unless he got on the tram without my seeing, concealed himself among the rush-hour throng . . .'

Surely it was ridiculous?

Attempting nonchalance, James sauntered towards a busy covered arcade in the street opposite. His mind was racing: of course, Karachan could have seen him jump onto the tram and then followed him in the saloon.

James shivered. *I can't take the chance I've been followed*, he thought. *I've got to sharpen up. Sharpen up, for God's sake!*

A pungent odour from a shop beside him caught in his throat, and on impulse he ducked inside. Most of the shelves were empty, but some were stacked with unattractive soaps in big medicinal bars. The people inside stared suspiciously, but James made a great play of clutching his stomach, groaning as if he were about to be sick. The horrified assistant tried to push him back out, but James twisted free and staggered across to a door at the back of the room, miming the urgency of his situation. Rather than risk any other outcome, the assistant grabbed him and propelled him through the door into a back room full of grime and cobwebs. A toilet with no lid stood behind a creaking door, and James blundered inside, slamming the door shut behind him and locking it. The angry assistant banged on the door, but James was already clambering onto the toilet to force open the narrow window above. He scrambled through it, wincing at the pressure on his bruised, battered body, and emerged into a quiet alleyway. A storm of flies flew up from the piles of abandoned rubbish.

'Spa-see-ba.' James muttered the phonetics of the Russian 'thank you' and allowed himself the smallest of self-satisfied smiles as he hurried on his way. There was no sign now that he was being pursued, no one in sight at all. James planned to keep it that way.

He ran to the end of the alley and onto the next street, hoping to hide himself in the growing crowd.

By lunchtime, the thrill that came with a challenge met was carrying James forward.

He had a map in his pocket. The newsagent's eyes had all but exploded at the sight of James's thin roll of US dollars; the returns of a black-market deal seemed to outweigh the fear of getting caught for it. Saying, 'Fair price,' over and over, he pushed five gold rouble notes into James's hands while trying to take as many of the dollars as possible. James had an idea he was being wholeheartedly cheated and was glad he'd kept a number of the dollar notes back. He demanded the map of Moscow for free, and the newsagent's willingness to accept this term confirmed his suspicions.

Still, what the hell. Right now the map was worth more than any money. James sat down in a dowdy restaurant on Prechistenskiya Pereulok and ordered today's special (which he suspected would be yesterday's 'ordinary' heated up): to start with, a *shchi* – a kind of thick cabbage soup served with rye bread – followed by leathery veal cutlets with fried potatoes and sour gherkins, and finally a slice of torte made with apricots, walnuts and meringue. Although he didn't feel hungry, he forced himself to eat: he didn't know when he might get food again, and knew he needed the energy.

The map was daunting in its detail. James noticed the numbers and letters that referenced each square on the grid, and remembered the letters and numbers on his father's coded memo. Could that be it – grid references on a map? But if so, *which* map? Perhaps there had been a map inside the backpack, a map long since lost, left behind in the chalet in Chamonix, overlooked . . .

Well, maybe he'd pick up more clues at his destination, which was about two miles away: ulitsa Bolshaya Ordynka was a long street that ran for well over a mile through the Zamoskvorechye quarter of Moscow, from the Moskvoretsky Bridge down to Serpukhovskaya. He tried to say the strange, exotic words aloud without stumbling. He thought of Elmhirst stalking around the major cities of the world, taking their customs and culture in his stride, executing his duty on His Majesty's Secret Service – and felt somehow like an apprentice, finding his dark little niche in a world that was growing smaller and more dangerous each day.

Draining his glass of tap water, butterflies fluttering in his stomach around the sunken wreck of the heavy torte, James set off for the mysterious address, keeping to the backstreets where possible, wondering if his quest could finally be nearing its conclusion. He kept glancing about for signs that he was being followed, feeling conspicuous in his scuffed and dirty clothes with the map in his hand. He found an old checked cap lying in the gutter of Lopukhunskiy Street and put it on, hunched his shoulders as he walked and changed his gait to make himself blend in better. He crossed the river, wider and bluer than the Thames he'd gazed out over just days ago, its shores choked with construction materials as the shabby wooden bridge, no longer strong enough, was reshod with cast iron. Had his father walked across this bridge, heart heavy with whatever business he'd become caught up in? Could James now really pick up where Bond Senior had left off and solve the puzzle?

Wrapped in his thoughts and fears and hopes, James trudged on through Moscow's demanding sprawl. A dark lane with slanting pavements cut onto a wide-open thoroughfare pocked with giant craters: either bombsites or foundations being laid. *Dangerous foundations*: his father's words in the letter seemed almost mocking now. He hurried on, past the baroque facade of an old red-brick church, muttering prayers and paranoid that danger would strike just as he stood ready to find the long-buried truth and drag it out of hiding.

At the end of that street he emerged onto the ulitsa Bolshaya Ordynka. The street was neat and ordered, but its rows of small classical and Empire-style mansions had seen better days. At this end of the street the house numbers were low, so he turned right, still unable to shake the feeling that he was being watched.

Finally, heart pumping faster, James found himself surveying number 67: an old, three-storeyed, cream-coloured dwelling, edged by a fancy cast-iron fence. Exploring further he found a quiet square courtyard to the rear of the house; large trees had grown carelessly tall in each corner, shaking untidy boughs of green confetti at the highest windows.

Did my father stand here? Somehow, right now, James felt closer to him than ever.

Returning to the front of the house, James climbed the steps to the imposing door. His knock sent pale-blue paint-flecks falling to the dirty doorstep, and jarred the door off its latch so that it swung open.

Drawing a deep breath, James walked out of the sunlight and into the musty shade of a huge, neglected front hall. A carbon arc lamp shone dimly, barely illuminating a ceiling that was black with grime. There was another door ahead of him, and stairs leading up into shadows.

James tried the door. It opened with a drawn-out creak, and he peered through into a mid-sized room crowded with furniture and strewn with clothes. An armchair placed beside a pile of blankets was crowned with a pillow – an impromptu bed. There was no one there. James closed the door again and ventured cautiously up the narrow staircase. He thought he heard movement further up round the corner – a stealthy, light-heavy retreat, as if someone had a limp or was carrying something bulky. But when he reached the next landing, there was no one in sight; another door stood closed and black against him.

James smelled cabbage and sausage coming from a room at the end of the landing. He walked cautiously across and looked in on a cramped kitchen, dominated by a black-leaded, wood-burning range that stood cold and empty, as if intimidated into silence by the three Primus stoves on the floor before it. Why so many?

A voice behind him made James start. He whirled round and saw a large, elderly woman in a grey floral dress that had seen better days. She looked indignant, and began speaking loudly.

'I don't understand you,' James said bluntly. 'English?'

The old woman stopped talking and stared.

'Do you know the name Andrew Bond?'

The woman muttered a curt dismissal that would be much the same in any language, and bustled off through the other door on the landing. As she left, James saw a shadow shift behind her. He walked out of the kitchen, but the shadow had withdrawn. There was movement on the stairs round the corner.

On instinct, James hurried up them in pursuit. 'Hello?' he called. 'I'm looking for something ... or somebody ...' He trailed off. What the hell *was* he looking for? Up ahead he heard a scrabbling on wood and as he burst onto the upper landing he saw a girl with a cane, long pale fingers grappling with a brass doorknob.

'Excuse me,' James said, politely but with force, leaning against the wall beside her, trying to get her to look at him instead of at the door. 'Do you know Bond? Andrew Bond?'

The girl turned to him now, slender and attractive, looking out from under thick black hair. Her eyes were wide and blue and guileless, round pools in a face like white stone scrubbed smooth by the sea. Her nose was as straight as a statue's and her lips were like those in a little girl's drawing: plump, red love-hearts split by the dark line of her mouth. And yet, for all her beauty, there was something in her being that James shrank from. It was like an absence of spirit; almost as if a part of her had broken once and in consequence the whole had ceased to work and held itself separate.

'Please, will you help me?' James said simply.

The girl looked at him, her thin brows knotted part way between startled and suspicious. 'English?' Her voice was unexpectedly deep.

'Yes. My name is Bond—'

'Go.' Her aspect hardened as she opened the door. 'Leave us alone.'

'*Us?*' James seized on the word like a dog thrown a steak, and he saw the blue eyes widen. 'You speak English. Who are you with?'

Saying something in Russian now, she slipped through the slender gap in the doorway.

'Wait.' James set his foot firmly against the door before she could bang it shut. 'I got this address from Andrew Bond.'

'There are many here, staying.'

'But you speak English. Could you help me—'

'We have rules. We do not talk to strangers. It is . . . *noticed.*' She brought the pointed end of her cane down on James's foot. He scowled, retreated – and the door slammed shut. His hand was reaching for the brass doorknob when he heard the turn of a key in the lock.

'Damn,' James breathed. What could he do now – kick the door down? He couldn't force the girl to talk to him . . .

Equally, he couldn't just walk away.

James put his ear to the door, but all he could hear were voices from the landing below: muted urgings, mutterings. James walked wearily back down the stairs to find the woman he'd seen before dragging an elderly man out of the room. He was wielding a poker in his hand, which was shaking badly. His squinting, red-rimmed eyes were magnified by thick round glasses so that they looked more comic than fierce. He took a short, warning stab at James, then broke off into a coughing fit.

Holding up his hands in apology, James backed away down the stairs to the entrance hall. What a curious arrangement! Were the old couple related to the girl? No, he remembered the portable stoves – they suggested different groups: *There are many people living here.*

Whoever had been resident when Andrew Bond made note of the address, they could be dead by now, or moved away, or 'disappeared' by the state into a labour camp in the distant east . . .

And I could go the same way if I'm not careful. James went out through the front door, but wasn't about to give up now. He would make a further visit when the working day was done, when the house was full.

Wave all the pokers at me you like. I will get answers.

James went down the steps and circled the house, peering up at the windows. The strains of some dramatic classical music floated down from an upper window, the flutes and strings overlaid by the crackle and scratch from a gramophone record. James had heard it somewhere before: an opera, perhaps, or a ballet? Dirty curtains blew at the window, hiding the view inside.

Frustrated, James stalked out of the courtyard and away back down the street. He didn't see the bearded man with the pockmarked face and the staring eyes who stepped forward into the sunlight from the front porch pillars of the property across the road, staring over at the many windows of number 67, Bolshaya Ordynka Street.

13

The Father and the Son

Impatient and nervous, and with hours to kill, James decided to pass the time in the large park that skirted the Moskva river to the west of the city. It would be hard for anyone to follow him inconspicuously there and, God knew, his aching soles could use a change from concrete and tarmac underfoot. Thoughts of Elmhirst and the man with the slashed throat, and the gunshot were pounding through his head to the same relentless rhythm. Then he pondered where he would go tonight. The hotel would doubtless be under observation, not only by the people who'd tried to kidnap him, but also by the secret police.

One step at a time, James told himself. *You can't control the future, so work on the present as hard as you can.* The girl who spoke English: judging by the way she'd avoided him, by the fear in her eyes . . . she knew something, James was certain.

With his legs worn out from tramping across Moscow, he decided to take the Metro. The gargantuan subway stations made impressive sights. Exiting onto the concourse at Park Kultury, James felt as if he was exploring a vast subterranean Turkish bath, with vaulted stone ceilings and immaculate walls. Giant murals in mosaic and brilliantly coloured paint adorned the walls, while Grecian statues stood in niches among the many-coloured marble pillars and arches, like would-be travellers turned to stone.

Finally emerging from below ground, James came to the Gorky Park of Culture and Rest off the busy Krymsky Bridge. Soon he was trailing through the cultivated fields and lawns. In the late afternoon sun, the deep green of the grass set off the whites of the balustrades along the embankment and the statues of sportsmen, and the cobalt blues of the lakes and ponds. On the banks, bushes covered in white and red blooms had been carefully pruned into likenesses – James recognized the great dictator, Stalin, and supposed the others were Soviet heroes or politicians. He walked on in search of more carefree sights. Boats were afloat on a lake, and James imagined being out in one himself, rowing across the water, relaxing. How long since he'd allowed himself the luxury of switching off like that, of letting go?

One more stab at finding the truth of this riddle. James rubbed the tired and aching muscles at the back of his neck. *If I still get nowhere, then I'll find a way to sneak back to the National and learn what's what; at least they speak English there.*

James soon found that the park was more than a green space – it proved to be a 750-acre demonstration of how good socialists ought to spend their leisure time. According to the notes on the tourist map, it had been conceived and built as a centre for health and recreation, catering for the cultural needs of millions of visitors, encouraging them to take part in artistic and sporting activities. In one vast enclosure James saw volleyball played with grace and skill, while beyond that an open-air chess festival was taking place. He felt a little calmer in this unexpected oasis.

City life cut in soon enough as a clock tower clanged five with monotonous chimes. James took it as his signal to return to the house on Bolshaya Ordynka and start his surveillance. The city was filled with evening life. Special constables in blue armbands directed the traffic as trams clattered past, and buses bore their passengers in all directions across the city. Again, James stuck to the quieter streets where possible. Windows stood wide open, and the strains of a stately dance in three/four time emanated from a score of wireless sets. The roofs and attics seemed alive with the scratchy music, and when a man began an operatic serenade twenty times over, it seemed a whole company was singing the city to rest.

Finally James turned onto Bolshaya Ordynka. He had not gone ten yards when he saw a thin, dark-haired figure walking towards him, leaning lightly on a cane. *The girl.* Immediately James dropped to one knee, pretending to tie his shoelace, then crossed the road between two parked motor cars. From the other side of the street he watched her walk by, an empty string grocery bag in her free hand. She was going shopping, then – perhaps fetching food.

James quickened his step. With the girl not around to observe him, he might get further in his investigations.

Fortuitously, the front door still stood ajar. James walked up the steps as if he owned the place, and went inside.

The house was quiet. The front hall was just as he had left it, and he could hear no sounds of life. He took the stairs up to the first floor and looked into the communal kitchen. A pile of old utensils lay scattered on the floor as if kicked, but everything else was just as it had been.

James went up to the next landing and knocked on the door the girl had slipped through. There was no response. He put his ear to the wood, heard nothing, and placed his hand on the brass doorknob; there was a quiet squeal as the handle turned, but the door didn't budge.

'Hello?' James tried. 'I'm here because of Andrew Bond. I've got a message—'

'*Bond?*'

James jumped back, almost crashing against the opposite wall. The voice that had come through the door was deep and loud. The man must be standing right up against it.

'Bond, for God's sake ...' The voice had dropped to a hoarse pantomime whisper. 'It can't be you!'

Hair prickling on the back of his neck, James took off his cap and stepped forward again. 'It is,' he said cautiously. 'I'm Bond.'

A key turned in the lock and the door opened to reveal a dishevelled, pathetic-looking man, perhaps in his early sixties. He had been handsome once, James supposed, but now the left side of his pale, lined face sagged as if the muscles had given up. His silver hair was thin and lifeless and his blue eyes looked rheumy, unseeing. The man's dark suit was of good quality, but too big for the spindly body it contained.

'Andrew Bond!' The man nodded, smiling – not so much at his visitor, James felt, as at his own cleverness in recognizing him. He spoke fluent English with a strong Russian accent. 'I thought you had died, but I should have known better: the dead do not stay buried. The past will not leave us in peace.'

James opened his mouth to speak, but no sound came out. He didn't know what to say. *How can this man think that I am Andrew Bond? Is he blind?* Yet if he admitted he was not, would the old man stop talking? *He doesn't just look sick in his body . . . His mind must be broken.*

'It's . . . been a long time,' James said, noncommittal.

'Has it? Has any time passed at all?' The old man shook his head, his fingers plucking nervously at his sleeves. 'You promised they'd never know I approached you. Promised that the woman in the veil would be stopped, that you'd get me out.'

'I . . . did my best,' James said with feeling, even as he remembered his father's telegram. 'You worked with the veiled lady?'

'Her sights were upon me.' The man looked troubled. 'You know, I was a great architect once. I took space and gave it purpose. Such . . . terrible purpose.' He gazed up into James's face, but again, he didn't really seem to be looking as he attempted a further smile. 'But, this is no place to talk, eh? Out on the landing! We will disturb the others. Three other families live in our house now. It's a good citizen's duty, eh? So much space here, while others crowd together, a family to a room . . . Come inside. Let no one say that Ivan Kalashnikov has no manners.'

That name. James almost jumped as he pictured the signature on the building designs in the planning files in London: *I. Kalashnikov,* the architect responsible for the Mechta Academy. 'Thank you . . . Mr Kalashnikov.' James followed him into a study with a dusty dark-wood table and chair, and even dustier books and papers on the shelves. Some of the books were in English, and concerned with architecture.

Andrew Bond had been trying to direct Max to Kalashnikov. Not only the mole in the Soviet scheme ... but its architect?

'Anya is out just now.' Ivan shuffled across the little study and gestured to a chair. 'We can talk more freely without her here. She still does not know. Not all of it.'

James took off his backpack, wincing at the ache in his muscles, and placed it on the floor with his cap. 'What doesn't she know?'

'The secrets I meant to take to my deathbed ...' Ivan laughed suddenly, turned to the shelves and felt along the books until he reached one so large it jutted over the edge. 'So many dead around me, and yet the grave eludes me still, Bond!' He heaved the book down onto the table with a slam and turned to the last page. James saw a newspaper clipping there from the *Daily Telegraph* dated March 1933, and quickly scanned it. The story concerned a group of eleven mystery men with no identity papers who had drowned together in the Thames. No one had reported any missing persons, but the article noted that each body bore large, distinctive tattoos – in Russian. 'When I saw this news, I prayed that the Project would be discovered, that my works would never stand complete. But no, the connection was not made.'

'Your four buildings in London, you mean?'

'Four entry points.'

'Entry to where?' James had no idea what he was talking about. 'Could you tell me more about the Project—'

'They were criminal tattoos on her workforce, of course.' Ivan tapped the side of his nose. 'They show what you did, and your ranking in the gulag. You know, the gulags, the Soviet labour camps? Criminals and political prisoners are sent there:

an expendable workforce. When I read that you had died, I felt sure that they knew I had contacted you . . . that I would be sent to the gulag myself.' James jumped as Kalashnikov's hand suddenly closed on his wrist. 'I should have died there, let Anya be rid of me. I should be set free, Bond, just as you were. Secrets weigh too heavily upon me, you know? You understand?'

'I understand,' James said, although he didn't. 'But the Project, and the way to bring it down – down with just one blow, you said. Can you remind me . . . ?'

'*Remind* you? What I did to Anya was *down* to you!' Kalashnikov's lips shrank back from his teeth in a feral grimace and he slammed the large book closed. 'You know the risks I took, approaching you, the big Vickers man? "We pay well for new weapons," you said. "Tell me everything; trust me," you said. I compiled all the information. You said you'd act on it. You knew the dangers, same as me, but—' He stopped suddenly as if a thought had occurred. 'Didn't you take my gun?'

James frowned, wrong-footed.

'I gave it to you. They say a gun is never the answer, don't they . . . ?'

'A gun is never the answer?'

'See?' Kalashnikov giggled. 'Oh, but that gun really *was* the answer. It really was . . .'

'Mr Kalashnikov – Ivan – please—'

'I read that you'd died.' Kalashnikov looked at him sharply. 'No way out for me then, eh? They used Anya's talent as cover: to fulfil her dream of dancing in London – *that* was the reason for my being in London, so far as SIS knew!' His voice was growing louder. 'So they smiled, those investigating agents at

117

the Russian Embassy, and they said how proud I must be, and let me build and create and prepare for the killing ... prepare for the river of blood that is coming.'

'I'm sorry.' James raised his hands, trying to calm Kalashnikov, feeling badly out of his depth. The man seemed lost in a world of his own pain, and James hadn't grasped enough of the situation to help him navigate it. He rose and went to the window, parted the curtains and looked down into the private courtyard, hoping that no one had overheard Kalashnikov's outbursts. The old woman who'd harangued James earlier, and her husband with the poker – they were both sitting on a bench now, taking the evening air. Another couple sat on the bench opposite, leaning against each other. No one seemed disturbed; perhaps it was safer to keep your eyes and ears shut in Soviet Moscow.

James turned back to Kalashnikov. 'I think it would help to talk things through from the beginning.'

'Help.' Kalashnikov stared at him for a few seconds, then burst into laughter. 'I begged you for help. "Trust me," you said. And you hurried away, and you never returned ...' The smiled faded as he hugged himself feebly. 'I was so afraid. I'd thought of a way to stop their plan, but I was so afraid they would discover it, afraid of what they would do ...'

'What way?' James urged him. 'How can it be stopped?'

'So afraid.' Kalashnikov didn't seem to hear him. 'And so I did it. I crippled my own daughter so we could escape.'

James stared. 'Anya ... ?'

'She couldn't stay dancing in London with her leg mangled, could she? It would have seemed suspicious had we stayed, so we were allowed to return to Russia ... Soviet doctors are the best in the world, they say, and I had hope, but ...' He was weeping now, tears as thin and grey as his hair. 'Some things cannot be fixed, eh?'

'No.' James remembered the hurt in Anya's eyes, her hands clutching the cane, and felt sick. 'No, I suppose they can't.'

'I thought it was over. I had destroyed Anya's dreams, but we still had each other. I remember how you spoke of your boy – John, was it ... ?'

'James.' He closed his eyes, not trusting his voice to hold. 'My ... son's name is James.'

'I hope you tell him you love him. There is so much we keep silent. So much we would rather not share ...' Kalashnikov's voice was hushed now. 'I think they knew that somebody had talked to you, Bond. A project like this requires many hands, many nervous men, and it only takes one to talk. A security risk, you know? Well, the lady with the veil, she can't have that, can she!' He shook his head fiercely. 'When the secret police came for me, they used the handcuffs. American handcuffs – do you know them? They flick onto your wrist and the little ratchet teeth, they lock in place. If you do not double-lock them, the little teeth will tighten with each movement ... and tighten ...' He was rocking gently, staring into space. 'As they pulled out my hair and beat my feet with brass rods ... I watched the skin on my hands burst ... the blood flow from underneath my fingernails. I could never draw again. I, who have pinned down palaces on paper ...' He smiled, shrugged. 'They must have believed me innocent in the end, but by then ...'

'I'm sorry,' James mumbled. He'd been so hungry for answers but, by God, now he'd heard some hard ones. If

Andrew Bond had lived, then SIS would have rescued this terrified little man, Anya would still be able to walk and dance, and the Project would be a distant memory, a failure. Instead ...

Kalashnikov has spat out the gristle of things, James thought, *but I need the meat of what happened, before he loses his mind altogether.* He placed a hand on Kalashnikov's arm — but the old man snatched it away with a shout as if woken from a nightmare, backed away and crashed against a sideboard. The decanters and glasses within rattled and shook, and so did Kalashnikov.

The brass knob of the door to the landing jumped suddenly. Instantly alert, James jerked round to face the newcomer, arms raised in a fighting stance.

It was the girl, Anya, leaning on her cane in the doorway, her string bag barely bulging with a tiny loaf of black bread. Her blue eyes flicked between James and her father; her face was hard and closed.

Anya put down the bag and pulled a knife from her pocket, the blade crusted with blood.

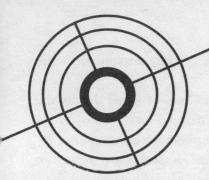

14
Death Has Many Voices

James eyed the knife and raised an eyebrow. 'Straight to the point?'

Anya's face didn't flicker. 'I warned you to stay away.'

'I'm only here to talk to your father,' James told her. 'Isn't that right, Ivan? I don't mean you any harm.'

'Of course.' Kalashnikov gave a wheezing laugh. 'They said Bond was dead. How can the dead harm the living?'

'Papa becomes confused sometimes. I do not.' Anya kept the knife pointing at James. 'You see this?'

James nodded. He could see that her arm was straight and steady. She wasn't afraid. She was prepared.

'A man tried to steal my bread in the street,' Anya went on. 'I persuaded him to leave me alone, but his hand will stay split for a week. Do I have to convince you in the same way?'

'Anya, please,' Kalashnikov said. 'Bond and I have finished our talk now.'

The hell we have, thought James. 'Well, actually, sir, I still need to—'

'Papa needs to rest.' With a cold look at James she put the knife back in her trouser pocket, then put an arm around her father, patient and dutiful, cooing to him in Russian.

'You think Bond will disappear?' Kalashnikov seemed to consider this. 'Or is it only the living made to disappear these days? And yet, we must forgive. Forgiveness is so important, Anya. I . . . I've always taught you that . . .'

'Yes, Papa. You've taught me that.' Anya sounded bored, distant, detached, but helped her father through the inner door. It led on to what might once have been a dining room; now a single bed, made up fussily with crimson bedclothes, stood against one wall, incongruous amongst the wooden furniture and the modernist paintings of skyscrapers. Anya sat her father down in an old green velvet wing-backed armchair that faced the window. She lit an oil lamp, replaced the glass chimney, and placed it on the windowsill where its flickering light played over Kalashnikov's palsied face. He was smiling like a child now, and seemed to have forgotten his visitor already.

Anya, however, had not. She limped over to James and pulled him through the door, back into the study. 'How dare you!' she hissed. 'How dare you make him relive those times, after all he's been through!'

'All I want to know is—' James broke off as he saw her reach for her knife, closed his hand on her wrist and shook his head. 'I need to know what your father told mine about this secret Project of his in London. Andrew Bond was my father. My name is James.'

'Then if you have come to gloat over your father's work, James Bond, you may leave content.' She pulled away from him, crossed to the door and opened it. 'Leave *now*.'

'Listen to me.' James's frustration was close to igniting into anger. 'A lot of lives may hinge on my finding out what's been happening. I'm here with the British Secret Intelligence Service.'

'Those liars and devils hire children now, do they?'

'I don't know what propaganda you've heard—'

'Just *get away from us*.' Furious, she limped through the door to the stairs leading up to the next floor. 'What little space we have left in life I will not share with the likes of you.'

'No. I'm damned if I'll go.' James followed her as she climbed awkwardly up the stairs. 'I've had enough of riddles and half-answers. I don't understand what your father was caught up in or what exactly he did to you—'

'Papa only ever wanted to protect me, you know.' Anya turned and sneered into James's face as she reached her door. 'He cannot see that I protect us both now. I have ever since . . . since the police gave up on extracting confessions and let him go.'

James nodded. 'It sounds like it was a terrible ordeal.'

She pushed out a deep breath and opened the door. 'They came for him one Thursday morning. I was left alone for five weeks. When he came back . . . his body was broken and his mind worse.'

As she went inside, James looked into her room. Damp speckled the old pink and cream wallpaper and the bare floorboards. A pair of ballet shoes hung by their ribbons from a post at the end of the narrow bed – each slashed all over, he noticed, as if by a sharp knife or razor.

She saw him looking, and something like shame flitted across her face. 'You will leave now,' she said. 'Please, before you make things worse, before the others talk to the police of this. I have seen them eyeing our space up here. They would not hesitate to betray us . . .' Anya parted the curtain, looking down, her face bleached of all colour in the sunlight. 'That is strange. *Everyone* is outside.'

'Having a house meeting without you?' James joined her in looking down into the courtyard, where three further people had appeared, now sitting on a third bench between the other two. He felt suddenly uneasy. 'Things seem very quiet out there . . .'

There was a loud thump from somewhere downstairs, and a familiar shout: '*Bond?*'

James jumped, felt almost dizzy with pure relief. 'Elmhirst!' he shouted. 'I don't believe it!'

'Who is this?' Anya rounded on him, eyes narrowed. 'Who have you brought here?'

'It's all right. He's with British Intelligence. I don't know how he found me, but—'

'To hell with you both!' As James left the room, Anya slammed the door shut behind him.

'Elmhirst?' In a couple of seconds James was down on the landing below, but his call, again, went unanswered. He ventured down the next flight of stairs. 'Hallo?'

'In here!' Elmhirst's voice rang out from upstairs now; he must have got into Kalashnikov's rooms.

James ran back up the stairs, puzzled, and entered the old man's study.

'There is so much we keep silent.' On the other side of the door Kalashnikov's voice sounded muffled. 'So much.'

James opened the door to the makeshift bedchamber. 'Elmhirst?'

There was no sign of the SIS man. Only Kalashnikov, propped up in the high-backed armchair, facing the window with his back to James. 'There is so much we would rather not share.'

Then James saw the body lying face up beside the bed. His heart jumped as he saw that *here* was Ivan Kalashnikov, his sightless eyes fixed on the ceiling, a gory smile carved into his throat, his white shirtfront now soaked crimson with blood. *He's dead*, James realized, feeling sick. *But I heard him speak from the chair . . . ?*

'He's slow on the uptake. Still, don't take a chance.' Impossibly, it was Elmhirst's gruff voice coming from the chair – but the figure that rose from the old patched velvet seat wasn't the British agent. It was a boy with taut skin as black as his cotton suit, and a shaved head, his oddly delicate features more beautiful than handsome.

It was the boy from the Mechta Academy on Millbank: the boy who'd been checking the explosives, who'd attacked him in the cellar and knocked him out cold. *He must have come out here with Karachan*, James realized.

White teeth shone in the boy's smile as he gestured to the corpse on the floor and opened his mouth. A short, horrible gasp burst from his lips to die out in bubbles. James's stomach turned: it could only have been an echo of Kalashnikov's dying breath.

The boy met James's horrified gaze and went on smiling.

'What are you doing here, you sick . . .' James couldn't find a word strong enough and simply stared at him in loathing. He was glad Anya had stayed upstairs, that she hadn't been confronted with this – not yet, at least. 'Who are you?'

The boy spoke back in a voice James knew and hated: '*Yo soy Imitador.*'

It was the voice of La Velada. *This freak knows her, then.* 'Shut up,' James snapped. 'I asked for *your* name.'

'Mimic.' The boy suddenly sounded young, fragile. 'I ... am ... Mimic.'

'Mimic? What kind of a name is—'

'I have a boy your age.' Mimic's voice grew deeper, with a kindly Scottish burr. 'His name is James.'

James couldn't breathe. That was his father's voice. The imitation was perfect: the accent, the intonation, everything. *Mimic must have met my father, heard him speak.*

'His name is James.'

And stolen his voice.

'Don't you dare,' James hissed at last.

Mimic only grinned and continued. 'I have a boy.'

'Stop.' It sounded as if his father were here, in the room, and after all he'd heard, James couldn't suppress an emotional reaction. 'When ... when did you meet him?'

'His name is James.'

He's getting inside your head. James gritted his teeth. *Keep him out.*

'James! James!' Mimic stabbed the air with the knife, froth speckling the corners of his mouth as he kept calling James's name again and again. 'His name is James!'

James couldn't take any more. A once-brilliant man, broken and lost, lay dead between them, and now this son of a bitch

126

stood here mocking James's father. James started forward, eyes on the knife. Mimic slashed at him as he approached, but James brought up his left hand, flattened it to a hard edge and chopped into the boy's wrist, then windmilled his other arm into a judo strike against his neck. Mimic staggered, threw back his head and dropped the knife. James kicked the weapon away and it skittered under the bed like a rat fleeing light. Before Mimic could recover, James punched him hard in the stomach, knocking him back against a dark-wood cabinet. The glass panels cracked and shattered; the belongings inside rocked and fell.

James was distracted by their motion for just a fraction of a second, but it was all Mimic needed. The boy threw himself forward, one arm striking up and the other down, the technique James had himself just demonstrated. Almost before he knew it, James found himself being driven back across the room. He brought up his arms to protect himself from the blows and cuffs raining down on him, but stumbled and put his hands out automatically to break his fall against the dining table. A dark fist struck his face. James felt heat as his nose gushed blood, saw sparks as the other fist struck his cheek. Head spinning, James tried to marshal a coherent attack, but Mimic was one step ahead now, anticipating his moves and performing them first. For every gasp or cry James uttered, Mimic returned a perfect copy, and the psychotic smile grew wider.

Finally James came up hard against the study door. Propping himself back against it, he kicked out savagely at Mimic's shin and scored a hit, then followed it up with a solid punch to the heart before striking again under the chin. Mimic tumbled to the floor, but immediately he kicked James's legs out from under him.

Now it was James's turn to go down. A dizzy blink later and Mimic was on top of him, knees squeezing at James's ribs, wiry hands around his neck.

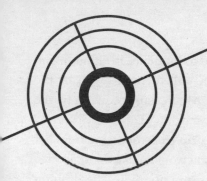

15
House on Fire

Desperately James twisted and bucked and managed to jolt Mimic clear. The boy rolled with the momentum and was back on his feet, his eyes shining murder.

But before he could resume his attack the door behind him burst open, slamming into his back.

'*No!*' It was Anya, pushing through, her blue eyes fixed upon her papa's grisly body.

The impact of the door threw Mimic forward, off-guard. James took full advantage and raked his knuckles along the boy's jugular vein. The effect upon this pressure point was decisive: Mimic fell like a dead weight, and as he tumbled, his fingers tangled in a lacy tablecloth and knocked over the oil lamp. In a moment, with a fierce kerosene *whoosh*, flames had taken hold of the old lace.

'Papa!' Anya tried to reach the crumpled, bloodied body on the floor, but was stopped by a rug in front of her, which erupted in flame as if it had longed to for years. Body smarting from the blows he'd taken, James pulled Anya away as the peeling wallpaper caught alight. Mimic lay sprawled in the corner beside the man he'd murdered.

Anya tore her arm from James's grip, tears squeezing from her narrowed eyes. 'I told you. I knew you would make things worse!'

'There's no time for this,' James said hoarsely. The draught through the window gave the fire fresh and vicious fuel, the heat driving James back, the smoke choking him. 'We've got to get out.' He retreated into the other room, picked up his father's backpack and started struggling into the straps.

So he was caught off-guard when Andrei Karachan thundered into the room. *Not you too!* James thought, no time to get clear as the man's steel-grip fingers closed on his throat and drove him back against the bookcase.

'Anya ... !' James rasped, hoping for her help and yet fearing for her life.

Karachan shook his head smugly. 'So kind of you to tell us at last who was our traitor ...'

Lights flashed behind James's eyes as the chokehold tightened. In desperation he groped wildly for a makeshift weapon amid the debris on Kalashnikov's desk. He found a dusty bottle of vodka and swung it against the back of Karachan's head. The bottle cracked and Karachan gave a high-pitched cry, his knees sagging. James propelled himself forward but couldn't break the man's grip; locked together, the two of them pitched into an awkward stagger that carried them out through the door and onto the smoky landing before finally both went crashing down the stairs. James gasped as the wooden edges of the risers bit into his body.

The Russian's stranglehold was broken as he and James struck the floor, but Karachan's big hand closed around James's ankle to stop him getting away. James kicked and struggled, but his throat was stripped raw, his lungs ached, his head was spinning, and he couldn't shake this damn grip on his leg . . .

Then Karachan gave a ghastly, choked-off cry as the end of Anya's cane thumped down into his windpipe. He released James, thrashing like a salmon speared in mid-stream. Only when his struggles ceased did Anya raise her stick and continue down the staircase to the ground floor, leaving James in a heap.

'Anya, wait . . .' He rolled back to his feet, weary as hell, but with the old dogged determination to outlive his enemies. He staggered down the stairs. The front door stood open, but Anya was making for an exit at the back of the hall; going for help from her housemates in the courtyard perhaps.

James started after her. 'You can't stay,' he panted. 'Come with me!'

'With you?' Anya spun round to face him and the look in her eyes was one of such hate-filled conviction that James actually shrank from it. 'I only saved you so the secret police get you in one piece.' She hobbled away to the back door. 'I have witnesses, and we'll tell the authorities *everything*.'

As Anya pushed through, James saw the path to the courtyard beyond. She limped quickly towards the rear of the building, through the white smoke gusting from the upper windows, shouting in Russian. At least all the other occupants of the house had been outside when the fire broke out. Sitting on the benches, so still and quiet . . .

'Oh, no,' James breathed, and again set off in pursuit.

When he caught up with Anya, she was standing before the benches like an actor addressing her audience, all eyes upon her. But these eyes weren't turned from the whirling smoke, or fixed on her in concern. They were dead jellies in sunken sockets: corpse eyes. James saw that the old man with the poker now wore a bloodied cheesewire around his neck like a grisly necklace; he saw a pouchy, blonde-haired woman gazing up at the stars, darkness dripping from the incision above her collarbone.

All of them. James looked away, stunned and sickened. *Murdered.* To stop them talking? To wipe away all trace of Ivan Kalashnikov and those who knew him?

Slowly Anya turned to James. 'You did not do this . . .'

'Of course I didn't,' James said brusquely. 'You must know now, you'll be next. We have to get away from here.'

Without a word she pushed past him, bolting from the courtyard back towards the front of the house and the street beyond; her limp wasn't holding her back now: she moved with a powerful, muscular grace. James thought for a moment that perhaps he should let her go. She was right – look at the hell he'd unleashed on her life. But he knew too that there were others crowding close who could bring worse . . .

He broke into a run and gave chase. *Do I really think I can protect her,* James thought, *or am I just hoping she knows whatever her papa knows – and that she'll share it with me?*

How far was he prepared to go for the truth?

James pushed the questions aside, quickened his step. He caught up with Anya in the middle of the road, facing down a fire engine that was racing over the asphalt, clanging bells shattering the calm of the summer evening.

At the same moment he saw Karachan stumble out of the old house with Mimic. They'd recovered too soon for James's liking; he still felt exhausted, his lungs turned inside out by coughing.

Anya had seen the killers too, and started to shake – from the look on her face, more with anger than fear. James linked his arm through hers and pulled her firmly away. The gathering crowd spared her a little shock and sympathy, then turned back to the show as the firemen connected their hose to a hydrant and unleashed a stream of water on the building's upper storeys. Mimic and Karachan were accosted by special constables, fresh on the scene, who knew nothing of the events that had taken place. But instead of arresting the murderer and his accomplice they simply steered them clear of the smoke to the side of the road.

'Anya,' James said as he marched her away, 'is there anywhere safe you can stay tonight?'

She didn't look at him, shaking as she walked. He took her silence for a 'no'.

'I was staying at the National Hotel,' he went on, 'but after what happened this morning I don't think I can go back ...' Mimic had impersonated Elmhirst's voice to lure James into danger, therefore Mimic had clearly come across the SIS officer: had he killed Elmhirst to stop him getting to the information they thought James had in his head, the means to solve Andrew Bond's riddle?

'You ask if I have somewhere safe to stay ...' Anya's walk was becoming robotic, her limp growing more pronounced. 'My papa has been killed. The people who lived with us, who hated and resented us, were killed with him. The men who did this . . . they are monsters without mercy.' She stopped suddenly. 'I have no one now. Nothing. Nowhere is safe. They must kill me too.'

James held her arm. 'I know you're in shock, know that after what you've seen—'

'Perhaps if I make it easy for them to catch me,' she broke in, 'it will be quick.'

'Perhaps if you make it hard for them, you'll stay alive.' James looked at her. 'You want to die? You want these killers to go unpunished?'

'There's nothing I can do.'

'You can get even!'

Anya looked at him, disconsolate. 'This is your way?'

James wiped dirty hands through his sweat-soaked hair. 'I'm still here, aren't I?'

'And this is good?'

'It's better than anything else.' But as James looked past her down the street, fear knifed its warning down his spine. Through the smoke, he glimpsed two figures coming their way: he supposed the police must have finished with Mimic and Karachan. 'Now we've got to run like hell.'

'But my leg—'

'Like *hell*.'

James snatched her hand and ran off, grateful that she was at least allowing him to pull her along. He turned left at a junction, past the pink-and-white frontage and grey-slate domes of a Russian church, and led the way west along Pogorelskiy Lane. They ran past a line of buildings with ground-level windows but no doors that he could see, as if they had sunk into their own foundations.

Anya's limp was growing ever more pronounced and her breathing shakier. *We're too damned slow*, James thought. *If we can't outrun them, we'll just have to give them the slip.*

A bare concrete courtyard led from the *pereulok* onto a smaller half-demolished alleyway, where workmen's huts sprouted from the pavement like canvas mushrooms. James pushed Anya inside one of them, and in the musty gloom they listened. The sound of pelting footsteps was approaching already. James looked around the hut for anything he could use as a weapon, but there was nothing beyond a small table and three dirty mugs. He held his breath, fists clenching, as the footfalls sounded louder, closer.

James wiped cold, dirty sweat from his neck. *They know we're here!*

16

A Walk in the Park

For want of a better plan, James readied himself to pick up the table, like a lion tamer warding off a lion. Surely at any moment Karachan and Mimic would both barge in and . . .

No. The rush of footsteps went past, and the canvas at the entrance to the hut flapped as if tugged by the slipstream.

'Back the way we came,' James whispered. 'Fast as you can.'

Anya nodded mutely.

A nightmare game of hide-and-seek began. James led Anya back to the lane they'd left, but Karachan and Mimic doubled back too, searching under cars and trucks parked at the side of the road. James began to look at his map, but Anya shook her head impatiently and took hold of his wrist, leading *him* down a small side alley onto a bigger street. Still panting for breath, wary and alert, James broke into a jogtrot alongside her; he wanted to push on faster but her limp seemed to be growing worse.

At the end of the street, overhead cables hung like industrial bunting, and a queue of people waited by a sign on a pole. 'Trolleybus!' James panted, pointing out the sight to Anya. The electric hum and whoop of an imminent arrival put hope into his heart. 'If we can get aboard . . .'

They ran down the urban canyon to the line of people filing aboard the red-and-cream crate. Looking behind as he joined the end of the line, James could see no signs of pursuit. *But I was wrong about that before,* he thought. *I could be again.*

He paid their fares, but there was standing room only. The trolleybus didn't move for some time, and James had nightmare visions of Mimic and Karachan climbing aboard, trapping them in the scrum of passengers. *Mimic* . . . His powers of impersonation were eerily accurate. When he'd spoken as La Velada, she might have been in the room.

Except I'd know if she was, he thought, *by the chill.*

Finally the vehicle jerked and hummed away, the collector pole on its roof drawing power from the overhead cables, pushing the wheels round. James waited for the thing to pick up speed, but soon realized with dismay that this slow trundle was as good as it got. 'Karachan and Mimic could walk faster than we're going.'

'That will make them less likely to believe you would be on board,' Anya said without emotion.

'I suppose so.' James nodded. 'Does this trolleybus take us near Gorky Park?'

'Why?'

'There's a Metro stop on the far side, isn't there?' James recalled. 'Takes us to the top of Gorky Street, not far from the

National Hotel. There's space to hide, crowds to blend in with. It will be harder for anyone to make a move.'

'Harder for them to kill us, you mean.'

'Or to catch us for questioning first.'

Evening was well advanced by the time James and Anya disembarked from the trolleybus on Krymsky Val street and made their way into Gorky Park. Anxious almost to the point of exhaustion, James looked around for signs that they were being trailed. He wore the backpack on his front so he'd be harder to spot from behind.

'I think we have "lost" them.' She spoke distantly, like a distracted mother indulging a fanciful son's game. 'Moscow is big. We are small.'

James looked at her sideways. 'Thank you for agreeing to stay with me.'

'These men killed everyone in my life for what they might know. They will kill me also, if they can.' She looked back at him. 'I stay with you until we talk. If I can tell you things my father did not, you will leave me alone for good, and I will leave Moscow and be free. We both get what we want.'

James shook his head. 'You sound so calm. After all you've just been through—'

'This day is good, perhaps.' Anya sniffed and straightened. 'The ordeal is over now.'

'Excuse me?'

'The slow death of many years was ended tonight.' She sounded so matter-of-fact as she turned her sad blue eyes on him. 'After all the things Papa did to me, do you think it is proper that I should grieve?'

James felt uneasy. 'Then you know about what he did—?'

'That he slammed the door of a motor car on my leg? That he crippled his own daughter to avoid having the death of strangers on his conscience?' Anya nodded, emotionless. 'Yes. He thought he kept the secret, but when he came back from the secret police . . . he began to call out in his sleep, each and every night. I learned just what he did, through the floorboards. Each night a new raving. The others in the house heard some of it too. They came to fear him.'

James frowned. 'Fear him?'

'Or to fear what he might rave of *them* in his sleep, if he was taken again.' She looked down, brushed grass from her cotton trousers. 'Well. They do not fear now. And if they go to heaven, I hope St Peter will allot them more space than the state's nine square metres.'

James noticed the absence of all emotion; was it shock, or something more ingrained − a way to cope? Whatever the case, right now he couldn't afford to antagonize her. For all her deadpan rationalizing, Anya had no reason to stay with him and several good reasons to run. He wanted to put her at ease, reassure her that he could bring more to her life than carnage.

Reassure himself.

He tilted his head to one side. 'Nine square metres, you say . . . ?'

'That is the permitted living space in Moscow today. As people arrive from the countryside to work in the factories, or build the new Metro stations, the population here has risen too fast.'

James thought back to the many Primus stoves in the kitchen. 'Your papa mentioned that.'

'It was once a house for Papa and me alone. When they turned it into *kommunalki* – communal apartments – it was a sign that Papa had fallen from favour. In the *kommunalki* everyone is thrown together: strangers from different backgrounds, different generations.' Her sudden smile was broad and bitter. 'It helps with the housing shortage, but better still, it means that neighbours spy on each other. They pass on every morsel to the house committees that take the rent, in the hope that Stalin's rats will bite and take away the "wrongdoers". Get rid of someone in your *kommunalki* and there is more space to share around.' She paused. 'I am sure there are many good citizens who cheer for what you did today. When my home has been cleared, so many more can move in.'

James flinched, stopped walking and looked at her. 'Please believe that I'm sorry, Anya. I didn't know I was being followed, and had no idea what I'd find at your address. My father knew what your papa risked by sharing his secrets, and was determined to protect his identity by encoding his notes ...' Briefly he filled Anya in on the chain of events since the discovery of the backpack and its contents.

'It is good, then,' Anya said slowly, 'that these men come after you.'

He shot her a glance. 'So they can kill me, you mean?'

'It means their project can still be stopped. And if it can be stopped ... if many lives can be spared ...' Anya tapped her fist against her injured leg. 'Perhaps this is a little bit more worth it?'

'Perhaps.' James smiled faintly, nodded. 'Your papa ruined your dreams and your life, and yet you still looked after him. Why?'

'He was still Papa.' Anya blinked. 'The love and the hate, James, they lie inside and fight. Fight so hard they wear out, so that in the end you feel nothing, and it is better. Better just to get on with things.' She shrugged and looked away. 'This is what I have learned.'

'I learned to be tough when my parents died,' James told her as they set off again. 'But I'd give anything for just five minutes more with them.'

'Then you are stupid.' Anya snorted softly. 'When the five minutes were up, your parents would be dead again and your pain worse.'

'Perhaps pain is what tells us we're alive.'

'You think so?' Anya's smile finally reached her blue eyes. 'You would make a good Russian.'

As they walked on, making for the park entrance, James looked around at the busy crowds. At home, the newspapers all screamed about the dangers of Soviet Russia, the implacable enemy. Articles warned of the 'red menace', of the threat that the Russian people posed to the British way of life, encouraging their readers to think of them as a solid, homogeneous mass, as steely and dour as their ruler. But in truth, they were just the same as any people, a mix of contrasts, good and bad, worried for their families, loving their children. It was their leaders who were dangerous.

The leaders, and their instruments.

Anya stopped suddenly. 'You need to rest?' James asked her.

She didn't reply, just stared at a children's dance display, where two women in their early twenties were panting and perspiring as they called out instructions over the tinny blare of a gramophone.

142

He tried again. 'Do you still dance at all?'

Anya turned to him, and James had never seen such scorn in a single look. He glanced away – and then quickly dragged Anya down to the ground, peering through the legs of the people around them.

'What is it?' Anya kept her eyes fixed on the display.

'Eleven o'clock. Karachan again.'

'He has seen us?'

'Not yet. But I doubt he's alone.' James looked at her. 'How far are we from the main entrance?'

'It is the other side of the parachute tower.'

James looked over. Peeping above the sculpted parkland was the rim of what looked like a helter-skelter, lit up like a lighthouse now as the skies geared up for the slow summer sunset. The cheers and squeals of spectators, and of those jumping from the tower to drift down beneath huge canvas parasols, carried through the deepening gloom.

Why can't we always have parachutes when we need to jump? thought James.

Abruptly, Karachan straightened, made a strange kind of high-pitched bird call – a signal of some kind, a direction or a warning – and then stalked away towards some large tents on the other side of the field.

'Time to go,' James whispered.

They moved slowly, drifting in time with the crowds. James found himself muttering directions and footsteps taken as if this was a game of Which Way Now? and his father was watching his progress. He walked hunched over, pretending he'd dropped something and was half-heartedly looking for it; Anya did the same. *Please God, let us make it*, James thought.

143

She allowed him to take her arm and lead her onwards. With every step he expected a shout of recognition, or the hand of the enemy to fall on his shoulder.

'Perhaps we should split up,' James murmured. 'We might be less conspicuous.'

'This is less conspicuous.' Anya slipped her arm around his back, pressed her head against his shoulder, slowed her steps. 'We walk like sweethearts taking the air. Not strangers thrown together by crisis. Not running afraid. We are lovers on a summer night.'

Surprised, James moved his left arm about her. Able to lean into him now, she could disguise her limp; it was a good cover, he had to admit.

'Clever,' he whispered.

She said nothing.

Even after they'd made it out of the Maxim Gorky Park of Culture and Rest, they stayed close together, and James brooded over the night's trials and terrors. Elmhirst or no Elmhirst, he knew he had to follow the rest of his father's clues, find whatever was hidden here in Moscow. Because whatever Andrew Bond and Kalashnikov had worked to suppress, their deaths had changed nothing.

The Soviet attack was still coming. And since the mere possibility of discovery had triggered such callous violence and loss of life, James could only suppose that its scale was bigger than he would want to imagine.

Anya might be a stranger, but as they walked together across the busy steel congestion of the Krymsky Bridge towards the Metro, James was glad of her arm about him.

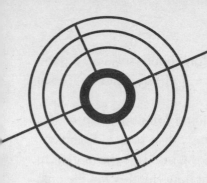

17

Sins of the Fathers

From his hiding place in a construction site off Gorky Street, hidden by shadows and tarpaulins, James looked longingly at the National Hotel. It was now after midnight, and Moscow's pale stone facades were aglow in the light of a full moon. All seemed quiet and ordinary: a thin stream of hotel patrons wandering in or visitors to the bar staggering out, the occasional taxi trundling into service. The most excitement there'd been in the last hour was when a small white lorry turned into a side street beside the hotel, only to re-emerge ten minutes later.

'Laundry truck. They take away the bedclothes for washing.' Anya shot him a sideways glance. 'No assassins. And no bar lady.'

'Not yet,' said James evenly. His plan was to lie in wait for the exotic Elizaveta, manageress of the American Bar, to finish her shift and close up. She seemed to know Elmhirst well enough, and had helped them before. James still had a good supply of roubles to buy assistance and information, if they could only get to her.

He surveyed the National building longingly. Up on the fifth floor was his unofficial room, with a bed and blankets, fresh clothes, a soft carpet, toothpaste and hot water – every comfort James could dream of right now. But this was the only place his pursuers could be certain he'd make for, sooner or later, and he didn't dare go inside. Not imagining all the other eyes that could be watching.

No one else is going to die because of me, he swore. He was tired of trying to manage this situation. If only he knew what had happened to Elmhirst! He and Anya could use an ally, an experienced officer to back them up.

'This Elmhirst may be perfectly well,' Anya said, 'and waiting for you to come back. Perhaps I can get inside, take him a message?'

'These people chased us both halfway across Moscow. You'll be no safer than me.'

'Out here, also. There are eyes all around, looking for those who stand out, who break rules, who flout authority.'

James snorted softly. 'I'm not sure I'd fit in very well here.'

'You are thinking this could never take place where you live?' Anya's smile was more of a sneer. 'Russia today is filled with those who told themselves, *It could not happen here*.'

A raucous shout went up from outside the National. Instantly alert, James peered out across the street through a hole in the tarpaulin. A large woman in a blue cocktail dress was struggling in the grasp of two suited men, her wild red hair like a raging storm over her head.

'Elizaveta,' James breathed, heart sinking.

'Now the secret police have her,' Anya said.

A black limousine parked in the street suddenly grumbled into life – James had thought it empty – and the two men forced the protesting woman into the back seat. A man appeared at the National's doors; swaying tipsily, he raised his hat in forlorn salute and then tottered back inside. A couple in the street hurried by, heads down, taking care to notice nothing as the limousine pulled away.

Anya seemed unsurprised. 'This is the way of it. After your friend makes trouble at the hotel, they investigate all who knew him. Or all who know you.'

'Most probably,' James agreed. 'I hadn't realized there was anyone in that limousine. There could be others watching.'

'Is there anyone you can call for help? You risk the British Embassy?'

'There's a mole there, and the telephone lines aren't secure.' James chewed his lip. 'I have to tell SIS what's happened to Elmhirst and the little I've found out. Go to the airport, get a flight back to London.'

'You don't think that the lady in the veil will be expecting this? That there will be agents watching for you there?'

James turned angrily. 'Well, what the hell else can I do?'

Anya considered. 'You could sleep. Regain the energy you have spent. Move in the morning when the streets are busy and it is safer.'

'Sleep?' James almost laughed. Exhausted as he was, and however much he needed it, slumber here in the fetid dark beneath the tarpaulin seemed unlikely. 'How about I tell you a bedtime story ...?'

He reached into the battered backpack, pulled out the telegram of the plaintext and the letters and numbers inked across the paper from Chamonix, and shared in more depth the baffling details of Andrew Bond's coded messages and exploits abroad.

'*Nash marsh*,' Anya read aloud. 'This means, *our march*.'

'Yes, but what does *our march* mean?' James shook his head. 'You see *Henson*, written there? He was my father's Latin teacher. He's a *talpid*, Latin for mole, in every other reference, but suddenly here he becomes a cardinal.'

Anya had already moved on to study the plaintext telegram. '*I left chapter and verse Moscow buried in James*,' she read crossly. 'Why could he not just say what he means?'

'Because he trusted only his brother to do something about it,' James supposed. 'Your father must have given him some very strong evidence of the Soviet plan.'

'I never found any evidence. I began to think Papa was mad all along.' She paused. 'He said he met your father through a mutual friend, a man who was an engineer for the Metropolitan-Vickers Electrical Company at Perlovka, and knew of your father's links to the British secret service.'

'Through my uncle. I never knew how strong those links were until a few days ago.' James paused. 'I do know that my father would have kept his word and helped Ivan if he possibly could.'

'So you say. Why? Because you loved him? Because your memories of him are tender and gentle?' Anya snorted. 'I loved my papa, and Papa loved me, but he still did what he did.'

'I'm not a child—'

'You sound like one.'

James bit his lip. He knew that arguing now, when they were tired and low, would be the worst thing to do; after all, he was trying to build her trust in him. 'Perhaps I do sound like a child. I suppose I never got to listen to my father speak his innermost thoughts to his pillow at night. I can only imagine how he felt.'

'That is how it should be,' Anya said. 'No one should have to hear their papa wake screaming each night.' She glanced over. 'You needn't feel bad for me, James. The screams, the babble in the dark, they upset me at first . . . but by the end it was just one more thing about him to hate.'

'Don't hate him,' James said quietly. 'Hate the people who did this to him. Who did this to *us*.'

'And what should we do to them in turn?'

'Stop them. However we have to.'

Fine words, Bond! James reflected. But how to put them into practice? What were the Soviet Union's true ambitions in this affair? Stalin had achieved so much for Russia and its satellite nations, but only through the most terrible means. What fresh targets had caught that implacable red eye?

Time passed, and James felt his eyelids grow lead-heavy. Anya yawned beside him and he found himself joining in. He shifted uncomfortably on the concrete floor. 'I'll never complain about my bunk at school again.'

Anya glanced at him. 'You wish you were there now?'

'I wish I was just about anywhere else,' he confessed. 'How about you?'

'I picture myself where I always am in my dreams: on a wonderful wooden stage in a marvellous theatre, like the Bolshoi.' Anya paused. 'You see, it is not *only* pain that tells us we are alive. I used to live when I danced. To dance is to *feel* alive; it is part of *tvorchestvo zhizni* . . . the creativity of life.' She paused. 'You know this too, I think.'

James frowned in the darkness. 'I don't dance.'

'Not true. To move because you must – because you may die if you don't – this is the dance you do, James Bond.' Anya's voice held a weary kind of wonder. 'The dance with death.'

'Well . . . if that's so, I couldn't ask for a better partner,' James joked uncomfortably. He remembered her reaction to the young dancers in the park. 'I . . . saw what was left of your ballet shoes in your room. Is there no hope you will dance again?'

'My right Achilles tendon was crushed, my ankle broken, the ligaments badly damaged.' Her voice was matter-of-fact, bled of all emotion. 'It was the end. The end of everything.'

'But I've seen how quickly you can move—'

'How quickly you can move, *considering*, you mean?' she broke in sharply. 'You sound like my doctors. "Ah, but you are still swift, *maryshka*! Keep up with your exercises. *Pliés* and *rises en pointe* – yes, I detect an improvement, a sure improvement! Apply yourself, good girl!"' Bitterness dripped from each syllable. 'A stray dog can lose a leg and still run. Her blessing is that she does not truly know what she has lost.'

'Perhaps *our* blessing is that we can find something new to replace it.'

'Ah, the English boy is so wise.'

'Your limp isn't that bad,' James persisted. 'At least, when you don't have time to think about it.'

'You think this is all in my head?'

'I only mean . . . I've seen you make running like hell look easy. There's speed and power and precision in you. Maybe you're capable of more than you think.'

Anya's face was stone-hard now. 'Tell me what you have found that replaces your dead parents, James, eh? That backpack you carry like an old teddy bear? Tell me you have not wanted to throw it in the river many times, even as you long for your father to be here beside you to carry it.'

James felt anger prickle along his spine, an itch he couldn't scratch — because he knew that, on some level, she was right. 'So, then, did you keep the remains of your ballet shoes just to torture yourself?'

'It is not so dramatic.' Her voice grew softer. 'They were my beautiful pointe shoes from Anello and Davide in Kensington ... I sewed on the ribbons myself. These shoes, they seemed so wonderful.' She laughed softly, scornfully. 'I used to look at them after the operations on my leg and remember: nothing good can last. They were relics. Like me and Papa, like everything and everyone else in that house.'

'I can see why you think nothing good lasts,' James said. 'But perhaps nothing bad will last, either. What we have — all that we *ever* have — is right now.'

'Perhaps.' Anya leaned back against a stack of bricks, and as she did so, pressed closer to him; deliberate or just a shift of position? Her scent — of Parma violets and musk — filled the darkness, and the heat of her body made him feel more conscious of his sweating.

He'd only just met this girl, and here they were! Damaged as she was, there was a darkness in her that he recognized, that he responded to. Life had thrown him together with so many girls. Roan. Boody and Wilder. Jagua, Kelly, Amy ... Kitty, of course, and that smile of hers ... He closed his eyes guiltily. In the end each girl became a confusion of friendship and fear, of memories, missed chances and moving on, the tender moments locked away for safety in his head and his heart.

Relics, he thought. *You keep the remains to torture yourself* . . .

'I . . . am glad that the old house has burned,' Anya whispered. 'Is it still burning, do you think?'

'The past never stops burning,' James said.

Worn out, lying under the tarpaulin, James was finally lulled to sleep. He dreamed of his childhood: a Christmas morning, tramping through thick snow with his mother and father . . . Running in a race, their cheers in his ears: 'Make us proud!' Dining out, going to the pictures, his father's hand ruffling his hair, his mother there too, smiling. They were all smiling, as if they knew the moment was perfect: to be cherished in remembrance always.

Less happy memories tumbled out of the darkness, but James reached for those too. He was small, tripping over the kerb, skinning his knee. 'Don't make such a meal of things, James.' There was a fierce burr to Andrew Bond's deep voice. 'Don't show it hurts.'

Then Mimic was standing behind him in the dreamscape, mouthing the words: 'Don't show it hurts!'

James turned to run and found he was riding on tweed shoulders through a sunlit forest. His father was laughing, shaking and jumping, pretending to throw James down onto the red-gold riches of the leafy ground. James's mother was laughing too, running alongside. But she hadn't noticed the men waiting at the edge of the clearing; only James had seen them from up on high. He opened his mouth ready to scream—

And James jerked awake, the shout escaping into reality, making Anya jump beside him. A stream of rapid Russian. James took in his surroundings: the stained concrete floor, the dirty grey of the tarp, the scraps of pale daylight peeping in through splits in the material.

'You scared me.' Breathing shakily, Anya looked out through one of the rips in the fabric and scanned the street. 'I think no one heard.'

'I'm sorry.' James checked his watch, which read almost five thirty, wincing at the stiffness in his limbs. 'Did you get any sleep?'

'I watched. I saw nothing.' She turned back to him. 'Will you try to get into your room now?'

Slowly James nodded. 'I think I have to. My aunt is staying at a friend's and her telephone number there is in my trunk.' He got up with a fresh comprehension of the expression 'bone-weary'. 'If I can tell her what's happened, she'll call SIS and get their advice on what to do next, I'm sure.'

'You will speak to her in code, perhaps?'

He scowled at the sarcasm. 'My uncle would've solved this puzzle if he'd received all the pieces. And I'll crack it yet.' He took a look out at the street for himself. Anya was right – the area was deserted; if they were going to risk getting inside, now was as good a time as any.

With Anya just behind him, James stepped out of the building site into the side alley; the suspicion that he was going to be caught at last made his legs heavy.

That was before he even saw the black NAZ-A parked at the other end of the alley. Before he saw the man with the bruised face and the black suit step out from the cover of some dustbins, just a few yards away.

The same glowering man who'd bundled him into a car outside the National yesterday. His kidnapper had returned.

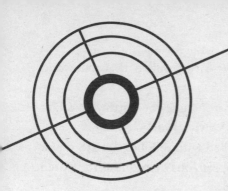

18

Cardinal Sins

The man's black brush of a moustache twitched as he spoke angrily in Russian.

'Finally, I find you,' Anya translated, holding herself tense as the man strode forward, still talking. 'He says that, to him, you are not worth the bother—'

A gunshot shattered the dawn stillness and the man's head jerked backwards as if tugged by an invisible wire. He twisted round, feeling for his spine with both hands. The fingers came away bloody.

Shot from behind? James instantly grabbed Anya and pushed her back through the gap in the tarpaulin. A second shot echoed off the alley walls, and Anya gasped as the man crashed through the ripped fabric after them. His eyes were glazed, his heart pumping gore over his shirtfront as he pitched forward face-first onto the concrete.

James recoiled in disgust. Who had killed this man, and where had they—?

'Bloody hell, Bond, get out here,' came the earthy East End holler. 'You waiting for a signed invitation?'

'Elmhirst!' James could've yelled with relief as the SIS agent burst through the tarpaulin, a worn-out grin on his face, grey fedora still jammed on his head.

He held out his hand to help James up. 'What time d'you call this?'

'Time to leave?'

'You're not wrong.'

'After what happened in the lobby . . .'

'Not here. We need to go. We'll take his car.' Elmhirst seemed to notice Anya for the first time. 'Who's your friend?'

'I am Anya Kalashnikova, and I am coming too.' She stepped over the corpse without a downward glance. 'Shall we?'

With a wry look at James, Elmhirst took the lead, making for the black car at the end of the alley. James followed with fresh hope in his heart that they might actually finish the job and make it out of Moscow alive. However, his optimism snagged on the sight of Elmhirst heaving out a corpse from behind the steering wheel. Looking up from the knife wound in the man's chest, James realized it was the dead man's driver accomplice from the day before.

'You did this?' Anya asked coldly.

'Both these men were watching the National for you, James, same as I was. When the first got out to investigate your shout, I took my chance. We need a motor, don't we? We'd stand out a mile on foot.' Elmhirst left the body face down in the dirt. 'Come on, those gunshots are bound to bring unwanted attention. Get in the back.'

James obeyed, remembering the rough feel of the old leather against his cheek. 'This is the car I was snatched in yesterday,' he announced, 'just after that man fell out through the National's doors with his throat slit.'

'All part of the same gang, the *Vorovsky* brotherhood. Proper psychopaths – so vicious, even the secret police balk at using them – officially, at least. Karachan must've put them on to us after he failed to do the job himself.' Elmhirst started the car and pulled away. 'Those two I went up to in the lobby, they were tooled up with Party specials – Nagant red star revolvers.' He turned left onto the main drag. 'I used a fruit knife I'd taken from breakfast on one of them, and nearly got blown away by the other.'

Anya sat stiffly, gripping the seat beneath her as if expecting the car to take off at any moment. 'You killed him also?'

'Needs must.'

With a shiver James thought back to his jump from the car yesterday. It sounded as if his escape had been narrower than he'd known.

Elmhirst shook his head. 'Anyway, couldn't stick around at the hotel after that, what with the police, Intourist and the hotel staff after me. So I've been roaming the city pretty much ever since, trying to find you, Bond. Heard news reports on the wireless about an incident in the Zamoskvorechye quarter yesterday evening. A boy of your description was seen fleeing the scene.'

'We nearly died there,' James said.

'About the only buggers who didn't, from the sound of things.' Elmhirst glanced at Anya in the rear-view mirror.

'Er – no offence, love. Sounds like another Great War broke out. Tell me what happened. All of it.'

Feeling a little self-conscious, James began. He had been waiting for so long to talk things through with Elmhirst, but now that the opportunity was here he felt more like a sinner making confession to his priest than any sort of hero. Anya made no comment on his story, staring out of the window, arms folded across her chest.

'So the Mimic showed up.' Elmhirst actually looked shaken. 'You're lucky you got out alive.'

'Without Anya, I wouldn't have,' James admitted. 'I saw this "Mimic" at the Academy – he must have come out with Karachan. He's uncanny.'

'So I hear. I only know him by reputation. No real brains but fiercely loyal, and a talent for impersonation like no one on earth.'

'His impression of you was so convincing.'

'I've snooped after Karachan enough times. Mimic must have heard me talking one time then.' Elmhirst shook his head. 'Whisper is, La Velada came across him when she was stirring things up in Ribeirao Preto, during the Brazilian revolutions back in 1930. Local robber gangs kept him caged up like a dog, used him to impersonate police officers so they could burgle without alarms going off. *O Imitador*, they called him; he didn't know any other name. La Velada heard rumours, and when she saw him in action, she killed his handlers and took him on.'

James shuddered. 'So the story had a happy ending.'

'Let's hope this one does.' In frustration, Elmhirst slammed a hand against the steering wheel. 'Why couldn't I have been there when you found Kalashnikov's address in that old souvenir! Things might have ended differently . . .'

'I'm sorry.' James looked down at his lap. 'You're right, I blundered in – didn't think what the consequences might be.'

'You could say the same for my father,' Anya said quietly. 'These killers only finished a job they started long ago.'

'It's the job Bond's father started that I'm keen to finish.' Elmhirst slowed down for a junction controlled by traffic lights, still quiet at this early hour. 'Which way now . . . ?'

Anya blinked. 'You do not know our destination?'

'Not until Bond works out where we're going. Then we'll speed straight there.' Elmhirst steered the motor car to the right. 'You sure there were no other clues hidden inside that little statue of St Basil's? Nothing about Cardinal Henson, or—'

'Nothing,' James broke in, disconsolate. Then he frowned. 'Cardinal is a high-up church official, right? Would St Basil's Cathedral have a cardinal?'

'There are no cardinals in the Russian Orthodox Church,' Anya assured him. 'The meaning of "cardinal" that *I* under-stand is that of a cardinal sin, like greed, or envy, or pride,' she said with sudden passion. 'Or a cardinal error: an unforgivable mistake.'

'We've all made a few of those,' Elmhirst murmured as the car ran into sudden traffic. 'For instance, why didn't I turn left instead of right?'

'Oh my God . . .' James started rummaging around inside the backpack. 'That could be it. That could actually be it.'

Elmhirst was deadly serious again. 'What could?'

'Stop the car a moment.'

Puzzled, Elmhirst did as James requested, pulling in to the

kerb beside a large vacant lot awaiting redevelopment. James pulled out his father's crumpled papers and riffled through them. It felt as if clouds were clearing at the back of his head. '*Play with James,*' he muttered. 'That's what Father wrote to my uncle. And you said, *Which Way Now*—'

'What are you talking about?' Elmhirst complained.

'This!' He read aloud from the Chamonix notes. '*Left for collection. Nash marsh! James and Cardinal Henson: Sep 42 Ori 33 Sep 31 Occ 57 Mer 21 Ori 18 Plamia 47 Occ 62 Sep 59 Iunoshei 45 ...*'

'Well?' Elmhirst grunted.

'When I was small, we used to play a game — a sort of treasure hunt using compass points. Dad would write directions for a certain number of steps north, east, south and west and I'd have to march about trying to find whatever he'd hidden.'

'All right, but what has this got to do with the clues you—?'

'*Cardinal*. North, east, south and west are called the *cardinal* directions!' James felt his heart hammer harder. 'And Henson – Father and Max's old Latin master – gets a mention because Latin is the key to it!'

Anya looked curious. 'The short words there mean something?'

'They're abbreviations: Sep, Ori, Mer, Occ stand for *Septentrio, Oriens, Meridies* and *Occidens*. In Latin, that's north, east, south and west.'

'Cardinal directions! Sneaky son of a ...' Elmhirst shook his head and laughed. 'All that Latin prep finally paid off, eh, Bond?'

Even Anya seemed drawn in. 'So the words are the directions, but the numbers—?'

'Are how many steps we have to take,' James broke in. 'The other words – flames, love, and so on – they weren't chosen at random, they'll be landmarks, or features of the architecture, something like that, helping us to stay on course along the way.'

'Along the way from where?' Elmhirst demanded. 'Where do we start following the directions?'

'Father wanted me to show Max the statuette of St Basil's Cathedral. Surely it's got to be there!' James said.

'Then the reason for all this violence, this pain ...' Anya leaned forward. 'We can find it now, yes? Whatever it might be.'

'Yes.' James pulled out the broken pieces of the little statuette and nodded. 'Whatever it might be.'

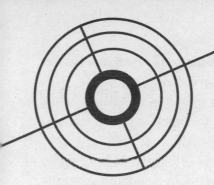

19
Red Treasure

Krasnaya Ploshchad, or Red Square, was a vast brick plaza surrounded by historic buildings and eye-popping architecture. Thousands of years of history had played out on this grand sweep of stone, and the population still gathered regularly to greet its rulers, cheer displays of Soviet strength and castigate past heroes, now fallen from favour. It was the centrepiece of Moscow, a symbol to outsiders of the Soviet Union's might and vision, red not only with the blood of former enemies, but with the blazing promise of power and prominence, of a colossal country on the rise.

Everywhere James looked there was a new draw to the eye: a miniature church here, an overly ornate mansion there, its clashing colours an affront to the greyness of the sky above. To the west were the dramatic towers of the Kremlin, while to the east stood the elaborate, elongated facade of Moscow's state department store, the GUM (pronounced 'Goom', Anya told him). Only the Soviet elite or visiting diplomats had wallets deep enough even to window-shop there.

'Their connections bring them treasures,' said Anya, 'while the rest of us take our places at the back of the queue and hope for whatever we can get.'

And whatever will we *get at the end of this treasure hunt?* James wondered. He suspected that Anya might be hoping for a new wardrobe. Since she and he both looked dirty and disreputable after their misadventures, Elmhirst had insisted on fresh clothes from a Torgsin store on Gorky Street, to confound any spies on the street. James now wore a red shirt and a tweed jacket a size too big, all he could find that came close to fitting, while Anya wore a shapeless grey cotton dress that came down to her ankles; the better, he supposed, to conceal the thick white scars he'd glimpsed on her slender right calf.

It was still early as they walked through the wide-open square. The cathedral was located in the forbidding shadow of the Kremlin's Spasskaya Tower with its shiny new red star, and seemed to rise up out of the Place of Skulls, a forty-foot-wide circular platform of stone, standing as high as two men. A gaggle of rotund women were busy cleaning the cobbles around it.

'So where exactly do we start?' Elmhirst asked.

'The entrance to the cathedral stands in front of the chapel of St Basil,' Anya said. 'This chapel was built over the grave of Basil the Blessed, the holy fool of Christ. In the end, his name was given to the whole church.'

James nodded. He felt that his father, never the most God-fearing of men if Aunt Charmian was to be believed, would have been amused by the notion of a 'holy fool'; as fair a reason as any for choosing Basil's final resting place as the point of origin for the trek to his own buried treasure.

From a distance, the cathedral looked huge – a colourful conflation of tent peaks and onion domes; but as James got closer, it seemed to diminish in size, though not in its curious, candy-box grandeur. Looking up at the cathedral – eight churches built around a central ninth – James was fascinated by the way the walls glittered thanks to a coarse-ground paste of enamelled fish scales, glossy mosaic tiles and dazzling jewels.

At the entrance, facing out to the north-east, James un-folded the paper from his backpack with no small sense of destiny. Years after the directions were written, it was he himself who would do the legwork on this final treasure hunt. He felt solemn and sad – and never more ready. Fears, fatigue and the memories of recent violence faded as he readied himself for the last march.

'Come on then.' Elmhirst had no truck with sentiment. 'What's first – north for forty-two paces?'

'My step is smaller than your long stride,' Anya pointed out.

'Between us we should make a good average,' James said. 'Besides, I told you, there'll be visual clues to watch out for.'

'So long as they're still standing,' Anya warned him. 'Moscow changes so quickly, and as the Metro was built this last year, so many buildings were pulled down . . .'

'Let's put it to the test.' Impatient, Elmhirst was already striding off in a northerly direction. 'You know, even as a kid, I never liked games with too many rules . . .'

The hunt was on. North, east, north again . . . The further James walked, the more his blood fizzed, uncertainty biting at his heels. He could almost imagine his father walking just behind him, smiling, knowing that his efforts in planning the march were being enjoyed and appreciated. *Amat victoria curam* – victory favours those who take pains . . .

'*Plamia!*' Anya pointed to a statue, the arm holding a burning torch above the porticos of a long white building on Razin Street. James led the way over and, once standing below it, read out the next distance and direction. He felt such pressure: the game might be childish, but the stakes were life and death. Whatever happened, James was determined not to let his father down in this, their final game together. A game he was determined to win for them both.

They moved on, counting each step, encountering a statue of solemn young people looking skyward in the well-kept grounds of the Anti-Religious Museum.

'There are your "youths", Elmhirst said, 'your *iunoshei*. Hey, that one looks a bit like you, Bond.'

James felt himself flush. Had his father thought of him when compiling the clues? Off they went again: east, north, east again and then south.

'What's this word?' James wondered. '*Opirat'sya* . . .'

'Leaning,' Elmhirst and Anya said in unison.

'It is there you should look.' Anya pointed to a custard-yellow tower some way across the street, visibly off-centre as it emerged from a smart white courthouse; James could tell from the red dots in her cheeks that she was as caught up in the excitement as he was. 'The Church of St Maksim's bell tower is famous here; we call it the "leaning tower" of Moscow.'

'Still on the right track then.' Elmhirst was tapping his foot impatiently. 'Next?'

Turning down an alleyway beside the leaning tower, James began to count out the next sixty-five paces. There were only three sets of directions left, ending in the words, *osculum pacis*: 'The kiss of peace,' he translated.

The last of the sixty-five steps took them to the junction of a quiet lane that bordered an overgrown grassy area, hemmed in by black railings. Beyond, weeping willows hid the terrain with great falling cascades of greenery. Forty-three steps eastwards and they reached a wrought-iron gate that led into this green space, which they now saw was full of slabs of leaning stone.

'A graveyard,' James breathed.

'He was looking to bury something,' Elmhirst noted. 'Where better?'

The gates were chained shut now, the padlock rusty; it seemed that the graveyard was no longer in use, its land earmarked for future development.

'Over we go.' Elmhirst looked around to make sure they weren't being watched, then vaulted the gates with an easy fluid movement. He reached his hands out to help Anya but she shook her head; she was so slender, she could slip through the railings instead. James took the time to check for watching eyes too, then vaulted the fence in much the same fashion as Elmhirst. 'Twenty-three steps west,' he read out, his heart crawling up his throat with every step.

Anya peered at the paper in James's hand. 'Now, fifteen steps north and we reach the kiss of peace.'

'I'll kiss anyone if we actually find the pot of gold at the end of this rainbow.' Elmhirst's dour expression couldn't hide the anticipation in his eyes, and he quickened his step. 'Well, well ... don't tell me that's it ...'

A cracked marble tomb, half covered in ivy, rose from the soil in a quiet patch of dappled sunlight. Abandoning his counting, James hurried over to study the figures carved out of the stone: a man who might have been a priest stooped over a woman on her deathbed; each figure held a small cross, lips pressed together, eyes closed.

Anya read the inscription on the tomb. '*Dimitry Yakov and his beloved wife, Vjatka ...*' She turned to James and Elmhirst. 'Yakov is the way Russians say "James".'

James felt a jolt as he remembered the coded words from the telegram. 'Chapter and verse buried in James,' he breathed. 'This is it. Whatever Father hid away all those years back, it's right here!'

Elmhirst gave a lopsided smile. 'Chapter and verse, safely hidden. The lowdown on the big bad plot your old man stumbled on ...' He gave a hearty laugh. 'Damn well didn't make it easy, did he!'

'But we've done it.' James's voice cracked as he gazed at the old marble, so skilfully carved, knowing that, years ago, his father had stood here studying the very same thing, burying his secrets beneath this depiction of love beyond death. James felt he'd made a pilgrimage into the past, and found himself moved. 'We've actually done it.'

'*You've* done it, Bond.' He jumped as Elmhirst laid a hand on his shoulder. 'I knew it was worth bringing you out here. Now we dig up whatever it is. Which means I'd better go and find something to dig *with*, hadn't I? Spades, trowels ... If I can't buy them from a hardware store I'll pinch them from a building site.'

'I'll go with you,' James offered at once.

'It's all right.' Elmhirst smiled kindly. 'Your part in this has been played, and played well. I won't be long. Stay here, stay down and stay quiet until I get back.' Without a backward glance, he disappeared through the weeping willows' waterfall of green.

'So.' Anya sank down onto the ground beside the little mausoleum, rubbing her bad ankle as she looked up at James. 'How do you feel now?'

'I'm ... not sure.' He sat down beside her. 'I thought perhaps by solving this treasure trail of Father's, I'd feel closer to him. But instead, I'm thinking if Father had never started this – or if I'd never been brought out here to help finish it – a lot of people would still have their lives.' He looked at Anya. 'No one knows that better than you.'

'When my father chose to defy the state ... he knew how dangerous it was, for him and for those around him. Your father too, in trying to help him. They knew there would be a greater cost if they chose not to act.' Anya folded her knees to her chest and hugged them. 'Let us hope that what we find here can stop this project.'

'Only then can any of this be worth a damn.' James looked at her, wanting to feel better, but not yet able to grant himself that privilege. Waiting around here was chafing at his soul. As the sun probed down through the dappling leaves, James began to explore the graveyard for something that might serve as a makeshift tool. When he couldn't find anything, he began tugging up weeds from around the mausoleum, checking the soil for a likely spot to start digging.

Anya was looking at the figures carved into the old stone. 'The Romans believed that a person's dying breath contained the essence of their soul,' she announced at length. 'Do you know the *Aeneid*?'

'Virgil's epic poem?' James thought of all the dry, dreary Classics lessons he'd daydreamed through at Fettes and Eton, and grunted. 'Sadly, yes.'

'When Dido commits suicide, her sister tries to take her soul into herself. "Let me wash her wounds with water, and with my mouth collect whatever last breath she has."'

James had to admit, the way Anya said the words, they sounded beautiful. 'So, in other words, her sister lives on inside her?'

'Yes. I was only thinking – in a way, this march of your father's, leading you here ... This was his last breath, and you have taken it.'

'So now he will live on inside me?' James grappled with the thick roots of a particularly tough thistle. *I spent so much more time with my mother, I can never forget her. But Father ...*

Even after all this, James still felt as if he barely knew him.

He threw the thistle away and wiped his sore fingers on his shirt. 'So ... either you have an extremely good memory, or you spend too much time reading long-dead authors.'

'One of my tutors – she made me study many works for when I played Giselle.'

'Where was that?' James started prodding at the earth he'd cleared. 'Paris?'

'London.' Anya looked a little shy, but proud to relate her story. 'I performed with the junior Ballets Russes de Monte Carlo at the Mercury Theatre in Notting Hill. Giselle is the most demanding part. And for a thirteen-year-old ...'

'I'm impressed.' James pulled a small, unassuming twig out of the soil. 'I'm also surprised that Russian ballerinas are allowed to perform in the west.'

'Since the start of the century ballet has been the visiting card of Russian culture,' Anya said proudly. 'It revived interest all around the world. Western Europe sees past the politics and celebrates our work.'

'Trust La Velada to exploit that — to use your career to place your father in the heart of things.' James studied the twig; it had no roots. Perhaps it had been placed in the ground deliberately. A marker? He began to scrape at the soil with his fingers. 'Your father drew up plans for those buildings, those four points around the Thames. I suppose they needed him close to the site in case there were any problems . . .'

'So he said. Although he actually specialized in subterranean designs,' Anya said. 'Underground, you know? He helped to plan many of the Metro stations, carving deep into the earth.'

'*Dangerous foundations*,' James muttered. 'That has to mean something more fundamental than a basement that can be used to store explosives. And why did Father focus on the Mechta Academy, and not the other three buildings?'

'In Russian, *Mechta* means "the Dream".'

'A Russian dream . . .' Both fearful of the truth and hungry for it, James plunged his fingers back into the earth and dug with more urgency.

'The dream was to create an international academy to promote Russian arts,' Anya went on wistfully. 'I was going to attend it myself when all was ready . . . to study once more under Madame Radek.'

'Radek, did you say?' James peered round the old stone to look at her.

'Gaiana Radek.' Anya's eyes were closed against the sunlight. 'I studied with her in Paris. Missed her terribly when I came to London. Why, what is it?'

'I met her,' James said. 'She's the Assistant Principal at the Mechta Academy.'

'I am glad. That role was promised to her by the founders. They thought her reputation would help cement the school's position.'

'I tried to warn her about the explosives I'd seen.' James went back to his excavations, clawing at the soil. 'All she cared about was this big gala show at the Royal Opera House. Thought I was trying to sabotage it!'

'Oh, Madame Radek.' Anya smiled fondly. 'Well, she can be fierce. But she adored me.' She opened her eyes, looked round at him. 'Hey, you are making good progress.'

'Elmhirst should've tested the ground first,' James agreed. 'This is coming away easily enough without a spade.'

Anya crawled round to join him. 'I can help. We should waste no more time here than we need.'

'I just pray we find it,' James said. 'We *must* find it.' The rumble of the traffic was both a comfort and a concern, reminding him that if they'd been followed here, anyone could be creeping up on them – and in numbers. He knitted his fingers together and made a scoop, leaning forward to clear away more of the earth. 'I only hope this is the right spot . . .'

'Surely your father would not hide this "treasure" too deep . . .' Anya was burrowing from the other side of the hole, little smudges of dirt on her porcelain face. 'He would not want your uncle to be here long.'

As she spoke, James's fingers touched something cold, flat and thin beneath the loose dirt.

A brown leather strap.

'Oh my God.' Anya looked at him, her blue eyes widening. 'This must be it.'

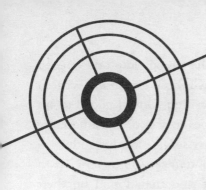

20

The Last Breaths of the Dead

James's heart was beating so loud he couldn't speak. For a few moments he could only stare down into the crater they'd made. Then, slowly, he reached down and tried to work his fingers beneath the strap. Suddenly it came loose, unwinding from the earth like some monstrous flatworm, making James flinch. He saw more brown leather beneath: there was a whole satchel buried down here!

'This is it, all right,' he said hoarsely. Scrabbling at the ground with fresh strength and raw fingers, he worked to loosen the satchel. Anya joined him.

'Come on.' James's nails broke and his fingertips grew raw as he tore at the leather bag. It stayed stubbornly in the soil. 'Come *on* ...'

Then, like a loose tooth prised free, the bag burst out of its earthy grave. With a start, James saw that it was one of his old school satchels; he fumbled with the rusted clasp and opened up the flap of leather – yes, there was his name inside, written in a child's attempt at best handwriting. Once hugged to his chest as he walked the snowy slopes to school in Gstaad, the old satchel had been pressed into service by his father in Moscow and buried in a half-forgotten cemetery ...

'From my papa to yours, lost and then found by their children ...' Anya put a hand on James's arm, her touch surprisingly tender. 'Are you ready to look inside?'

He opened the satchel's main compartment. A large manila envelope filled the space, and as he pulled it out he found his hand was shaking. Inside was a thick sheaf of papers, documents of some sort. James flicked quickly through them – damn it, they were in Russian, of course: he couldn't read a word. He handed them to Anya. Then he realized there was something else in the satchel, right at the bottom. Something harder, oddly shaped ...

It was a gun. A Beretta 418 in a flat, chamois-leather holster.

So the promised buried treasure had some unexpected bite! James removed the gun from the holster with reverent care. He saw that the barrel had been cut off immediately past the end of the slide, making it even smaller and easier to conceal.

'Your father's gun?' Anya whispered.

'*Your* father gave it to him, so he told me. For protection, I suppose.' James prised out the magazine and saw the eight .25 calibre bullets in their copper jackets nestled inside. 'He said that on this occasion a gun was the answer ...'

'There may be better answers in the papers, no?' Anya was already leafing through the musty pages.

176

Carefully James slotted the magazine back into the Beretta, and made sure the safety was flipped on. He turned the weapon over in his muddy hands; the side-grip panels had been removed, and it felt snug and secure in his palm, almost as if it was meant to be there. *This isn't the time*, he told himself, and made to slip the gun back inside its holster. As he did so, he saw something etched into the thin leather. 'Wait. Anya, look at this.'

She leaned in beside him as he turned the holster inside out. There was a map drawn there, or a plan of some sort – a simple maze of straight black lines with numbers inked neatly beside certain junctions. A wavy line in deep blue had been drawn over the top of them, with a single word beside it.

'I recognize Papa's handwriting.' Anya spoke softly. 'That says, "fleet".'

'The Russians are sending a fleet?' James looked at her sharply. 'A gun is the answer, your father said. A way to stop the fleet, maybe? But, then, what do these lines and numbers represent?'

'There must be a clue in the rest of those papers.'

Anya returned to them, while James put the gun back into the holster and placed it carefully at the bottom of his father's backpack. When he glanced back at Anya, he saw that she had stopped shuffling through the papers; on top of the pile was a buff manila file, stamped in red ink.

'Some of these are marked *Revvoyensoviet*,' she said quietly. 'That's the Revolutionary Military Council of the Republic – the supreme military authority of the Soviet Union.'

James scanned the page, noted a small black signature at the bottom. '*Colonel . . . Irena Sedova*,' Anya read.

'Otherwise known as Babushka,' James breathed.

'Grandmother?'

'That was her nickname.' A tingle of fear explored his backbone. 'I've run into her before: a Soviet spymaster, working throughout Europe to undermine foreign governments. I should've known she'd have played a part in this.'

'Whatever *this* is! These papers show only Papa's designs for the Mechta Academy, two office blocks and a theatre. There is also mention of a tower ...'

'No plans?'

'Not with the others.' Anya kept looking, scanning the yellowed pages. 'There *are* reports on flood damage near the sites to be built on ... water volumes the length of the Thames ... predicted highest and lowest tides up until 1936 ...'

'The land came up for redevelopment after the great Thames flood.' James recognized the plans of the Mechta Academy building he'd seen back in London. At first sight they looked identical – but then he noticed something he certainly hadn't seen at the planning register. 'Wait. That looks like ... a *sub*-basement floor. I've seen the official blueprints, and it wasn't there.' James found a map over the page, and felt cold despite the morning sunlight. 'That little cellar space where I found the explosives – it's linked to a secret passageway that must go on for miles ... *That* must be the Project, building beneath the Thames.' He looked at the map more closely; the path of the tunnel was annotated with algebraic equations and scribbles that James couldn't understand. But one thing he saw plainly. 'Anya, this underground passage connects those four buildings together beneath the Thames.'

'But what is its purpose?' Anya frowned. 'There must be many tunnels there already: for electricity, subways, sewer systems . . .'

'Those predictions you saw on the level of the River Thames.' James looked at her. 'What if your father was tasked not with protecting his buildings from floods . . . but with using them to make sure that the floods would happen.'

She stared at him. 'What?'

'There has to be a reason why they're digging in secret so close to the course of the Thames.' James felt sick. 'If you plant explosives above ground, they can be seen and defused. But if you place them underground, you can use more of them. You can seed an area of several square miles with hexogen, or whatever those explosives are called, put them in just the right place to do maximum damage – if your architect is clever enough.'

'Oh, Papa,' Anya breathed, flicking back through the papers. 'Hexogen, did you say, James? That word is here. Formulae and quantities, calculations and . . . Oh, I don't know.'

James looked too, though the notes were all in Cyrillic – until Anya moved her hand to reveal some words written neatly in English:

Hejnał from Krakow to Jericho
J6 14–15
Holster

'Holster,' Anya noticed. 'This is linked to the map drawn inside it?'

'Must be. The wavy blue line could be the Thames. Perhaps when it floods, they'll send in their fleet . . .' James wished that

Elmhirst would get back. 'Jericho's in Oxford, I think – does the Thames reach that far?'

'You expect me to know?' Anya snapped. 'J6 sounds like it could be a map reference.'

'And the Hejnał is that bugle call blown by the Trumpeter of Krakow in the book. But as for the numbers . . .'

'We do not need to understand it all.' Anya set down the papers. 'Just get this information to people who will.'

'*Shhh,*' James hissed. He could hear furtive movement through the trees. 'Someone's coming.'

Anya's pale blue eyes widened. 'Elmhirst?'

'The very same,' came the low reply. James and Anya let out deep breaths as Elmhirst pushed through the hanging veil of the willow trees, a rusted old spade in his hands. 'Sorry I've been gone so long. I found this, but now I reckon I've been on a wild bloody goose chase. What've *you* found?'

'Secret tunnels underneath the Thames!' Triumphant, James quickly bundled the documents together and held them out to Elmhirst. 'With these, we can expose the Soviets' plan – bring it all down.'

'Is that right?' Elmhirst beamed, tossed the spade away and grabbed the wad of papers. 'Well done, Bond. Good God, this is a proper haul.' He gave an earthy chuckle. 'I'll bet this little lot could've stopped the Soviets and their plot years ago . . .'

As the sun manoeuvred its way clear of cloud, James caught a gleam in the leaves behind Elmhirst, and stiffened.

Sunlight on gunmetal.

He got up casually, his heart hammering. *Elmhirst was seen; someone's followed him.* He picked up the spade – then turned and hurled it into the undergrowth like a javelin. A gasp was eclipsed by a gunshot, and bark exploded from the tree trunk high over Anya's head as the shot went wide. James was already sprinting for the point of origin, diving through the willow's leafy curtain.

It was Karachan, flat on his back beside the spade, one hand clutched to his chest. At the sight of him, and the Browning revolver he carried, James was gripped by a deep and weary hatred. *You again.* He kicked the gun savagely out of the assassin's grip.

'Good work, Bond.' Elmhirst picked up the Browning and covered Karachan with it. 'You did well.'

'Listen!' James heard a faint clunk – the sound of a heavy chain falling. 'The gates. Someone's cut off the padlock.'

'They're coming in.' Elmhirst folded the manila envelope, pushed it into his jacket's inside pocket and raised the gun. 'And you can bet your backside that's not the caretaker . . .'

A dark, furtive movement from just behind him made James turn – and a fist struck him just behind the ear. Realization rocked him with the impact: *Someone else came in with Karachan – and that's their back-up at the gate!* He staggered and turned as the hateful face of Mimic thrust up against his own.

'No!' James brought up the heel of his hand, full force, under Mimic's chin, knocking him back. He saw Anya, slumped on her front over the gravestone, apparently out cold, and a wave of anger came over him: after all this twisted little freak had done to him, after all the people he'd killed, the lives he'd destroyed . . . He kicked Mimic's feet from under him; when the boy fell on his front, James readied himself for a 'bronco' kick: to jump, draw up his knees and then drive his boots into

181

the small of Mimic's back; to stop him hurting anybody ever again—

'No! Please!'

The voice burst from Mimic's lips, but it was not his. James was stopped in his tracks, incredulous and chilled.

The voice begging him now was his father's.

'I've not told anyone, I swear.' Mimic turned over onto his back, his dark eyes rolling in a weird ecstasy as the words tumbled out. 'Get your hands off her—' The boy jerked, as if emerging from a trance, looked straight at James and screamed.

Screamed with the voice of James's mother.

'No!' James put his hands to his ears as the scream went on. *This creature was watching when Mother and Father died!* He was about to throw himself at Mimic, to smash him, punish him – *kill* him – just to make him stop.

Then stop Mimic did, and switched straight to another deadly accurate impression: 'Damn it, Bond, you unhelpful bastard. You weren't meant to die till you talked!'

James felt his world shake as the voice cut through him.

It was a perfect impression of Adam Elmhirst.

Stunned, James was starting to twist round towards Elmhirst when something hard came down on the back of his neck. Karachan loomed over him, back on his feet with the Browning again in his hand, held like a club.

This can't be happening, James thought desperately. *None of it!*

'Well, boys,' Elmhirst said mildly. 'I'm sure you'd like to thank Bond here, as I would, for delivering the goods.'

James stared at the agent's rueful smile, the hint of apology in the pale-blue eyes. At the gun trained on his heart.

'All along,' he murmured. 'You. A double agent at the heart of SIS.'

'Now you get it. And I get this.' He pulled the manila envelope out of his pocket and kissed it. 'I work for SIS, but my loyalties are to the Soviet Union. And now there's no chance of *anyone* stopping the Project.'

By now, James could hardly hear him; overcome by his enemies, his only ally out cold, James found his thoughts slipping away into one dark centre in his head.

His voice cracked as he said to Elmhirst, 'You killed my parents.'

'It was tough, Bond, watching your mum and dad fall from that rock face, watching them kick and scream — until they bounced, at least. That's haunted me, that has, through the years.'

James couldn't speak. He was actually grateful for the tears that came, blurring his sight. Mimic took James's wrists and pulled them hard behind his back, whispering tenderly into his ear in Monique Bond's lilting accent: 'Please. We've got a son.' He giggled, then resumed: 'A son who needs us . . .'

James closed his eyes as a needle penetrated his wrist, and he finally fell from the precipice of his sanity into nothing.

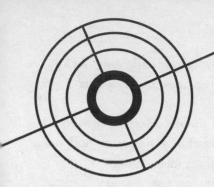

21
To Break the Bond

A spray of saltwater on his face woke James. *Where am I?* His eyes were crusty and wouldn't open. He shifted, and found that the ground was hard beneath him. A steady mechanical growl carried under the wash and lap of water, and the cool wind blew gusts of spice and diesel fumes past his nostrils.

'Come on, boy, give me your Jimmy Cagney ...'

James held still. That was Elmhirst's voice. Then, a moment later, he heard the voice of the tough-guy actor; it could have come straight from James Cagney's gangster picture, *The Public Enemy*: 'Why, that dirty, no-good, yellow-bellied stool! I'm gonna give it to that Putty Nose right in the head ...'

It had to be Mimic, of course. Laughter followed, men's laughter. How many people were here – wherever *here* was? The ground seemed to tilt underneath him. *Am I on a boat?*

Slowly, sluggishly, James's senses were hardening, seeking out clues while he feigned unconsciousness. *How did I get here . . . ?*

In an awful rush, memories of the old Moscow graveyard returned. The horrible realization that his parents had not died in a straightforward climbing accident at all.

James fought to keep his body at rest, his face neutral. He'd seen so much horror in his life: death and disaster of all descriptions. It was as though steel shutters came down inside, fenced off his feelings, allowed adrenalin to do its job – to get himself and those he cared about the hell out of danger. But this time he was far too late to save the people he loved. They'd died years back, at the hands of someone he'd thought he could trust. At the hands of someone whose life he'd saved in Los Angeles last year . . .

'Now give us your Jean Harlow,' Elmhirst beseeched Mimic.

The boy obliged and reproduced the actress's voice without hesitation. 'You want things and you're not content till you get them! You don't give. You take . . .'

Ragged applause followed, and a sardonic wolf-whistle – James estimated three other men were present.

'Movies are fine, but now let's have some real-life drama,' Elmhirst drawled. 'I know! How about the day we met Andrew and Monique Bond?'

James fought desperately to show no reaction.

'*Get your hands off of her!*' came Andrew Bond's cry, and James's heart ached. If he opened his eyes, surely he'd see his father standing there. '*Damn it, Elmhirst, I haven't talked to anyone. I don't have any evidence! Please, my love, don't cry . . .*'

'Stop it!' James shouted. 'For God's sake!' He jerked his

body up into a sitting position, gasping as nausea spun from skull to stomach.

Elmhirst was crouching over him, a grin on his doughy face. 'Welcome back, Bond.'

James tried to get up, but found that his wrists were handcuffed and his ankles chained together. He saw a conning tower rising amidships and realized he was not on a ship, but a submarine that had surfaced to utilize its powerful diesel engines, charging its batteries as it sliced its way forward, buffeted by the choppy waves which formed the only landscape.

'Where's Anya?' he demanded.

Elmhirst ignored him. 'Did you not like Mimic's little historical re-enactment, Bond? He's got an eidetic memory to go with his knack for voices – never forgets a thing – makes him quite an asset. Didn't you just love his impression of your aunt Charmian on the phone at the airport?'

'That was Mimic I talked to?' James shut his eyes. 'Of course. You told me she was staying with a friend so I wouldn't query the different telephone number.'

Elmhirst smiled. 'Mimic could do her voice because he telephoned her the night before last, pretending to be *you*. Told her you were staying with your old mate Hugo for a few days, so she wouldn't miss you.'

Bastard, James thought. 'Tell me where Anya is.'

'You trying to act tough, Bond?' Elmhirst straightened up. 'Well, listen. You've been flown from Khodynka aerodrome in Moscow to Esbjerg in Denmark, and transferred to a Soviet submarine we met off the coast. You're in chains in the middle of the North Sea and dependent for your survival on the whims of your worst enemies.' He shook his head. 'So do me a favour: drop the tough-guy act, and maybe think about begging.'

'Go to hell,' James muttered under his breath. Through the pelt and bluster of the spray and wind, he saw the captain at the helm station, and guessed that the other two men were the watch officer and a lookout. He guessed too that Elmhirst and Mimic were more than just passengers; they were here as honoured guests.

But where is Anya? James wondered uneasily. *Why am I being held on deck instead of down below?* He needed more time to recover, time to think; perhaps appealing to Elmhirst's sense of vanity would buy him precious minutes. 'I suppose Karachan attacking us at the hotel was staged to make me trust you more. But what about those men you killed – the ones from the brotherhood who were trying to get me?'

'Your trouble, Bond, is that you don't pay attention.' Elmhirst's smile was sickening. 'I told you, out in Russia Great Britain's resources are limited; if we need a job doing, we often employ locals.'

'What job?'

'SIS have no idea I've been in Moscow – I told you, I used a fake passport. As far as they're concerned, I'm currently undercover, investigating the whereabouts of that stolen Blade-Rise hexogen – stolen by myself, of course.' He tutted. 'Unfortunately Karachan was clocked at Croydon Airport's passport control on his way to catch the plane before us. That led to SIS checking passenger records to look for known accomplices. And, of course, they found your name on the manifest: the boy who delivered fresh evidence on a Russian cold case straight to their door.'

'SIS thought I'd been kidnapped … so they hired some freelance muscle to find me?' James felt sick, remembering the thick Russian accent in his ear: *You come with us . . . you not hurt.* He bowed his head. 'They grabbed me like that to take me to safety.'

'Off for tea and crumpets at the British Embassy, yeah. And they all knew me, of course, from past dealings, which is why I had to kill them. If it got back to SIS that *I* was in Moscow with you, well . . .'

'They would know that you're a lying, murdering, traitorous—'

'As it is, one of my fellow agents has already been assigned to investigate what happened. He's on his way from London now.' Elmhirst tutted wistfully. 'I knew they would send someone, of course. I'm only one agent of many on the Karachan case; I put them off for as long as I could. And they won't know he's being smuggled back into Britain the slow way, by submarine . . .'

James was still getting his head round the deceit. 'You took me to Moscow to make sure you found the evidence first?'

'I don't like loose ends,' Elmhirst agreed. 'That's why I've tied you up.'

James looked him in the eye. 'Are you just gloating for fun, or is there a reason why you haven't killed me?'

'I don't do anything without reason, Bond. I want information, so I'm offering some in exchange.' He held out his arms. 'The Revolutionary Military Council of the Republic has invested years in this project, waiting for the perfect time, building up to the biggest coup in history. Then, just weeks before we're ready to go, evidence turns up that could blow the whole thing. If your old man had just handed over said evidence to me when I asked for it, maybe your mummy would still be alive today.'

James felt his guts clench. 'What do you mean?'

'On your father's last visit to Moscow with Vickers, La Velada learned that he had evaded his official party escorts three times. I was stationed there – asked him what he was up to. He wouldn't talk.'

'*SIS suspicious.*' James remembered the coded message from Chamonix. 'That meant he found *you* suspicious – he must've thought the only way you could know so much was if you were involved. That's why he encrypted the message in a different way.'

'Typical Bond. Too clever by half.' Elmhirst looked out across the churning ocean. 'I eased up, played dumb, let him think he was in no real danger. But I followed him home with Mimic.'

James closed his eyes. 'Yes. I heard.'

'We confronted them. Your mater and pater made a run for it, got away into the mountains ... When I caught up with them, they still didn't want to play. They were roped together by then, tried to climb too far, too quickly, and . . .' Elmhirst looked across at Mimic. 'How did it go, again?'

Mimic screamed the scream of Monique Bond, his eyes as wide as his grin. Sickened, James looked away.

'I've done so many things to safeguard this project,' Elmhirst went on, 'so many. Now there's just one last dangling thread I need to tie up. For my peace of mind, you know?' His eyes were cold as the ocean as he regarded James. '*Hejnał from Krakow to Jericho, J6 14–15, Holster.* Words I found written on a page of your daddy's buried notes. He's gone back to that bloody Trumpeter book again, hasn't he? Another clue, tied in with you. So, what does it mean?'

James stared back, his face impassive. The message related to the map in the holster, of course, but he wasn't about to reveal *that*. Elmhirst hadn't been there when James discovered the Beretta in its chamois case, and didn't seem to know that James had placed them in the backpack. If only he had that backpack now!

Elmhirst nodded to the watch officer and the lookout, who moved forward and grabbed hold of James by the ankles and armpits.

'You know what?' the agent called. 'Killing Bonds prematurely? It's habit-forming.'

Without further ceremony, the crewmen tossed James off the deck.

Shocked, James had time to draw only the quickest breath before he crashed into the cold, churning grey and sank, unable to swim properly with his hands cuffed together, weighed down by the chains. Pain bit into his ankles as the chain grew taut and tugged him through the water. Choking, struggling to reach the surface and spluttering for air, James saw the bulk of the sub loom up to his left and fought to get away from it, pushing wildly against the water with both bound hands. If he was drawn into the propellers . . .

No good, he thought desperately as he went under again; pressure, the sub's engines and the buffeting current roared in his ears. *Can't swim like this, can't—*

He felt another jerk on his legs; the chains that held him were being hauled in by the two crewmen. While Elmhirst watched, James found himself pulled out of the sea feet-first and dumped once more on the deck. Retching, gasping for air, he turned onto his side and glared up at the rogue agent defiantly.

'Try again, shall we?' Elmhirst walked closer. 'What does that message mean?'

'I'm not sure.' James swallowed hard, still panting for breath. He had to play for time – time to think. While he lived, there was just a chance he could do something to stop Elmhirst; right now, to him, nothing else mattered. 'I ... I know that the Hejnał is the tune the Trumpeter played in the book.'

'And the "J" has got to be you, right? J for James.'

'Perhaps. As for Jericho ... it's a suburb of Oxford. We ... had relatives there. On my mother's side.'

'Names?'

James didn't answer. Elmhirst nodded to the crewmen, who lifted James back up again. He thrashed angrily in their grip as they took a menacing step closer to the side of the U-boat, like fishermen about to throw a disappointing catch back into the sea.

'Well?' Elmhirst called.

'If you kill me,' James shouted back, 'you'll never know!'

For the longest moment he was suspended in mid-air, dripping wet, staring at the whipped-up white of the propellers' trail through the ocean. Then the captain called something in Russian, and James was thrown onto the deck as the crewmen ran to join him at the helm station. One by one they ducked down into the belly of the sub, before Mimic followed suit.

'Shipping sighted,' Elmhirst said. 'We have to dive.'

James felt the heat of relief in his cold, wet, aching body. 'So you're postponing your little poolside party?'

'It gave some amusement to the men. I didn't expect to get much more out of you than that. You're too much the natural hero: with so many more lives at risk back home, your life means nothing, right? Which is why, since time is short, I thought I'd bring some extra leverage.'

James stared up. 'Anya?'

'Anya.' Elmhirst hauled James to his feet. 'Keep any details back from me, Bond, and you'll watch me do a proper number on her legs. I'll make sure she never walks again.'

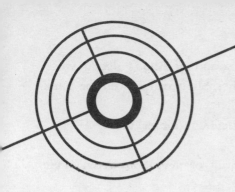

22
Truth and Blood

Wet and shivering, James was lowered down into the belly of the sub. At the bottom of the conning tower, two of the ratings caught him and swung him round into a narrow corridor. James's head smashed against the bulkhead; the pain was blinding, and he must've passed out. When he came to, he was lying on a narrow bunk. The atmosphere was dank and stale and salty. Through the throb of his headache he heard the hissing of pipes, the deep diesel drone of engines and the *pat-pat* of water dripping.

He was lying down, and still wet, so he couldn't have been out for long. The light came from a red bulb bolted into the ceiling, like the one in the underground chamber beneath the Mechta Academy's basement. James tried to sit up, but found that while his legs were now free, his hands had been cuffed behind his back.

'James?'

His heart jumped at the sound of Anya's sleepy voice. *Leverage*, Elmhirst had called her. She was lying on the bunk below his. 'Are you all right?'

'My arms are tied behind me, I cannot feel them.'

'Mine too.'

'I've been slipping in and out of sleep. You weren't here before – where did they—?'

'Elmhirst had me chained up on deck, but then we had to dive.' James turned onto his side, pins and needles prickling through his wrists. 'I reckon we're approaching England.'

'Why is Elmhirst even keeping us alive?' Anya said. 'He has his information now.'

'Not all of it,' James muttered. 'Not yet.' As his headache ebbed a little, he took in the tiny cabin properly. There was room for the two bunks, a folding sink, a toilet – and his father's battered backpack, lying discarded on the floor.

The gun and the holster, he thought. *I pray they're still there.*

The thought of prayer made a connection in his mind. *The Bible. That reference, J 6 14–15: it could mean chapter six, verses 14–15. And Jericho ...* He'd lived through so many dusty sermons at Eton and Fettes, there couldn't be a schoolboy alive who didn't know the story of how the Israelites had brought down the walls of besieged Jericho with the sound of their trumpets, to break inside and destroy their enemies ...

He was about to say as much to Anya when it occurred to him: *Elmhirst's told me where I am and what he wants, wound me up like a clockwork mouse, and now he's put me in on my own with Anya. What's the first thing we're going to do? Talk. Plan.*

What if this room is bugged?

'James?' Anya prompted.

Awkwardly, he managed to swing himself down from the bunk to the cabin floor, leaned in to her ear, spoke in a whisper: 'Assume we're being spied on. Toe the line. Say *nothing* about the gun.'

Anya pulled away, then put her lips to James's ear. 'Do we even have it?'

'I'm going to see. It might be our only advantage,' James whispered. Then he looked away and raised his voice. 'Nothing to do but wait, I suppose.'

Anya sighed. 'I wonder where we are going?'

'Somewhere on the English coast, I assume, if Elmhirst wants to go to Jericho.' James leaned towards her, lowered his voice to a murmur. 'We need to talk — if we *are* being listened to, it'll cover the noise of me trying to open and search through a backpack with both hands tied behind my back.'

As he rose and crossed to the backpack, she nodded her understanding. 'I liked England,' she began. 'It was such a joy to study there . . . I was to be the next Mathilde Kschessinska. Do you know of her?'

'Happily not,' James said, fumbling behind him for the backpack's straps. 'I don't imagine she'd be happy with the hash I'd make of pronouncing her name.'

'My tutors all said that I was a future *prima ballerina assoluta*, perhaps even greater than Mathilde . . .' Even in the crimson gloom James could see animation return to her face; he needn't have worried about slow and halting conversation, for Anya was warming to her theme. 'Even at thirteen I could master twenty consecutive *fouettés en tournant*.'

'Is that a type of food?'

'Philistine! It means "whipped turns" done in one place and on one leg.' She seemed to luxuriate in the memory, moving under the bunk's rough blankets as though they were silk.

James freed one of the straps with his swollen fingers and began on the other, nodding at Anya to carry on. 'You must have started young ...'

'From the age of five I was taught in Paris by Madame Preobrajenska, a former Russian ballerina with the Imperial Theatre. She gave evening classes in a big studio on the Rue de la Pompe. Father was always so busy, but I barely missed him: from the age of eight I trained with Madame every day after morning school.'

'Single-minded,' James observed, freeing the second strap so he could reach inside the backpack.

'Have you never found something you excel at, James? Something that defines you?'

With a jolt he remembered Elmhirst discussing something similar. 'Nothing very worthwhile, I'm afraid.'

Anya closed her eyes, and James held still. 'You know, if I try, I can still see Madame's studio, just as it was when I was small.'

'Take me there.' James reached down inside the backpack, exploring with his fingertips, pulling at fabric. 'Anywhere beats this hole.'

'I can see the watering can she used before every class to dampen the floor and create grip,' Anya went on, 'and the long stick she used to beat time.' She smiled at her imaginary surroundings. 'There were barres along three walls, and the fourth wall was a mirror from floor to ceiling. I would watch my reflection turn and point ... Back then I had grace, and beauty, and power.'

You still do, James thought, *if you could only see it*. Finally his fingers brushed the soft chamois of the Beretta's holster, and a wild pulse thumped triumph through his body.

'It's like I'm there, Anya.' He pulled out the gun and holster and manhandled both into the back pocket of his trousers. 'Yes, the view is suddenly so much better . . .'

The sudden scrape of a bolt made them jump in panic. James scrambled to his knees as the second bolt screeched across the iron bulkhead door. Whoever came in couldn't fail to see that he'd been through the backpack. What if they searched him—?

Anya sprang up from her bunk. 'I will buy you time,' she hissed and, as the door swung open, jumped bravely forward and swept her leg upwards.

It was Karachan standing in the doorway with a tray of food. Anya's pointed foot knocked his wrist and the tray went flying. His face twisting with rage, Karachan grabbed a handful of Anya's hair and hauled her outside; with her hands cuffed behind her back she was powerless to stop him.

James was scrambling up to help her when Mimic leaned in and slammed the door shut.

'The view is suddenly so much better,' Mimic called mockingly in James's own voice.

James guessed he'd been right about the listening device in here – or just outside the door. Who needed a hidden microphone when you had a bug as big as Mimic? 'Anya!' he shouted, fumbling to close the flap on the backpack. 'Are you all right?' He heard her scream, scrambled up and kicked savagely at the door. 'Leave her alone!'

'All right,' came Elmhirst's hateful voice. 'Let him look.'

Trembling, James stepped away from the door as it opened, the Beretta in his back pocket, afraid of what he might see. He felt helpless. If only his arms were free!

'I'm all right, James.' Anya was on her knees in the cramped, whitewashed corridor, bread and broken crockery on the floor around her. Karachan still held a big clump of her hair in one hand but her face was full of pride and defiance.

'How long she stays all right depends on you,' said Karachan.

Elmhirst came into sight and stood beside Anya. 'I give you a chance to spill the beans between you, and what do you do? Talk about the good old days at Madame Up-Herself's in belle Paris.'

'All right, I'll tell you.' James's eyes met Anya's, dark and wide in her pale china face. 'Tell you everything.'

'Yes, you will,' Elmhirst assured him. 'Because, let's be clear here. You're St George, she's the damsel – and I'm the dragon.' He slapped Anya's cheek with the back of his hand, and she gasped.

James felt anger flare. 'I said I'd tell you—!'

'So tell me.' Elmhirst smacked her cheek again, harder. 'Those relatives of yours in Jericho . . .'

'My – my uncle Perry and aunt Kitty,' James blurted, looking down at the floor. *You can do this. Think.* 'There's a funny-shaped flowerbed in their garden. When I was little, I thought it looked like a big gun, and when the flowers bloomed . . .'

'That made the holster?' Elmhirst surveyed him coldly. Then he nodded and Karachan pulled more tightly on Anya's hair. Elmhirst took a handful and did the same. 'I said, was that flowerbed—?'

'Yes, that was the holster!' James said quickly. 'Let her go.'

'Now tell me about Krakow. About J6, 14, 15 . . .'

James cleared his throat. 'In *The Trumpeter of Krakow*, I remember the Hejnał was played four times each hour to each cardinal direction in turn, starting with the east.' He swallowed hard. 'So the numbers must fit the same code as the first treasure trail.'

'Six steps east, fourteen west and fifteen north?' Elmhirst sounded dubious. 'How could your dad have hidden something in Jericho while he was in Moscow?'

'I don't know,' James said, and wished he didn't mean it. 'He sent that postcard to Max; perhaps he sent one to my uncle and aunt in Jericho too? SIS could be asking them about it right now . . .'

Elmhirst said nothing for several seconds.

'It is possible,' Karachan conceded.

'Yes. It's *just* possible.' Elmhirst heaved Anya to her feet by her hair. She whimpered with pain, but didn't cry out.

'I'm telling you the truth!' James shouted desperately.

Elmhirst picked up the metal tray from the floor. 'Remind me, which one is her good leg?'

'Damn it, Elmhirst—'

James broke off as the agent swiped down savagely with the tray; the edge sliced into Anya's left calf, just below the knee. She cried out with agony and Karachan let her fall to the floor. James started forward, but Mimic scurried in and shoved him back into the room. Then the door swung closed on him with a metallic boom.

'Just a love tap. Like I said, Bond,' Elmhirst called. 'Leverage.'

James turned away from the door, fighting to stay calm. What would Elmhirst do to Anya next? *He's playing mind-games*, he told himself. *He wants you to think you're beaten.* He fished the gun out of his pocket, felt for the safety catch on the back of the handle. *Well, I'm not beaten just yet. When this journey's over . . .* He practised unlocking the gun. Eight bullets, but how many enemies? Under wartime conditions an ocean-going sub on patrol might have as many as eight officers and twenty ratings; there might be fewer for a one-off transport mission, but James had no way of knowing.

What he *did* know was that if you brought a gun to a confrontation, you had to be ready to use it. And was he? Could he shoot to kill, in cold blood?

'Sleep tight, James,' Elmhirst called from outside.

James felt the skeleton grip press against his sweating palm. 'You too,' he breathed. 'While you can.'

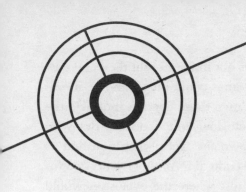

23
Homecoming

In the crimson gloom, James felt a sense of unreality as time washed past. He laid the gun next to him on the bunk; then, lying on his back, he was able – with some difficulty – to tuck up his legs and bring his bound wrists up and over his feet so that his arms were in front of him once more. He found his watch had been removed, presumably when the cuffs were fitted, so he had no way of knowing how long the voyage was taking.

He took the Beretta and placed it more comfortably in his front right pocket, got up and tried walking about. The handgun was so light and unobtrusive his clothes gave no hint that he was armed. It was the slightest of comforts.

Again and again he studied the map on the holster, trying to make sense of it. The defensive walls of Jericho were blown down by the repeated blasts of the trumpet – over six days, if he remembered rightly from the book of Joshua (*J for Joshua?*

he thought), and the Israelites got inside to rout their enemies. What was the connection? James could only imagine it was *flood* walls – a plot to bring down those barriers that held the Thames in check, to devastate low-lying London. But who needed trumpets to bring down the walls when you had as much RDX as the enemy already did? All those years ago his father couldn't have known just where the explosives would be stored, so what exactly *did* the map show?

He hid the chamois-leather holster in the backpack again, then wearily strained to get his arms back in place behind him. His hands throbbed and his wrists were raw, but somehow, between that, fear for Anya and his growling stomach, James actually managed to fall asleep; a natural, more replenishing rest than his earlier drugged oblivion.

He woke to find that the constant rush and hum of the engines had slowed to a sinister whirr. A heavy knock on the door. 'Nearly there, Bond,' Elmhirst called. 'Thought you might like to come and see the view. Stand back from the door.'

So! James felt a tremor through his body. *We're close to land – and a chance to get free.* He swung his legs off the bunk and waited while the door opened. Karachan stood beside Elmhirst, the Browning revolver clamped in his fist.

'Where's Anya?' James demanded.

Elmhirst smirked. 'Come on.'

With Karachan's gun pointing at his head, James ducked through the doorway into the narrow corridor and quickly got his bearings. He realized he'd been locked in an officers' mess in the sub's forward battery, so called because below the floor panels were almost 150 batteries, the life force of the ship when travelling below the water – when the air-sucking diesel engines could not be used. He was led aft into the cramped main control room where a skeleton crew, led by a captain and an engineer, was running operations. Each square inch of wall was covered in cables, gauges, dials and instruments, piled in big boxy stacks. Key levers controlling the various vents, safety tank, gears and so on were crowned with different-shaped handles so they could be identified even in darkness should lights fail during an emergency.

The captain barked something in Russian and the boat shuddered as the ballast tanks were blown, compressed air pumping out to displace the ballast water. Bow-first, the sub began to rise.

'Periscope depth,' Elmhirst announced. 'No point having a fantastic view if you can't appreciate it, eh?' He stepped over to the periscope shears and raised them, moved himself and the stubby handlebars through 360 degrees, looking through the world above the water.

'It's Anya I want to see,' James said. There was no sign of her, or Mimic, and he felt the bite of nerves. 'Well?'

'You don't want to get too fond of that one, Bond. She's the sort who'll get under your feet.'

Looking down, James saw a perforated floor panel covering the crawlspace beneath: Anya had been crammed in there like a medieval prisoner into an oubliette. A gag had been placed around her mouth and her eyes were closed.

'Anya? Are you all right?' James started forward, but Karachan shoved him roughly away towards Elmhirst.

'That's close enough.' Karachan unpinned the floor panel, reached inside the crawlspace, grabbed Anya by the hair and hauled her out. She stayed icy silent, eyeing her captor with undisguised hatred.

'Come on, Bond.' Elmhirst patted the periscope. 'Distract yourself. I want to share that glorious view.'

James didn't move.

'Seriously? You don't think you Bonds have put Anya through enough?'

Karachan let her fall to her knees. But as she looked up at James through her dark, lank hair, he saw strength in those blue eyes. She had been through hell, just so he could get hold of the Beretta, but how could he repay that sacrifice – how could he even draw the gun with hands cuffed behind his back?

Telling himself that the moment would come, James shuffled over to the periscope. Elmhirst checked the view first, twisted on the right-hand grip to flip different lenses over the 'scope, then on the left to choose a filter that would best suit the light conditions on the surface. 'There, you see? Perfect.'

James put his eye to the eyepiece; he supposed the sub must be snorkelling, only its periscope visible as it swam slowly beneath the surface of the water like a watchful predator. He saw churning grey beneath an evening sky. The view swivelled to port and James felt a jolt jump through him.

The magnificent classical buildings of the Royal Naval College were sliding slowly past.

'We're in Greenwich.' Slowly James looked up from the periscope. 'We're travelling right up the Thames.'

'Breaching the mighty heart of London.' Elmhirst nodded. 'I thought you might like to see it. Because after tomorrow night, no one's ever going to see it this way again.'

James was about to demand some answers when a cultured, effete voice behind him made him jump. It was the voice of the King, George V. 'My subjects, a great calamity has befallen our proud nation ...' James turned to find Mimic standing behind him, the soft, curious face gazing his way. 'The time it will take to rebuild London – and our lives – cannot yet be calculated ...'

'Why is he speaking like the King?' James asked. 'Don't tell me he's met His Majesty as well?'

'He's heard broadcasts like the rest of us. He's the voice of them all!' Elmhirst's lips twitched, but the rest of him wasn't smiling. 'All right, Your Majesty, hope you slept well. You're doubling as planesman today so take your seat.' At once, Mimic seemed to shrink back into himself, nodded and hurried to his position. 'We'll be docking soon.'

'Where?'

'You saw Kalashnikov's architectural plans.' James hadn't really expected a reply, but Elmhirst seemed happy to tell him. 'At each site, a secret underground level has been built to accommodate the submarine pen and the storage holds.'

'So that's how you got the men and materials in to make the tunnels connecting Ivan Kalashnikov's four buildings,' James said. 'Direct to the workplace by submarine.'

Elmhirst actually looked impressed as he nodded.

'And those storage holds must be linked to the cellar where I found the explosives, as well as the under-Thames tunnels,' James added. 'Isn't that right?'

'They link to all kinds of places,' Elmhirst said. 'Now, you'll have to excuse us ...' He nodded to Karachan and spoke in Russian.

'Take them to crew quarters,' Anya translated.

The two of them were herded further aft to the forward battery. James was trying to picture the map on the chamois leather, wondering if it related to the submarine pens in some way. Was that what Ivan Kalashnikov had been trying to draw attention to, or was there something more?

Karachan pushed them through the door to the cramped crew quarters. With space at a premium, the bunks for the less-privileged ratings were three deep. The thick thrum of the generators filled the stale air, but James could still hear commands and answers firing from the control room in Russian. There was a sharp hiss as the ballast tanks were emptied of air and took on water, and the floor beneath them lurched; James imagined the hydroplanes outside, fore and aft, angling up to drive the sub downwards ... downwards into a manmade channel of water that led to a hidden dock under the Thames, so craft could come and go in absolute secrecy. James marvelled, trying to imagine the sheer scale of the operation: how many tons of sand, aggregate, cement and timber had been diverted here? How many men had been forced to work the huge, heavy-duty machinery – excavators, pile drivers, cranes, floodlighting – worked to death, perhaps, their bones tossed into the foundations as a fresh intake came to build over the top of them ... No wonder the Project had taken years!

'It was Papa's designs that made this possible.' Anya was sitting on the lowest bunk, gingerly flexing her legs. 'He had no choice but to follow the military's plans, I know, but—'

'He left clues behind as to how to sabotage those plans,' James said quietly; 'how to bring the walls tumbling down.

And if we could only get hold of some of the explosives I saw stored at the Mechta Academy, we could make Jericho more than just a metaphor . . .'

'Provided we could ever find the place he has marked,' Anya added.

The sub manoeuvred its way slowly, carefully – a truly secret weapon, at liberty to strike right here in the precious heart of England. *And if no one can stop them, it's my fault,* James thought dismally, *because I trusted a man I thought believed in me. A man who tricked me with lies and half-truths and set me loose to betray my country – then brought me back to watch it burn.*

James thought of the slim Beretta in his pocket and imagined pumping all the bullets into Elmhirst's chest. The realization struck him, hard as lead: *If I possibly can, I will kill you.*

Over several noisy minutes, the rigmarole of surfacing and then docking unfolded: systems shut down, flywheels were turned, terse orders given. The door to the crew quarters was reopened, and Karachan beckoned out James and Anya at gunpoint. He ushered them back into the control room, which was lit up in Christmas red and green. Hatches had been opened and air let in.

'We have returned to the Mechta Academy,' Karachan announced, unlocking first James's handcuffs and then Anya's. 'It ends for you, boy, where it started.'

Gingerly massaging his raw wrists, James didn't bother to reply. He realized the cuffs had been removed so they could follow Elmhirst and Mimic as they scaled the ladder to the conning tower and from there through a hatch that led onto the bridge.

The submarine had risen up from black water into a shadowy concrete cavern. The sharp stink of sewage, diesel and paint turned James's empty stomach; the stale air seemed more fit to be chewed and spat out than breathed in. The walls of the pen were rough, unfinished concrete, lit by comfortless lamps that seemed almost scared to shine in so bleak a space.

The rest of the crew stayed aboard – James supposed the submarine must have other trips to make – and Elmhirst led the way onto a kind of long stone jetty. James traipsed along beside the limping Anya, shivering and silent, appalled by the mere existence of this underground abscess in London's mighty heart. He thought of all the millions of people above him and wondered whether Aunt Charmian was all right.

The concrete walkway led to a set of huge blast doors, as heavy and cold as the atmosphere itself. Once through, James and Anya were led through a complex of stores and corridors carved crudely from the bedrock and embellished with steel. At last they reached a lift, its door a criss-crossed concertina of metal struts. They piled inside and Mimic stood disconcertingly close to James, staring at him.

'What are you looking at?' James growled.

'Looking,' came the uncanny echo, and a broad grin followed it. 'Looking at.'

Anya placed her hand against James's arm, in sympathy or comfort perhaps, until Karachan yanked it behind her back. She groaned as he fitted her with handcuffs once again. James gasped as his own red-raw wrists were seized by Mimic, and fixed once again with the iron shackles.

The lift slowed with a sickening lurch and Elmhirst opened the door onto what seemed like a different world: an ordinary bright corridor with whitewashed walls, frosted-glass windows and polished floor tiles.

If we could only get out somehow, James thought. *Fetch help . . .*

'This way.' Elmhirst turned left, boot heels ringing out as he strode towards a grey door set into the right wall. He turned a heavy key and pulled hard on the handle, then stood aside, gesturing that James should enter first.

As he did so, James started in surprise. The room looked like a boardroom, windowless and dominated by a long wooden table in its centre. A familiar needle-thin woman sat at the table's head. Demir, the man he'd fought when he'd first broken into the Mechta Academy, was standing over her, his nose red and swollen, his eyes dark.

The woman watched James and Elmhirst approach, her dark eyes half obscured by her silver-flecked fringe.

'Madame Radek?' James frowned. 'Then . . . they've got you too?'

'James?' Anya's voice was low, cautious. 'James, that is not Madame Radek.'

'Not . . . ?' James frowned. 'But I met her—'

'I was *taught* by her in Paris. There is a similarity, but nothing more.'

The woman rose slowly from her seat, her dark silk dress spilling softly over her body. 'Don't you recognize me . . . ?'

'You are not Gaiana Radek,' Anya insisted.

'I was talking to young James Bond here.' She turned to Demir. 'Go and ready the motor car. This won't take long.' As

211

Demir nodded and left, she reached down for something on the chair beside her. 'I have an appointment at the Opera House, and must dress accordingly . . .'

James saw her take a black felt hat – simple, but stylishly cut with a tailored bow of moire ribbon – and place it on her head.

From the narrow brim, she turned a black veil down over her face.

How did I not see it? The world seemed to tilt around James. *It's her. La Velada. Here, all the time.* He stared, his jaw shifting wordlessly.

'What are you looking at?' Mimic turned James's voice back to him, and gave a high-pitched giggle. '*What are you looking at? What?*'

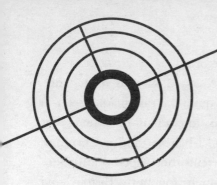

24

Invasion by Stealth

'Hello, Bond.' La Velada's own voice was higher, softer than the one she used for 'Madame Radek'; more considered, more conniving. 'You've been most helpful to our enterprise. How fortunate that I didn't kill you in Cuba after all.'

'What is she talking about?' Anya said. 'Where is the real Madame Radek?'

'Oh, she's quite dead, my dear. I had her walled up in her shut-down studio when I adopted her identity three months ago, to fully immerse myself in our plans here.' La Velada's smile was like a vivid red hook plucking at her face. 'Now, you'll let me enjoy my little reunion with Bond without interruption – won't you?'

'La Velada was very interested to hear that I'd run into you professionally last year,' Elmhirst said, 'and that you were getting involved in SIS business abroad.'

'That was by chance,' James retorted.

'Was it?' Her insufferable smile stayed stitched to her face. 'You can't deny you're becoming quite the unofficial asset. You wrecked our operations in Cuba, forcing us to change our schedule and revise our plans. And I believe that at Christmas you were involved in a chain of events that wiped out millions of pounds' worth of arms research for both Britain and Germany.'

'For which we thank you,' Elmhirst chipped in.

'Indeed,' La Velada said. 'It is as though you're being bred for battle. Small wonder that there have been close eyes on your future.'

'I thought the only reason I even had a future was because I can make sense of my father's riddle,' James said. 'If you're this desperate to know what he meant with his note, your *own* future must still be in jeopardy.'

'If we grow complacent, we are weak. If we are weak, we can fail.' La Velada moved slowly towards James. 'You walk that sharp line between insight and bravado with impressive talent, Bond. I suppose you've worked out what we've been up to?'

'Sitting on your backsides?' James suggested. 'How can it take three years to construct a few buildings around the Thames, dig tunnels underneath and set off some stolen explosives?'

'Ah, but that supposes our end is to level a city – when in fact this is merely our starting point.'

James's attempts at further bravado died in his throat.

'I can assure you, I've been most active since we met in Cuba,' La Velada went on. 'I have overseen construction work here and the distribution of materials and personnel via submarine, enabled Karachan to develop the nationwide network of communist cells around the country, *and*' – she gestured to herself – 'still I find time to masquerade as a famous dancer and spend many months arranging a gala show, to be performed tomorrow night before royalty and the most important of VIPs. Why would that be?'

'Royalty . . .' James looked across at Mimic. 'He impersonated King George on the submarine. You're going after him, aren't you?'

'James,' Anya said quietly, 'I do not think the date for this performance was chosen at random. Those tide tables in the buried files say that in August 1935 the Thames was at its highest.'

'And reaches its peak as our performance begins. Very good.' La Velada held her palm almost sensually to James's cheek, and he flinched. 'I fear you struggle with scale, Bond. "Set off some stolen explosives," you say? There is nothing random about the positioning of each stockpile of hexogen, nothing imprecise about the tunnel's path through the strata of London's underworld.'

Karachan couldn't stay silent a moment longer. 'Kalashnikov designed it so that the force and pressure waves from each explosion would travel through the network and trigger the next,' he said, 'turning London's foundations to rubble and the Thames into a tsunami.'

'Embankments will fail all along the river, and fifty square miles of the most densely populated part of England will be flooded.' La Velada bestowed a warm smile upon James. 'In the aftermath, as the waters settle, our submarines will leave their pens and advance along the Humber, the Tyne, the Mersey, the Forth . . .'

'You can't just invade England!' James cried. 'We have allies. You'll start a second world war.'

'The submarines will not attack,' said La Velada. 'They will seem to offer protection against further incidents. Our presence will be welcomed by a frightened people.'

James stared at her, shaking his head. 'You mean, you'll blame London's destruction on the Nazis or something?'

'Adam Elmhirst, last surviving operative of the British Secret Intelligence Service, will make a most convincing case.'

'You are mad,' said Anya. 'I have lived among the British people. They fear Russia. They will never accept her rule.'

'Not overnight, perhaps,' said Karachan. 'But over many years we have covertly placed loyal Soviet sleeper agents in key positions of authority, to minimize resistance.'

'And when the King broadcasts to the nation that, with Westminster levelled, the Soviet Union has rushed to Britain's aid to help form a new emergency government in the north, well ...' La Velada gave an elegant shrug. 'How can the powers of the world protest when the sovereign warmly welcomes his invaders?'

'King George would never do that ...' But then James turned to Mimic, and his heart plummeted. 'But you don't need the King, do you? Not for broadcasts on the wireless. You've got *him*, ready to read out whatever he's told.'

La Velada nodded. 'And the real King will be in no position to gainsay us ... Because you'll never guess who's returned from a *fruitless* search for Blade-Rise's stolen hexogen, just in time to take up his role as one of the King's personal bodyguards, working with the Met at the Opera House tomorrow ...'

Elmhirst grinned, saluted and then mimed firing a gun with the same fingers. 'At the first sign of trouble I'll whisk him away so he's seen to escape, through an emergency exit underground.'

'Another of your tunnels?' Anya spat.

'Another of your *father's* tunnels,' La Velada corrected her. 'But no one will see us execute the King, deep beneath the theatre.'

'In the confusion of London's destruction we will ensure that all members of your current parliament are also exterminated,' Karachan said casually, 'so that a new era can be ushered in.'

La Velada looked proud. 'Of course, we cannot maintain the illusion of a king in voice alone for long, but then we won't have to. Frightened people adjust so very easily. It is Soviet money that will help Britain rebuild the terrible damage that has been done ... and Soviet rule that will bring communities back together.'

The wave of realization crashed hard over James. 'You're not starting a war. You're staging a coup.'

Karachan's dark little eyes twinkled. 'You might call it an invasion by stealth.'

'And the peace we make in the aftermath will give the USSR a satellite state in the heart of Europe,' La Velada concluded, 'bolstering our strength.'

'You've forgotten Jericho.' James licked his dry lips. 'You can still be stopped.'

'Ah, yes. Your relatives in Jericho.' La Velada shook her head. 'They don't exist.'

'What ... ?' James stared at her, his last hopes sinking. 'You don't know what you're—'

'Elmhirst radioed me the details of your charming story and I had them checked against your file. A weak lie. We're very disappointed in you, Bond.'

'Remember how Mimic slit Mr Kalashnikov's throat?' Elmhirst grabbed Anya by the back of the neck. 'How would you like him to have a go at hers now?'

Obligingly, Mimic recreated Ivan Kalashnikov's death rattle in Anya's ear. She shuddered, turning the movement into a convulsion as she tried to break free. It only made Elmhirst grip her harder. James bowed his head, knowing he was helpless and defeated. He hated that feeling; there had to be some last trick he could pull, some way to turn things around . . .

A change of tactic, perhaps?

'I don't *know* what it means,' James said. 'I've been racking my brains, but . . . it must have been meant for Uncle Max to understand.' He turned a piteous gaze on Anya. 'I didn't want them to hurt you, so I made something up.'

'You hear?' Karachan sneered. 'We've wasted enough time on this bourgeois blunt instrument. It's too late for anything to stop our plans now.'

'Yes,' said James quickly as Anya went limp in Elmhirst's grip, 'it's too late.'

'Is it, now.' La Velada stared at him. 'I find your capitulation a little out of character. But at this moment I have more pressing business. The dress rehearsal for tomorrow's performance will be starting soon at the Opera House.' She looked at Elmhirst and Karachan. 'Detain them for now. Since their fathers have helped secure our final victory, it seems only right that they should witness the dawn of our new order. With appropriate re-education, we may find useful roles for them in the coming administration. And if they will not learn, they will die.'

'Yes, they will die.' Elmhirst smiled at James. 'And her before you.'

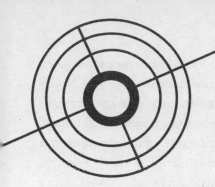

25
One and Only Chance

La Velada left to join Demir for her appointment as Madame Radek, while Karachan excused himself to make telephone calls to the heads of his communist network, ensuring that the final preparations for the coup were complete. *If only I could steal that list of Soviet moles*, James thought, *take it to SIS, get them to act* ... But as he and Anya were marched from the room at gunpoint by Elmhirst and Mimic, he knew it was fantasy.

'Why did you betray Britain?' James said bluntly.

'Why has Britain betrayed the working man?' Elmhirst retorted, unfazed. 'Just as the nineteenth century belonged to the British Empire, so the twentieth will belong to the Soviet Union. The way forward, the way to lasting peace, is through a well-planned global society. A communist future is more important than clinging to the old, outdated loyalties of king and country.'

'I don't care what you say, Elmhirst.' James shook his head. 'The people won't fall for your fairy stories.'

'You think not?' Elmhirst's smile was back, and cockier than ever. 'If a lie's presented in the right way, anyone will buy it.' He unlocked a door on the opposite side of the corridor and pushed it open. 'Case in point . . .'

James stopped dead, incredulous.

'What is it?' Anya asked as Elmhirst shoved them both forward into the room.

'It's . . . the police cell they put me in.' James stared at the narrow bunk he'd been lying on just days ago, at the cayenne pepper still scattered on the floor. 'This is where I was held after Mimic caught me in the school. I thought I was in another building altogether.'

'Because you were told by people you believed were in authority. Your being there made sense, so you didn't question it too closely. This is actually where we put up the men who undertook the excavation works. Imported slave labour. They thought it was luxury after what they were used to in the Soviet penal camps.' Elmhirst smiled almost sadly. 'See, people are happiest when they're told what to think. Only, now you know that it wasn't exactly in our interests to take you to a real cop shop, was it?'

'And when you came to get me out, I had to be blinded,' James realized. 'Otherwise I'd have seen you stage the fight, realize where I was and known you were lying to me from the start.'

''Ere, hold up!' said Mimic, in the voice he'd used as the duty officer James had heard as Elmhirst set him loose. 'You can't just take him out of here!'

'Tough, isn't it?' Elmhirst looked mock-sympathetic. 'When you finally work out you're not as smart as you think you are.'

Let Elmhirst call me names, James thought, *let him think me beaten. I'll get my chance.*

There's no time like the present.

'Please,' James said. 'Can you take off my handcuffs ... just for a little while?'

Elmhirst pulled a face. 'Wrists sore, are they?'

'Please? I wouldn't try anything. I mean, you've got a gun.'

'So I have.' Elmhirst walked over to James. 'And I've got fists, too.'

By way of proof, he smashed his knuckles into James's left cheek. James gasped as the world blinked out about him, snapping back on as he hit the floor. Anya stifled a cry.

'Never stop trying, do you, Bond?' The toecap of Elmhirst's right boot cannoned into James's stomach, kicked the breath out of him. 'Still think that you can turn things around?'

James gasped as another kick sent fire through his ribs.

'You lied to me on the sub. You wasted my time. And for what?' Elmhirst kicked him in the back; James gasped for breath, afraid he might throw up. 'Trying to live up to the daddy who was hardly ever there – is that it?'

'Go ... to hell,' James hissed.

'I reckon you saw me as a bit of a father figure. Bet you thought we made a good team.' Elmhirst hunkered down beside him, wiped blood from the cut on James's cheek with his thumb and studied it thoughtfully. 'You were drawn to me, like you were drawn to that silly bitch Roan back at Eton. Someone older; someone who'll throw themselves in deep, who knows they'll have to find a way out or cope with the consequences.' He shook his head. 'You invest yourself in them, you commit, because you think they'll pay a fine return. But not every investment comes good, Bond. Sometimes you lose it all.'

He stood up and stamped his heel down on James's left arm. James couldn't contain his shout of pain as the handcuffs scissored through his wrists, opening the skin.

Elmhirst crouched again and tweaked James's cheek almost fondly. 'Now, are you ready to tell me what your dad meant by those notes? The truth this time?'

James made no answer, shaking and wheezing for breath.

'Leave him alone!' Anya snapped. 'How can you expect him to answer questions when you do this?'

'I expect *you* to coax some life back into him. I told you, I don't like loose ends. I want them all tied up ahead of the final act.' Elmhirst rose, blew a sarcastic kiss at Anya and nodded to Mimic, who left the room. 'We'll be back. Tomorrow is a big day, and we don't want anyone to spoil it . . . do we?'

The door slammed shut behind them, and a key turned in the lock.

Anya rushed over to kneel beside James, and overbalanced with her own arms still tied behind her back. She was close to tears as she put her face against the back of his neck. 'Oh, James.'

'I . . . I'm all right.'

'You are not. *I* am not.' She shook her head. 'You know now that I am not the stone I try to be. That I am afraid.'

'You . . . and me both.'

'These people, they'll kill us both when they're through with us.'

'They're . . . fanatics . . . They'll do anything for what they believe in.' James clenched his teeth and rolled over onto his back so he could look up at her. 'So . . . we must be fanatics too.'

'Fanatical about what?'

'Living.' James coughed, his ribs agony, and swallowed down the taste of blood. 'We're fanatical about staying alive, hear me? And we'll do anything, risk anything, to keep living. While we live, we can fight.'

Anya looked down at him, and James saw a fierce light in her eyes. He felt it too, tasted it, when she bent down and kissed him fervently on the lips. To share something other than fear and pain felt good. He was sorry when she pulled away, breathing shakily, licking her lips. There was something he couldn't define in her clear blue eyes. Vulnerability, perhaps; a different kind of fear.

'What . . . are you thinking?' she asked softly.

'Two things. Firstly, that I'm glad that bastard didn't punch me in the mouth.' James managed a smile. 'Secondly, I think it's about time you reached into my trouser pocket . . .'

'And pulled out your gun.' Anya raised one eyebrow. 'The kiss was not that bad, I hope?'

James explained his plan. 'A bullet fired point blank through the handcuff chain might be enough to break it.'

'But the sound of the gunshot might bring Elmhirst and Karachan.'

'Then we'd better make damn sure the chain breaks first time,' James said, 'so that one of us can defend the other.'

'Yes. Each defends the other.' She leaned forward again, put her face to his. 'About this, I will be the fanatic.'

'Good. Just let me get my strength back.' James was desperate to escape, of course, but still felt weak from his beating, and if the gunshot did bring their captors running . . . Well, to get out of here alive, he needed to be ready to fight as never before.

James chewed over his father's riddle like a starved dog with a bone, as the night turned slowly dark through the small, high windows. 'If Elmhirst *does* come, I think I'll ask him for a Bible.'

'Ha,' said Anya mirthlessly. 'For we are close to our maker.'

'I just want to find out what verses fourteen to fifteen of Joshua chapter six actually say. *Blessed are they who remove their handcuffs, for they shall inherit the earth*?'

'It would make a change from having their faces rubbed in it,' Anya declared. 'Are you ready now? Shall I get the gun?'

James nodded.

Anya lay on her back, lifted her legs in the air, and contorted until she was able to bring her bound arms up over her feet and hold them in front of her (James noticed she took perhaps a tenth of the time he'd taken to do this). Then she reached carefully for the Beretta and pulled it out.

What shape was the gun in? Rather better than his own, James hoped; he could barely feel his fingers, which had swollen up like German sausages, and wasn't sure he could even fit his index finger around the trigger. So Anya was to take the gun in both hands and fire at the chain, point blank.

She looked grave. 'What if the bullet . . . bounces?'

'Ricochets, you mean? Or blasts shrapnel from the floor straight into us?'

'Yes, this.'

'We'll put the pillows underneath the chain. It might help.' He turned to look at her. 'It's a risk, I know. But we have nothing left to lose.'

Once Anya had retrieved two pillows from the bunks, James placed his hands flat over them and pulled his wrists apart to create tension in the chain. He gasped as the raw, sticky wounds burned. 'Ready?'

She paused. 'If I blow off your hand, do not blame me.'

James couldn't manage a smile. 'Just take your time,' he said. 'Try to squeeze the trigger rather than jerk your finger on it—'

The gunshot was like thunder clapping in his ear. James gasped.

'I jerked my finger. Did it work?'

James tried to pull his hands apart but he couldn't, and swore. 'No. Did you miss?'

She leaned forward. 'The links are made flatter, but did not break.'

'Then try again.' James's hands were shaking and he willed himself to calm down. 'That gunshot could bring someone running; if we're not ready . . .'

He looked back at her, ready to attempt an encouraging smile, but Anya, holding the gun barrel a half-inch from the chain, put her head back and closed her eyes. Before James could protest she had fired again.

With a violent convulsion, his wrists jumped apart. *Yes!*

'You did it!' James turned and threw his arms around her, then winced as the metal bracelets scraped his raw flesh. 'But will anyone come to check on us?'

They held their breaths, listening. Five minutes later, James decided that no one had heard. 'All right, your turn.'

Once Anya was positioned just as James had been, he fired the Beretta. The links in the chain were only warped by the impact, but after some determined chipping with the gun barrel they came apart.

'We did it!' She squeezed James's hands. 'Getting hold of that gun was worth the consequences.'

James winced in memory. 'I forgot to ask. How is your leg?'

'It did not hurt as bad as being pushed under the floor.'

'You stayed strong.'

'It is suffering that makes us stronger.' Anya chewed dead skin from her lip. 'I fear I will be strong as an ox before this night ends.'

'To live through it, we need a plan,' James said.

They got busy, talking and arguing over the best course of action. But as the long dark hours stretched on, James began to fear that no one would come at all. *Perhaps Elmhirst has gone home to get a good night's sleep*, he pondered, *ready to take up his place as the King's bodyguard – and murderer.*

Finally the sound of footsteps carried down the corridor outside. Heart flying, James got up and looked through the grille. 'It's Karachan, with a tray of food.'

'He is alone?'

'Well, you know how boring his conversation is.' James checked the gun for the hundredth time, making sure to squeeze down the safety catch, backing away to the far wall. 'Get into position.'

Anya nodded and slumped back on the bunk, arms behind her back.

The key turned in the lock. Karachan stepped inside, a tray with slices of bread in one hand, the Browning in the other.

'Bond,' he said. 'Elmhirst and I wish to see you.'

'Must be hard for someone as powerful as yourself,' James said, 'reduced to running his errands.'

'We share the work as we share the goal. How else can we find fulfilment?' Karachan put down the tray, but the Browning stayed levelled at James's chest. 'Besides killing non-productive capitalist garbage, that is.'

'You're wasting your time. I told you, I don't know what Father's notes mean.'

Karachan nodded. 'Then you will know what pain means.'

'What about Anya?' James demanded.

Suddenly Anya opened her eyes and screamed. Karachan turned to look at her.

Even as he moved, James whipped his right hand from behind his back, aimed quickly and fired the Beretta. He felt the recoil curve up his arm to his shoulder, but held the gun steady. Blood stained Karachan's shirt cuff as his arm jerked, and with a bloodcurdling cry he dropped the gun.

'Now, down on your knees!' James shouted, gripping the little Beretta with both hands. 'Do it!'

Cradling his wounded forearm, Karachan slowly knelt. Anya rose from the bunk and performed a stiff but satisfactory *rond de jambe*, her right leg straight while her left foot extended to the gun and moved it out of Karachan's reach. But as she stooped to pick it up, she blocked James's line of fire just for a moment.

It was all Karachan needed. He lashed out with his good hand and shoved Anya into James. James was knocked backwards, and before he could bring the gun to bear, Karachan had jumped up and cuffed the Beretta out of his grasp. James brought his hand down on Karachan's bloodied wrist — too late to stop his opponent's knee slamming into his solar plexus. Gasping, he fell backwards against the wall.

Karachan was on top of James in an instant, grabbing for his throat.

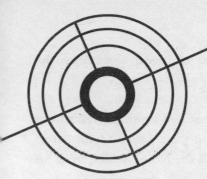

26
Into the Tunnels

The sudden bang of a more powerful firearm reverberated through the holding room, and one of the high windows exploded in a hail of glittering shards. James found himself released, gasping, as Karachan turned to face Anya, back on her feet with the Browning clutched in both hands; she'd let off a warning shot.

'I've not waited this long to lose now,' Karachan warned her. He lunged with horrible speed but, in a blur, Anya turned round on one leg and kicked out with the other to catch him in the chest. Karachan staggered back, slammed against the wall. A jagged length of glass teetering in the window frame above was dislodged and fell.

With the noise of a kitchen knife meeting a cabbage, the sharp point of the broken glass embedded itself in the back of Karachan's neck. He groaned, eyes widening. 'You'll die for that.' Slowly, as if disorientated, he reached behind to pull out the glass. As he did so, a jet of blood spurted up the whitewashed wall.

'You before me,' hissed Anya.

Repulsed, James turned and snatched up the Beretta from the floor, waved it in warning. But there was no fight left in Karachan now – it had gone with the blood spilling from his body. He fell heavily to the floor: a truly dead weight.

James wiped his hands through his hair and put a hand on Anya's shoulder as she lowered the gun. 'You're all right?'

Anya looked paler still, but she nodded and took a shaky breath. 'We should check him for things that may be useful.'

'I'll do it.' Taking a deep breath, James approached the body, his shoes splashing in the dark-red puddle still spreading from the severed artery. He searched all Karachan's pockets and had soon made an inventory: one pack of Russian cigarettes, a pack of dog-eared playing cards, a silver lighter, a dirty silk handkerchief and a brass fob-watch that looked as if it belonged to one of the ruling classes the man professed to despise. James pocketed the lot, but his most interesting find was in the outside lock of the door: a brass ring onto which over a dozen keys had been loaded. His battered heart thumped harder at the thought of finding freedom. If they could only get out and warn somebody . . .

Anya pocketed the Browning and gnawed at the bread, passing a slice to James. He stuffed it into his mouth hungrily, pulled the bunch of keys from the cell door and, chewing together, they ventured out into the corridor. James closed his eyes, swallowed down his dry mouthful and tried to remember which way he'd been dragged out after being blinded.

The sound of a slamming door echoed from somewhere close by. Elmhirst was coming.

'This way,' James muttered, and went in the other direction, clutching his painful ribs, Anya hobbling along behind. They came to a plain white reception room, the walls dotted with small, heavy lead-glass windows that let in the light but would never let anyone out. James tried the heavy oak door but the handle wouldn't turn; it was locked.

James sorted through the keys and shoved a likely-looking contender into the keyhole. It didn't budge. 'Damn it.'

'Try again,' Anya urged him.

He did, pausing as he caught a distant sound from somewhere inside the building. The second key did not fit either.

'Karachan?' came Elmhirst's bellow.

Rattled, James passed the keys to Anya and raised the Beretta as the booted feet came closer. 'I'll get him,' he muttered. 'I'll damn well get him.'

'And if he gets us first? You have seen how I shoot. We could die before we can warn anyone.' Anya tried another key in the door, with no success, then turned to a plain door on the internal wall to their right. She pulled down on the metal handle and the door opened onto a concrete corridor.

'Elmhirst said the labourers were put up in this part of the building,' James remembered. 'There can't be a way out here, or they would have just run.'

'But the foremen had to inspect what the workers did, no?' Anya argued. 'Perhaps they had a private exit, and one of these keys will fit.'

It had better, James thought, hurrying Anya along the passage, which soon resembled a graveyard for tools: dirty picks and shovels and drills left lying around, caked in clay. They passed several doors, but they were locked . . . all but one, which gave onto an old, disused shower block. The air smelled stale and rank, and James glimpsed a pile of perhaps ten mouldering bodies abandoned on the tiled floor.

Beside him Anya retched, and they retreated, slammed the door shut.

'How many have died for this "Project"?' Anya whispered.

James looked at her. 'How many are going to?'

There were old clothes discarded on the floor, and Anya quickly pulled on a pair of canvas trousers with braces and a thick woollen jumper against the cold. They moved on, down a flight of stairs to another grey, unfinished corridor. Anya's limp had grown more pronounced and was slowing them down, but James didn't say anything for fear of shaking her confidence. She had to believe that they could do this.

And I have to believe it, he thought.

Behind them he heard the distant slam of a door. *'Bond?'* came Elmhirst's angry shout. 'There's no way out!'

Anya hissed, 'He tries to scare us.'

'He succeeds.' James grabbed her hand and pulled her onwards, his heart quickening at the sight of a lift door standing open up ahead. It was like the one they'd taken to the school from the submarine pen. James ran into the metal cage and studied the controls. There was just one brass button inside. Might it lead up to another part of the school?

Anya was already closing the doors, so James hit the button with his palm. He swore as the mechanics juddered into life, shaking their little cell, and they began to descend with what felt like horrible slowness.

'How far down are we going?' Anya wondered.

James knew she was thinking the same thing he was. 'If

Elmhirst reaches the lift and hits the button to call it back again . . .'

The lift lurched, and James's heart almost stopped. But an additional thud followed, signalling that they had arrived. James slid open the concertinaed doors and dragged Anya out into another bare concrete area. The corridor to their left had been walled up with breeze blocks and timber planks while, to their right, the dripping black maw of a tunnel entrance offered the only way forward.

Anya opened a door beside the lift. 'Stairwell,' she said uneasily. 'So Elmhirst can take the stairs down after us.'

James was already studying the planks, trying to find one that could be wedged between the wall and the door handle, something to slow their pursuer down. But how long would that take? Elmhirst could crash in on them at any moment – most likely with back-up.

'We'll have to take our chances in the tunnel,' James said, pulling Karachan's lighter out of his trouser pocket. 'Perhaps we'll find a way up to the surface . . .'

'We know there *is* one,' Anya reminded him, 'leading up to the Royal Opera House. Perhaps we can get out and warn people of what's coming. There's still time . . .'

'The Opera House is only a mile and a half north of Millbank as the crow flies.' James flicked on the lighter, and its flame danced as he headed for the mouth of the tunnel. 'It's just a shame that down here, without a compass, there's no way of knowing which direction north is.'

'There may be markers in the tunnels,' Anya said, limping into the gloom beside him. 'The men who worked here would need to navigate too.'

James held up the lighter, hoping she was right. He was horribly aware that whoever came after them would have a lot more knowledge of the tunnel layout than they did.

After only a few yards the electric lights dwindled to a pale haze, and James and Anya were crunching concrete dust underfoot as they ran into the darkness. James tried looking at the walls, but the wavering flame was too bright, searing his sight so he couldn't see beyond it.

Anya stopped suddenly. 'Is that something on the wall?'

James peered and found a hurricane lamp hanging from a nail. He pulled it free and lit the wick inside with the lighter. A comforting, smoky orange glow rose from the lamp and they proceeded with more confidence.

'Elmhirst hasn't come after us,' James said. 'What does that suggest to you?'

'That he is fetching help,' Anya said. 'He means to organize this properly. We shall have a small head start.'

'Let's try to make it larger.'

James was glad he'd taken Karachan's fob-watch; time passed oddly in the thick underground darkness, and each time he took a guess as to how long they'd been in the tunnels, he found he was wildly out. At last they came up against a thick, solid steel door in the rock. James had hopes it might lead to a lift shaft to the surface – but, no, there was only another tunnel on the other side. James supposed the door was to isolate the Mechta Academy section from the rest of the tunnel network, so the explosion of fire wouldn't channel into the school. And small wonder the flood-protection buttressing was so pronounced on the outside of the building; it had been designed by Kalashnikov to withstand the coming destruction, as well as to help disguise the submarine pens.

'This feels so strange,' Anya said quietly. 'To know that Papa designed all this. I feel like I am walking around inside his head.'

'None of it would exist,' James replied, 'if my parents had only got away from Elmhirst.' The harder he tried not to imagine the two of them running through the snow, hunted and afraid, the clearer the image became. But had a part of his father relished the danger, felt himself to be indestructible; a man destined to go on for ever?

Nobody can, James supposed. *But, please, let me go on long enough to make a difference now.*

In time, a thicker darkness loomed to their left. James held up the lamp. 'A junction,' he observed. 'Looks like a passage leading off from this one. D'you want to stay here while I explore it?'

Anya shook her head. Cautiously they went down it together, the crunch of their feet on the concrete the only sound. It led to another tunnel, running more or less parallel to the first.

James lifted the light to reveal a sinister obstruction in the tunnel ahead – a huge stack of crates and boxes dominating the space like some primitive, unsettling sculpture. The whole affair was held in place by thick steel netting, pinned to roof and floor with monstrous, immovable bolts. James knew what he would see stencilled on the side of the crates. He'd seen it already, in the under-basement at the Mechta Academy.

'Hexogen,' he breathed. 'A miniature mountain of high explosives.'

'How many of these piles have been assembled down here beneath London?' whispered Anya. 'Twenty? Thirty?'

'Chained and netted like that, they'll be impossible to dismantle without heavy-duty machinery.' James chewed his lip. 'We've got to get help. We've got to stop that first fuse being lit, whatever it takes. If we can't, the chain reaction begins tonight. The design of the tunnels directs the force of each explosion so that when one blows, it sets off the next in sequence.'

'Until they have all gone,' Anya agreed. 'And so has London.'

James nodded. 'Leaving Britain to become one more republic of the Soviet Union.'

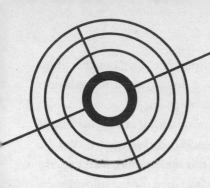

27
Expected to Die

On and on James and Anya wandered along tunnels carved through clays and sands, the ancient elements upon which London lay. They rested only briefly, straining to catch the faintest sounds of pursuit. James began to realize just how vast the scale of the Soviet plan really was.

'Something's bothering me, Anya.' He stood up with the lamp. 'The Project was built around four buildings and a tower – but you said the designs for the tower weren't there in Father's buried papers.'

'Perhaps I missed them,' said Anya. 'Or perhaps it had not been designed at that time?'

'Perhaps,' James agreed. 'I wonder where it stands now?'

The fob-watch said it was close to noon as they passed another huge pile of explosives, secured near another junction. As they crept past, James cupped a hand around the storm lamp, kept as close to the wall as possible. The concentrated power in the explosives would be colossal, and an explosion here could trigger the entire chain reaction.

He quickened his step until the mountain of crates was out of sight. Twinges of claustrophobia plucked at his resolve, and he took deep breaths. To be trapped in this underworld, with the city above in such danger . . . His father had died for the information he'd gathered. For James there could be no peace, no hope of rest, until he knew he'd done something to make a difference.

'Wait a moment.' James stopped abruptly. In the glow of the lamp, he could make out characters chiselled into the stone. 'Junction two,' he read. 'And look, what is that?'

Anya peered at the stonework. 'A three?'

'Oh my God . . .' James dropped to his knees and put down the lamp, scrabbling for the map on the chamois holster. 'Anya, that *has* to be it! *J6* isn't a grid reference, or a Bible chapter – the "J" stands for *junction*, don't you see? And the number is the number of the tunnels.'

Anya had got to her knees next to him. 'You mean, *6 14–15* would be the *sixth* junction crossing tunnels number fourteen—'

'And fifteen, yes.' James nodded, his heart quickening. 'So the detail of the map must show the precise point to bring down. And that blue wavy line above the tunnel—'

'Is water.' Anya gripped his arm. 'When we lived here, Papa told me there are thirteen rivers and streams buried beneath London's streets. Perhaps water runs at the weak point above that stretch of tunnel. An underwater stream?'

'Or a tributary, or . . .' James groaned. 'Fleet! That wasn't some early warning of Soviet submarines travelling north, your father meant the *River* Fleet. It still runs underground, marks the border of Westminster and the City.' He paused. 'Do you think it's just coincidence, or can we blame your papa's sense of humour for designing and numbering his weak point for a biblical reference?'

'I am afraid we can.' Anya half-smiled. 'But, James, these tunnels are like a labyrinth. We are in the second junction of tunnel three – who knows how we get to fourteen or fifteen . . .'

James studied the map for any further clues, but there were none; it was really just a detail from some larger plan to be used as reference.

Anya stood up uncertainly and brushed bits from her trousers – a futile but endearing act given how filthy they were already – and they set off again, bearing left along the tunnel. The floor was submerged, and soon they were wading through water that was almost knee-deep, as quietly as possible.

Within minutes, James stopped at the sound of movement some way ahead of them.

Anya had heard it too. 'Rats?'

'Too big.' James peered into the gloom ahead, lowered his voice. 'Must be part of Elmhirst's search party.' Anya made to move away, but James stopped her. 'How are *they* navigating these tunnels . . . how are they dividing the space up to search?'

Anya caught his gaze and understood. 'They must have maps.'

'And if we want one, we'll have to help ourselves . . .' James blew out the lamp. A brief whiff of kerosene filled the stale air – then there was nothing but the cold darkness and the endless drip and plop of water. 'If we're going to deal with this man we have to be quiet. We can't risk anyone else hearing.'

He saw a torch beam play from the darkness, and he and Anya flattened themselves against the wall. The light was strong, and there was nowhere to hide from it.

'Follow my lead,' James whispered. He slipped down into the cold, disgusting stink of the water, lying on his back, grimacing as it sucked at his skin through his clothes. Anya did the same. The man with the torch came closer, sliding his feet through the silty water so as to make as little noise as possible. The torch beam swung over James's chest and, with a gulp of air, he sank his face under the water, save for his nose and mouth. Silence thickened with the pressure in his head, and he felt the eddies in the water increase as the man approached. The torch beam must have revealed Anya, for he heard a voice shout out in Russian.

Hold still, Anya, James thought, bracing himself as the man splashed closer.

When he was alongside, James lifted himself on his elbows, raised his legs and thrust both feet into the man's groin. With a strangled cry and a crash of water the man went down. Anya jumped up and flew forward with the Browning. The crack of stock against skull rang out over the wash and lap of the freezing water.

Shivering, James reached beneath the surface to retrieve the man's stubby silver torch. He saw that their hunter, as big and black as the tunnel, had been knocked out cold. Anya was already tearing at the insides of his coat, trying to find—

'A map!' She held a folded piece of paper out to James, triumphant. 'Now, we must go – this noise may bring others.'

James nodded, his heart thrumming with excitement – until it stopped still as a gunshot crashed out in the confined space. Mouldering brick exploded from the wall behind him.

'It's brought them, all right!' James shouted. 'Run!'

Another shot saw a pack of rats break cover from the slimy water. James and Anya turned and splashed away after them through the murk, the torchlight flaring over water and walls. They turned right along the junction and into the next tunnel. But the water here was up to James's waist, deep enough to swim in – an underground tributary perhaps.

Anya shone the torch around desperately. 'Which way now?'

James turned right and found the water became deeper still. 'Swim for it?'

'But if the map gets wet ...'

'I'll take it; you use the torch.' James grabbed the map from her and clamped it in his teeth. Then he launched himself into the water, propelled by his most powerful front crawl. The torch beam lanced through the pitch-darkness as Anya kept close behind. James angled his chin to the tunnel roof, trying to keep the map as dry as possible. Another gunshot boomed above their thrashing in the water.

James came up hard against something ahead, stood up anxiously and found that at this point, the water came up to his chest. Anya shone the torch over some timber shoring. To the left was a crude archway hollowed out of the rock, mostly blocked by building debris: rubble, steel mesh, the bent and severed blade of some sort of earthmoving equipment.

'We're trapped,' James breathed. 'We can't climb over that.'

'Maybe ... we do not have to.' Anya ducked beneath the stagnant water, exploring the submerged landscape. James frowned, and when she didn't reappear called her name as loudly as he dared, wondering how long it would take for their pursuers to trap them here and—

A loud splashing on the other side of the barrier signalled that Anya had found a way through. 'It is narrow,' she hissed, 'but you can swim through.'

James glimpsed torchlight playing on the walls. 'Where does it say we are now?'

'Junction six. Tunnel fourteen.'

'Then – this is the place,' James realized. 'The start of the weak point in the network. Hold on, let me pass the map to you . . .' He climbed awkwardly onto the rubble, found a gap large enough to push his hand through to her on the other side. Anya took the map. 'Wait there,' he said. 'I'll join you.'

Even as he spoke, wet splinters burst from the timber beside him as another gunshot reverberated around the tunnel. James ducked down beneath the stinking water without another thought, arms outstretched and feeling through the blackness for the same path through the debris that Anya had found. He pushed forward between two chunks of stone, but his build was bigger than Anya's. His chest felt wedged, his back scraping against the stone.

James found that he was stuck fast between the abandoned concrete blocks.

Fighting to keep calm, he tried pushing against the stone to free himself. His movements grew wilder, more desperate. *I have to get through here before I drown*, he thought. *Or before I'm shot*. He almost opened his mouth to cry out as something took hold of his wrists and pulled.

From the reassuring squeeze of her fingers, James guessed it was Anya reaching through from the other side of the underwater obstacle, trying to pull him free. The blood began to roar in his temples. James felt like a cork in a bottle, a cork that didn't want to give. *Come on!* he willed himself, fighting harder, pressure building behind his burning eyes. *Now! It's got to be now . . .*

But the concrete did not give.

James heard another gunshot echo weirdly through the water. The blackness was absolute, the all-pervading cold had stripped all sensation from his skin. He stopped his struggles; the world felt suddenly peaceful, after taunting and hurting him for so long. A part of James wanted to give himself up to the peace and the dark, to drift to the bottom and know nothing more. But then he heard his mother's scream, imagined his parents falling.

'*Snap out of it, James!*' his father would tell him.

Twisting as if jerking awake, a terrible tightness in his chest and behind his ears, James finally felt the concrete shift a fraction. With fresh hope and desperation, he kicked his legs as hard as he could and struggled and scraped his way through the narrow gap. Hands closed on his forearms; *Please let them be Anya's.* He needed air, needed to surface—

Finally, retching and choking in the blackness, he broke from the water and recoiled from torchlight, bright in his face. Gulping at the stale air, he clung to Anya, shivering, wiping his eyes.

'We've got to go,' she said – as another bullet thumped into the concrete in the barrier behind them. Too exhausted to swim any more, James waded through the water, leaning against Anya for support. The tunnel led to another junction – numbered 16, he noted – and it sloped upwards so that the water level soon got lower. With this knowledge, James found the strength to quicken his step.

'Why do you think that barrier was left there?' asked Anya.

'To keep people like us out,' James panted. 'The excavators must have known that this area is particularly vulnerable if a part of the Fleet is running just above.'

'Causing a flood they do not want?'

'And enough damage to stop the chain reaction,' James agreed. 'I wonder how much force would be needed to "bring it all down with one blow"?'

'We need experts to tell us this,' Anya declared.

'And a way out to reach them.'

Once he and Anya had made it round the corner with no sign of further pursuit, they rested, shivering against a filthy wall. 'The map got very wet,' Anya apologized, smoothing it out against the wall. 'Let us hope it shows us the fastest way to reach the Opera House. We have to raise the alarm before the King arrives.'

She trained the torchlight on the map. A black cross was marked in the centre of a radial grid of several tunnels, and a large square nearby was marked ROH.

'There,' Anya noted. 'Things go our way, at last.'

James was too disquieted to feel much optimism. He and Anya began to calculate the quickest path through the maze of junctions and tunnels.

28

The Rise from the Underworld

There was no note of scale on the map, but James and Anya's ultimate destination proved to be barely a quarter of a mile away. The walls to the approach were smooth and polished, clearly carved out of the rock with precision and care.

To better channel the forces of the blast, James supposed.

The tunnel stretched downwards before opening out into an enormous, cavernous space, perhaps as large as the hall of an Underground station. James stopped dead at the sight of a colossal assortment of crates of prime Blade-Rise hexogen and boxes of TNT, double the size of the other stacks they'd seen. Like the others, it had been smothered in steel mesh, chained and netted together to prevent tampering – but from this one a wide trail of gunpowder stretched away along an adjoining passage.

'The fuse,' James breathed, 'waiting to be lit.' His skin prickled with fresh sweat. 'X marks the spot. This has to be the trigger to it all.' He tried to kick the black powder away, but it had been combined with a greasy glaze of some kind and plastered to the ground, making the fuse part of the rock they walked on. 'It can't be disarmed.' He checked Karachan's watch. 'And look – it's after two o'clock in the afternoon. The show will be starting in about five hours.'

'We have time to reach the Opera House,' Anya declared. 'Show the police all this.'

'Assuming they even start to believe us.' Studying the damp map and the square marked ROH, James noted a small dotted path stretching away from it. 'Come on; let's get the lay of this land.'

Exhausted, but driven on by nervous energy, James led the way out, this time climbing up the sloping passage. He realized he was following the fuse from the RXD pile, for a good hundred yards. How long had it taken to burrow out this impossible space, and how many had died to make it a reality – while above, London danced on in ignorance?

But after tonight . . .

James hurried along, splashing through the puddles at the right-hand side of the passage, checking the map in Anya's hands. The tunnel opened up into a smaller, roughly circular cavern perhaps thirty feet across. The weak torchlight was hardly enough to see by, but soon he spotted it – the door in the cavern wall, an oak panel barely wider than a man with a single brass keyhole below the handle.

'The way into the Opera House,' Anya said.

'And the way out,' James supposed. 'That dotted line on the map ...' He crossed to a different door in the wall opposite; it too was locked. 'This must lead somewhere so they can light the fuse and retreat.'

'After the royal execution,' Anya added.

Grimly, James rejoined her by the oak door. He pulled the ring of keys out of his pocket and tried each one in turn. Nothing ... nothing ... 'Come on!' He went on switching through the keys, hands slick with sweat. But it was no good.

'All that we have done,' Anya said bitterly, 'and we are just as trapped as before.'

James felt for the Beretta in his pocket and pulled it out. It was wet through, but the barrel seemed all right; it ought to function. He raised the muzzle to the lock, and aimed carefully.

'Get behind me,' he told Anya, and fired.

The retort rolled like thunder, as if the ancient clay was groaning in pain. The lock jumped as the bullet hit, but stayed strong in its housing. James fired again, with the same result. The door stood fast.

'Your gun is too small calibre,' Anya said, producing the heavier Browning. She aimed and squeezed the trigger, but heard only the empty click.

'Out of ammo,' James breathed. 'And out of luck.'

'Wait ...' Anya took the ring of keys from him. 'I wonder.'

'What is it?' James found himself jogging after her as she retraced their steps to the huge stockpile of explosives.

'The steel nets are tethered to the chains with padlocks, all the way around!' She was already sorting through the keys. 'If one of these fits, perhaps we can start to dismantle this pile ...'

247

The thought was hardly appealing, but James willed her to succeed as he watched her work, carefully and methodically trying each key in the lock, her tongue caught between her teeth as she concentrated. His guts turned with the tension, until finally, with a metallic click, one padlock popped open! Anya pulled away chains, and a section of the steel net loosened just enough for her to gain access to the pile. She looked up at James, eyes all but outshining the torch with pride.

He was about to congratulate her when he heard movement from further along the passage, and words in Russian.

Anya's eyes widened. 'They heard the gunshots.'

'Quickly,' James hissed. 'Get inside the mesh.'

Silently she turned and lifted the edge of the net she'd freed. James held it up for her while she climbed inside, then followed her into the shadowy edifice, squeezing into a space between two crates. They held silent and still, crushed together there as footsteps sounded in the cavern space outside; voices called out, echoes deadened by the strange acoustics.

James could feel Anya's heart chiselling at her ribs. 'What are they saying?'

Anya took a shaky breath. 'One says the other only imagined gunfire,' she whispered. 'He thinks we drowned back at the barrier.'

A man came into sight, holding up a lamp in one hand and a semi-automatic pistol in the other: it was Demir, La Velada's bodyguard. He spoke in deep, resonant Russian, and his bright torch beam struck the crates. To James, the light felt bright enough to ignite the explosives. He held his breath, waiting for Demir to circle past. His friend called across to him and a conversation ensued. When it ended, both men laughed.

'He said: *I tell you, they must be dead*,' Anya whispered once the light had faded, along with the footsteps. 'The other said, *If they are still wandering round here tonight, that will make certain.* But he will check the doors to the Opera House and the ... the Shukov to be sure.'

'Shukov?' James echoed, edging out from the hiding space after Anya. 'What is that?'

'It is strange to translate,' she admitted. 'The Shukov Tower is in Moscow – a radio mast. It is tall and powerful enough to broadcast across the nation ...'

Even as she spoke, James could tell from her face that she knew what she was saying. '*That's* the tower,' he breathed, 'and why we didn't see designs for it. It's not a proper building, it's a *transmitter* tower, a metal framework.'

'And that second door you found in the cavern leads there?'

'It fits,' James agreed. 'The dotted line on the map: a swift, safe route to a big radio mast for "King" Mimic to broadcast propaganda to the entire nation once the Thames breaks its banks.' He wondered exactly where above ground the transmitter tower was located; how far away it was from here. 'Well, when they find the lock's been tampered with they'll know we're not dead.'

'We may as well be,' said Anya with sudden bitterness. 'Those men laughed because they think Elmhirst is crazy to send them after us. Because there is no way to stop this.'

'Well,' said James, giving her just the smallest of smiles, 'we'll just have to see about that.'

They waited tensely while the men pressed on towards the cavern and its locked doors. Ten minutes later, only Demir's friend returned, gun drawn, playing his torch beam all about.

He cast a fearful look at the mountain of explosives, but gave it a wide and sensible berth.

If we only had that choice! James thought.

Only when the man had moved well on did he feel able to breathe again. 'He must think we doubled back through the tunnels.'

'What of the other?' Anya asked.

'Demir? Perhaps he's standing guard by the door.' James felt his heart quicken. 'If we can only overpower him, he might have the key—'

'Come on, then.' Anya was already extricating herself from the mesh and led the way along the tunnel. James followed, senses knife-sharp despite his fatigue as they neared the cavern.

There was no sign of Demir.

'He must have gone through one of these doors.' James muttered a prayer as he tried each in turn. But it was no good; they still stood stubbornly locked. 'Back to your plan, then. We dismantle the trigger.'

Anya nodded slowly. 'And hope Demir or his friend do not return.'

It was nerve-jangling work, unlocking the mesh surrounding the monumental pile of explosives and trying to remove the heavy crates as quietly as possible. Hours passed as they carried the boxes between them back the way they had come, hiding them in the submerged tunnel where James had almost drowned; the water, he hoped, would both hide their sabotage and render the hexogen useless. Every few feet they stopped to listen out for Elmhirst's men in the tunnels, but Demir and his friend did not return. Although James checked them many times, the narrow oak doorways in the cavern, those tantalizing escape routes, remained locked.

By six o'clock, for all their careful labours, they'd disposed of only a dozen crates.

'It is hopeless.' Panting for breath, Anya lowered her end of the thirteenth crate, forcing James to put his down too. 'Hopeless.'

He shook his head. 'We must dump it in the water with the others. Come on, it's just around the corner—'

'What difference does it make?' Anya wiped her forehead in the half-light. 'We can never get enough of the explosives away to make any difference to the trigger.'

She was right, James knew. 'All right. Let's leave this one here. I'll free another from the pile. Try the doors again, just in case.'

Anya limped away with no further comment. James walked with her as far as the trigger, then busied himself with liberating a further crate of hexogen while she went on to the cavern. Every thirty seconds he stopped work to listen for the sounds of approach. Before long he tensed as limping footsteps beat a swift tempo on the sticky clay.

'It's open!' Anya's face was triumphant in the dim glow of the torch as she ran back to join him. 'Open!'

'What?' James felt the warmth of hope flare inside. 'You mean—?'

'The door opens. There is a stone staircase on the other side. The way has been lit!'

'All right. All right.' James tried to rein in his runaway thoughts. 'For all we know, this could be a trap. Elmhirst can't find us down here, and time's getting short. But he knows where we want to go, where we'll be making for, and so . . .'

'His men leave the door open and wait for us up top?'
Anya's face crumpled. 'I had not thought of this.'

'I'd better look into it. Alone.'

'I am not a child to be protected!'

'I know, and I'm not trying to patronize you.' James
took hold of her elbows. 'If anything happens to me, you'll
still be free – and you'll have to end this on your own. Wait
here, out of sight. I'll come back and fetch you if the way
seems clear.'

She nodded, uncertain. 'Be sure that you do.'

James followed the path of glazed fuse through the tunnel
leading up to the cavern. The door that must lead to the
transmitter tower was still closed, but that to the Opera House
did indeed stand ajar. The staircase beyond was steep and
rough-hewn, lit by candles flickering in small alcoves gouged
from the rock.

Heart beginning to pound, James cautiously made his way
upwards. It soon felt as if he'd been climbing for ever. The steps
grew rougher, the nearer he got to the Opera House; perhaps
the excavation work had risked raising attention from the
staff and clientele.

Finally James reached a long ramp that led to another
metal door. Bracing himself, he tried the handle. It was
unlocked, and slid open, giving onto a dark space the size of
a cupboard. A large, hulking contraption filled the space,
which stank with the same smell as the submarine: diesel. *An
emergency generator,* James presumed.

Cautiously he felt his way around it and located a *further*
door in the wall opposite. This opened onto a much larger
space given over to storage; props and scenery from past

productions were held here for future reuse or cannibalization. *I'm out!* James thought with fleeting elation.

Now the hard work really begins.

James paused beside a pile of crates and tea chests filled with all sorts of strange paraphernalia. He started towards a door beside some scenery flats ...

Just as Demir burst out of a crate behind him.

James jumped and turned at the noise – just in time to see a hunting knife flying his way. Desperately he threw himself aside and the knife whistled overhead to stick into a wooden backdrop with a hollow thump.

It's a trap, all right, James thought, trembling. *I took the bait and walked straight into an ambush.*

Demir was already running for him. James scrambled up and tried to feint past the big man, but exhaustion made him slow and a heavy hand caught his face; he was sent reeling against one of the chests. Demir retrieved his knife from the scenery flat and now ran at James, wielding it viciously. James grabbed an oversized child's wooden building block to use as a shield and thrust it into Demir's face. Demir staggered backwards towards the door to the generator room. Just as he reached it, it burst open and slammed into the back of his head. He gasped and sank senseless to the floor – as Anya slipped into the props room, panting hard, out of breath.

'Good timing.' James crossed to take her in a tight embrace. 'But I thought I was going to let you know the way was clear ...'

'Yes, you thought that. But I think together we are better, no?' Anya extricated herself from his hold. 'Be careful. I have brought evidence that will help us be believed.'

'Evidence?'

'You said it yourself, who would believe a story like ours with no proof?' Anya opened her tunic to reveal a stick of hexogen explosive stuck down the waistband of her trousers. James recoiled automatically, feeling sick: it looked like a bullion bar made from modelling clay. 'We show the police this,' she went on, 'and warn them how much waits below at the end of the secret stairs.'

'Do you know how powerful that stick is?' he whispered slowly.

'When the police or SIS men see, they will listen.'

'More likely shoot us on sight! Elmhirst might not know we've found the weak point in his precious tunnels, but he'll have prepared for the possibility of our escape. He might even have circulated our descriptions among the staff . . .' James gently took the hexogen and placed it inside the nearest crate of abandoned props. 'I think we'd best keep this here, along with our other piece of evidence: Demir.' He took a length of silk wrapped around a mannequin and used it to tie the man's hands and feet. Then Anya helped him manhandle Demir into one of the crates.

'So, then,' Anya said. 'Who *can* we bring here?'

'It'll have to be someone in authority who can act quickly and whose mind isn't entirely shut,' James said, praying such a person could be found. He crossed to the far door to see where it led, but Anya's hands lingered in the crate for a moment, then pulled out a long, full tutu made of white silk tulle. She looked at it, and couldn't resist hugging it to her, nuzzling her face into its ruffles.

As he saw it, James frowned. 'Wear it.'

She shook her head fiercely. 'I cannot.'

'Smelling like we do and dressed as we are, we'll stand out a mile,' James reasoned, 'but if you look like you belong here, we're less likely to be challenged.'

'James, no. I have not worn such things since—'

'Since your leg was broken, and your life with it?' James shook his head impatiently. 'Then it's about time you did, isn't it?'

Her eyes flashed. 'Pig.'

James came up close to her. 'Anya, we're running out of time and we've pushed our luck to the limit already. Any advantage – *any* – might make a difference. I'll try and find something too.' He looked at her pleadingly. 'You'll fit in. No one will look twice at you.'

She nodded, looked away, and James got a sudden sense that it was *this* that she feared most. Once, she'd been a prima ballerina in the making, and then ... her dreams had been snatched away. He remembered the slashed ballet shoes hanging from the bed in her apartment in Moscow; then he remembered the gash carved into her papa's throat, and thought of his own father and mother falling through space past sheer rock, until ...

'Put it on,' James told her brusquely. 'The past's had too tight a hold on us both for too long. Tonight, we put things right.'

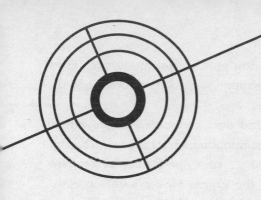

29
Countdown

I was wrong, James thought as Anya emerged in a white leotard matched with a bell-shaped, calf-length ballet skirt. *People* will *look twice.* She'd found some ballet shoes, the ribbons crisscrossing her bruised and battered calves, vanishing into her netted silk tutu. For his part, while he'd decided to pass on the male tights, he'd found a white shirt and a leather jerkin to go with his muddy trousers and shoes. In one pocket he carried the Beretta, in the other, Karachan's service pistol: the Browning.

He and Anya moved through the backstage warren of stores and passages of the Royal Opera House, passing stagehands and electricians and workmen and dressers in maid uniforms: black with white aprons. There was a buzz in the air. It was close to seven o'clock and the show must have been getting close to starting. The gala production might be based around children performing, but the care and attention to detail seemed equal to any professional production. How many hundreds – or thousands – would be packed into the auditorium tonight?

Anya looked nervous and uncomfortable as they passed young female ballet dancers mingling, stretching or exercising, together with male *danseurs*. 'I came here once before,' she said quietly, 'on a tour of the Opera House with my class-mates. I dreamed of dancing here one day.'

This used to be her world, James realized. *Now she can only haunt it.*

With a chill, he knew that La Velada must be somewhere close by, overseeing her show – and readying herself for the *real* main event: the catastrophes that would shake London to its hollowed-out core. This was her night, and if they stumbled into her path she would have them removed in moments, no matter what their protests. It would be the same if they accused Elmhirst, well-respected within SIS and entrusted with the King's safety. What officer of the law would ever believe their wild accusations? Until the horror started, and it was far too late to stop it . . .

We'll have to take matters into our own hands.

Just round the next corner James noticed a fire alarm on the wall. 'Anya, if we set that thing off . . .'

'The theatre will be evacuated, and the King with it. The Project will be spoiled.' Anya's smile faltered. 'Only . . . Elmhirst will still be guarding him . . .'

'I suppose so. But at least he won't be able to deliver the King down into the tunnel like a tenth-rate Phantom of the Opera . . .' James studied the alarm. It was a momentary contact switch where the glass panel held down the button: break the glass and you released the switch to set off the sirens.

Taking a deep breath, James sidled over to the alarm, discreetly raised his elbow and brought it down on the glass . . .

Nothing happened.

'What is wrong?' Anya asked. 'Why are there no sirens?'

'They've disconnected the circuit.' James felt fatigue pull at his fading hopes. 'Must have thought someone might try this.'

'Then we shall try something else,' Anya said, steering them away from the stage area.

She led him down a white-painted passageway, through a door onto a quiet classical staircase made of York stone. Then they tramped up several storeys into the highest reaches of the theatre. 'The carpenters have their workshops up here,' Anya explained as they walked, 'built into bays in the iron roof. In the middle, above the rear of the stage, is the scene-painting room, yes?'

'We can't see through the ceiling,' James pointed out, a little testily. 'How will that help?'

'The scenery does not *fly* down to the stage,' Anya retorted. 'There is a special goods lift that descends to the auditorium, and a smaller platform for the workmen. If we take it down just a *little* way . . .'

'We'll have a bird's-eye view of the Opera House.' James nodded approvingly. 'Get a feel for the geography . . . and see how many SIS men on the lookout for trouble are standing between us and our doing something about all this.'

The scene-painting room was a large and lofty space, the lean-to roof studded with skylights. Long Acre and Bow Street shone in the streetlamps outside, steeped in grandeur, and the moon shone a spotlight down on James and Anya as they picked a path through scenery flats to a platform lift. James led the way aboard and pressed a button. With a sharp *thunk*, the lift began to descend towards the rear of the stage, but when he removed his finger, their movement stopped.

Anya lay down on her front, peering out through the crack between the ceiling and the top of the stage curtain.

James joined her and stared out over the main auditorium with its sea of people. A quick calculation told him there were over two thousand people seated here tonight, with more standing at the very back. So many Very Important People, as smart as their surroundings: rich deep-pile carpets of rosy pink, and crimson walls with Regency stripes. The seats were crimson too, and the curtains that hung from the proscenium arch before the stage . . . It was as if La Velada had chosen a location that would hide the blood she was ready to spill.

Cream and gold balconies in the shape of horseshoes rose from the stalls in four main tiers. Fine branched candle-holders with shades of deep pink pleated silk cast a gentle, bewitching light over the stage. In the orchestra pit, at least thirty musicians were tuning up, the first murmurings of their instruments rising up in a haze of dusty beauty. An ornate brass clockface on the wall was ticking off the surviving seconds till the first act began, and the hum of excitement was palpable.

James looked up at the magnificent Royal Box to the left of the stage, decorated sumptuously in white and gold, with marbled ornamental columns.

'It has its own lobby, smoking basement and drawing room,' Anya said quietly, 'and a private entrance on Floral Street.'

'I suppose a king isn't allowed to queue with the hoi polloi,' James said. With a tingle of excitement, he recognized

George V in the box now, entertaining the Prime Minister and attendant diplomats and a uniformed policeman and—

Yes, there he was. Elmhirst, guarding the double doors that must lead to the anteroom beyond, hovering at the King's back like the shadow of death. James shrank back, worried that he might be seen even from all the way over here. At the same time he was gripped by a fresh determination to act. This was his country, and this was his war. *There has to be something I can do!*

The hushed mumble of chatter died away as the lights dimmed and a susurration of applause rose in its place as, with a sudden roll of drums and a swell of strings, the orchestra burst into the national anthem. The audience stood in respect and began to sing for their monarch – all save the security men in the auditorium, dressed in smart uniforms and looking around alertly for possible trouble.

'God save the King,' James muttered under his breath, 'or let me have a go ...'

The King stood graciously at the front of the box to receive the audience's tribute and, as singing gave way to thunderous applause, he raised an arm in royal greeting. Then the lights dimmed, the curtains opened and the show began. A clutch of young dancers dressed as cygnets took to the stage, while the orchestra sent Tchaikovsky swooning from their instruments.

'It is beautiful,' Anya whispered, and there might have been tears in her eyes. 'Is it not beautiful?'

'For how much longer?' James pressed the button that sent the platform lift juddering upwards. 'Come on, we've got to do something.' He led the way back into the scenery store. 'We don't know when the "trigger" will be pulled—'

''Ere. You two meant to be in here?'

James stopped still. A doorman – his rumpled, florid face in direct contrast to his impeccable dove-grey uniform – stood in the doorway. James caught a glimpse of the shoulder holster hidden under his jacket and realized that here was no ordinary member of the Royal Opera House staff.

'Well?' the man prompted them.

'Are you with the police or SIS?' James spoke with all the authority he could muster. 'If you are, we need to speak with you. If not, we need to find someone who is.'

The man looked unimpressed. 'What the hell are you talking about?'

'Please, this building has to be evacuated right now. The King is in danger.'

Anya nodded. 'There is a secret tunnel that leads to explosives . . .'

'Your voice. Ruskie, are you?' The doorman's look of incredulity hardened to suspicion. 'Elmhirst warned us you might find your way in here. The anarchist couple . . .'

I knew it. James's heart sank. *He's already turned everyone against us. However much we protest, we'll never be believed.* 'Listen, I can prove what I say,' James said quickly. 'We have a stick of hexogen hidden in the basement storeroom, right next to where the emergency generator is kept—'

'That's enough.' The doorman reached under his jacket for his gun, but Anya launched herself forward and grabbed his other arm, spun him round in a tight circle – and James's fist connected hard with his jaw. The man staggered back and James followed up with a punch to the solar plexus that brought the man to his knees. Anya snatched up the

Derringer pistol and brought the butt down on the back of his neck.

James felt a twinge of guilt at their systematic destruction of the doorman, but quickly removed the uniform. 'There's no time to convince anyone of the truth,' he said, mind made up. 'We're going to have to think of something else.'

Anya didn't answer. She had noticed a playlist pinned to a board on the wall beside her, the scenic designer's varying needs scrawled beside each point. 'At the end of this act,' she said, 'after the soprano has sung "*Un Bel Di Vedremo*" – "One Fine Day" – there is a ballet performance. An extract from the second act of *Giselle*.'

James was only half listening, struggling into the doorman's jacket. 'The one that you danced in before?'

'Yes. It is the scene where Giselle's spirit rises from the underworld ...' Anya frowned. 'The lady with the veil, she thinks she is clever. All these performances concern death – the Dying Swan, "When I Am Laid in Earth" from *Dido and Aeneas* ... and, James, look.'

'What?'

'The first act will close with Queen Gertrude's monologue from *Hamlet*, Act Four, Scene Seven.'

'So?'

'The announcement of Ophelia's death ... by drowning.' Anya looked at James. 'Could that be the moment when the fuse is lit?'

'Perhaps ...' James imagined the scene as the explosion rocked the auditorium, shook the chandeliers from the ceilings; as mass panic broke out, Elmhirst would seize the advantage and hurry the King away via the 'approved' escape route, where there would be no witnesses – to his death.

'How long will this first act last?' James asked quickly.

'Perhaps forty-five minutes?'

'Damn it, is that all?' He winced. 'Well, I can think of only one way to upset La Velada's plan right now.' He nodded slowly. 'It won't stop her, but until we find someone who *can*, it's the only thing I can think of.'

Anya looked at him. 'Well?'

'I . . .' James took a deep breath and looked down at the Derringer. 'I'm not sure you're going to like it.'

30
World and Underworld

Dressed in his stolen doorman's uniform, despite the short trouser legs, James had not been challenged as he moved through the Opera House. Now he stood on the mirrored first-floor landing, overlooking the busy entrance foyer. Glittering chandeliers, looking like diamanté spinning tops, lit the spacious, eggshell-blue Crush Bar that ran across the front face of the building.

As quickly and discreetly as he could, James was pouring the dregs of several leftover brandies into a single glass. He prayed that Anya would go through with his plan, that she wouldn't baulk at the last moment. If they didn't act in concert, they would fail.

James knew that a second chance was unlikely. The act would close as planned, and Ophelia's drowning could well trigger London's.

Boldly, he picked up a silver tray, placed his highball glass upon it, then carried it down the grand staircase, through the ivory and mahogany lobby with its bronze-capped pillars, and out onto Bow Street.

Such sweet air! The evening was warm, the night kept at bay by the electric brightness from windows, headlights and streetlamps. The sounds of music, street traders and traffic filled his ears as the mingling smells of Covent Garden Market, florists, tea shops and exhaust fumes caught in his nose. A London night like so many others: familiar and exciting – and precious too, James realized, because if he couldn't succeed, there might never be another.

Quickly he turned the corner onto Floral Street and approached the Royal Suite's private entrance. A stocky man, in his thirties perhaps, with a round face and neat ginger hair, was standing inside in a dress suit, black against the white and gold, his arms folded in a forbidding manner.

James didn't hesitate. He walked up to the door and pulled it open.

At once the man stepped forward to challenge him.

'Someone ordered this,' James said.

'No drinks in the auditorium,' said the doorman.

James lowered his voice confidentially. 'Bar got the order from one of your lot ahead of the interval – a Mr Adam Elmhirst? Said he could get away with bending the rules.'

'That sounds like him. Bloody SIS, treading on our toes, pleasing themselves.' The man smiled and gestured to the staircase. 'All right. Take it up to my colleague on the door upstairs.'

'Thanks.' James kept his face neutral, but inside, fear and adrenalin sent electricity through his body. As he climbed the splendid white staircase, he thought again that his timing would have to be perfect, and if Anya didn't come through for him . . .

It'll be the death of me.

James felt in his pocket for the old Beretta that had passed from Anya's father to his. As he gripped it, he felt a real connection to Andrew Bond. He could almost imagine him standing here now, watching this drama, begun four years ago, edge second by second to its final act.

I wanted you and Mother to live for ever, James thought. *Every child wants that, don't they? Think of all we could have done and shared together.*

But it's not only the way we live that defines us; it's what we die for.

He climbed to the top of the stairs.

In the gloom of the under-stage area, Anya dabbed tears from her eyes with dirty fingers. She'd knocked out a stagehand, his body sprawled at her feet, but her tears were not for him, nor for the violence she'd been made to witness and, in turn, perform.

Her tears were not for the beauty of the music score she knew so well, but had not listened to in years, nor even for the principal dancer who would soon join her down here in the darkness. The girl must be making ready for her grand entrance as Giselle, all set to rise up through the trapdoor beside her grave as if summoned by the undead spirits of the Wilis, the dancing spectres who clung to an afterlife, driving men to their deaths. Anya knew this moment would be the high point of the young girl's life, the start of a glittering career. No, Anya cried because she would soon overpower this girl and take away her dream, and she was afraid for herself, that she would feel nothing.

A soft movement stage right. Ah, here was the girl! Tall and beautiful, no doubt dressed in her white tulle like Anya, her face covered with an ivory veil. She looked like a virginal La Velada.

'Who are you?' the newcomer asked.

Anya pulled the Derringer from the waistband of her skirt and pointed it at her. 'Be silent,' she hissed, wondering how she would bind and gag the girl while holding the gun. But the problem was solved when the prima ballerina fainted dead to the floor.

Anya couldn't help but scoff a little as she pulled away the veil and looked at the girl's dark hair and fine cheekbones. 'Yes. Very young, very beautiful.' She closed her eyes, but a tear squeezed out just the same. 'I'm sorry, little girl. It is not your fault. I *am* sorry.' Anya wiped fiercely at her eyes, placed the veil over her face and pulled a decorator's dust sheet over the bodies before calling backstage, 'Hello? There's no stagehand – how am I to make my entrance above . . . ?'

Another man appeared, looking around crossly for the person she'd already dealt with. 'He should be here. I'll kill him.'

'No, you won't,' Anya said quietly, standing in place on the platform. The stagehand didn't suspect the switch – why would he? On a one-off night like this the stage was dizzy with dancers. But those above her on the stage now, those trained, hungry, ambitious ballerinas, they would know.

And they'll see, Anya thought. *See that I cannot move as they do. Not any more.* Nerves began to buzz fiercely, and she felt her neck flush. Her legs ached and throbbed, suddenly worse than ever.

No, she thought fiercely. *I have carried myself this far, run all the way from the jaws of death and back again.*

I can do this.

'Break a leg, love,' the stagehand murmured as he pulled on the lever working the pulleys that propelled Anya upwards from the darkness, like Giselle, into . . .

Into the glare of the footlights, blazing like suns, and the shrouded shape of the seated audience beyond. For a long breathless moment she stood there, adjusting to the shock. The other girls, the Wilis, had turned from her as the age-old choreography dictated: only Myrtha, the Queen of the Wilis, was facing her from across the stage, summoning her to the shadow world.

Become the character, Madame had always said. Anya knew that Giselle's first movements as she emerged from her grave were always very slow and measured. Just as well, since her legs felt like they would drop her with each step. But as she looked out over the sea of people, felt the gaze of rulers and royalty upon her from the finery of the Royal Box, it was as if something was coming back to life.

As she paused in the middle of the stage, with one arm raised and leaning forward with one leg bent *à fondu*, it was as if the moment was gathering itself just as she was. She couldn't remove her veil, not without giving herself away, but almost on instinct as the music swelled around her, Anya – *Giselle* – launched into a series of hopping, spinning movements with one leg raised behind her. She felt heavy and clumsy, but her legs held. They *held*. The dance was trapped in her muscle memory, and the joy she felt as she released it . . . From stage right to left she performed small, quick jumps in series, ending with the two turning leaps at which she had always excelled. But she stumbled on the second *jeté élancé* and felt herself waver as she launched into the quick series of *chaine* turns. Her veil fell away, and her face was revealed. The other dancers, the audience, the orchestra, the King of England, they were all watching Giselle become Anya. Poor, ruined Anya.

No. That is not true. She abandoned her final arabesque, sprang back to her plywood gravestone and pulled out the Derringer she'd hidden there. Giselle only ever saved one soul, her beloved Albrecht, before returning to the grave. Now, perhaps, Anya Kalashnikova might just save thousands.

She made for the front of the stage.

James found a security guard standing outside the panelled doors to the anteroom that led to the Royal Box. The man had his fists clenched, keeping an eye out for trouble.

'You,' he called to James. 'What do you want?'

'Brandy.' James checked the fob-watch and pointed to the drink on the tray. 'Ordered by Adam Elmhirst.'

'You sure?' The man eyed the drink, licking his lips. 'He can't drink on duty. He's guarding the King . . .'

'All I know is, I'm meant to deliver this for Mr Elmhirst to enjoy in the interval.' Inside the auditorium the music of the orchestra was faltering, dying out in confusion. *Something's happening on stage*, James thought. *Anya's doing it! Just as I knew she could.*

'Give that here,' the man said. 'I'll make sure he gets it.'

'That's good of you.' James smiled. The time had come. 'I

really want to let him have it ...' He started towards the man and raised his voice. 'Drink for Adam Elmhirst – with the compliments of Andrew Bond!' The sentry brought out his gun to challenge him, but James threw the drink in his face and smashed the tray down on his gun hand; the man fired but the shot hit his foot and he fell backwards with a cry.

James kicked open the doors to the anteroom, saw the entrance to the Royal Box. A large mirror hung on one wall, affording a reflected view of the stage for those seated at the rear; in it James glimpsed the King himself, with Elmhirst and his men just behind, whirling round to face him.

Elmhirst held his weapon at the ready to gun James down.

On the stage, the other dancers milled about in disarray as Anya barged through them. She glimpsed the dark, gaunt figure of La Velada in the wings, stage right. Sick with fear, tears threatening to overwhelm her, Anya raised her gun in the air and fired it. The crack of the pistol echoed out, silenced the orchestra, brought a sharp and dreadful hush down upon the auditorium.

How ironic, she thought, that the only thing that might save King George was for Anya to fake a threat to his life.

She bellowed into that silence, '*Death to the King!*' and fired again. A collective scream went up and shook the auditorium, twisted applause for her performance. Anya stood, staring up at the Royal Box as its occupants were either brought down to the floor or hauled away. The front rows erupted, well-heeled figures scrambling for the aisles in horror.

Anya had fulfilled her side of the bargain. Her performance was ended. *Be on time, James*, she thought, and leaped from the stage in a *grand jeté* before security could catch her.

At the sound of Anya's gunshot and rallying call, Elmhirst turned back in surprise, gun lowered for a moment. James flipped the round tray through the air and struck him on the side of the head. The agent staggered back against the mirror, cracking it, and James turned and ran out of the anteroom. *Catch me if you can* . . .

A bullet blew splinters from the top of the ornamental staircase as James hurled himself down the stairs. 'Priorities, Elmhirst!' he shouted. 'While you're shooting at me . . . what about your day job?'

'*Death to the King!*' Anya's shout electrified the auditorium, and – in Elmhirst's absence – the King's remaining bodyguards acted to protect their charge. James stopped halfway down the stairs to the lobby; the red-haired doorman had heard the disruption and brought his gun to bear, ready to fire. But he had no choice but to lower it again as King George V himself appeared, bundled away down the stairs by two loyal men. As they pushed past James, intent on their rescue, the doorman ran to the ornate lobby doors and opened them so that they could race straight out. James ran after them as if towed along in their wake.

'No!' Elmhirst now appeared at the top of the stairs, ashen-faced at the loss of his prize. The rattled doorman swung round at the noise, gun at the ready – only to be blown backwards as Elmhirst fired again with a bellow of frustration. James glimpsed the man land on his back – eyes staring, a hole drilled through his chest – and kept running, out into the night.

Was that bullet meant for me? he wondered. *Either way, the next one will be.*

James watched gratefully as the King was borne into the back of a Rolls-Royce Silver Ghost parked across the street. The first stirring winds of a summer storm plucked at James's hair and clothes as, with a throaty roar, the motor car tore away, taking the monarch to *real* safety even as Elmhirst burst out of the private entrance. He ran after the vehicle, frantically waving his gun arm. *Don't stop for him,* James willed the chauffeur, *whatever you do . . .*

The Silver Ghost turned the corner, and Elmhirst abandoned his mad flight. Other dignitaries from the Royal Box were starting to emerge into Floral Street with the sentry who'd shot himself in the foot. James turned smartly away, making for the main entrance. *We did it,* he thought breathlessly. *We saved the King, just me and Anya—*

His elation faded as a panicked crowd came bursting out of the main auditorium, stampeding through every exit in a wild rush for the safety of the blustery night. James marshalled the little energy he had left and began to push his way through this desperate monster of his own making, back inside the foyer. The sheer volume of people, pushing, clawing and trampling each other, intent on escape at all costs, left him shaken and frustrated as he shouldered his way through a choked doorway, back inside the auditorium. Someone was on stage appealing for calm and order, but no one was listening – least of all James.

He had to find Anya. He had no idea if she was at large or had been captured by security, but he decided to make for the set shop where they'd first emerged into the Opera House, the gateway to the underground passage leading down to the trigger and its colossal fuse … It had to be shown to the proper authorities. If Anya was able, she'd surely be making her way there now.

Keeping close to the side walls, forcing his way through the throng, James supposed with a cold dread that La Velada would be headed there too. And what of the other players? Where was Mimic now – and Elmhirst? He'd lost the King but was still at liberty.

And beneath the Opera House, the fuse that would ignite this last great wickedness was still waiting to be lit. He couldn't imagine his enemies cutting their losses to escape into the night.

The endgame, James knew, had finally come.

31
To Pull the Trigger

James made his way through backstage chaos, tripping over ballerinas and pushing past panicking stagehands, sweating, exhilarated, praying that he would be in time to finally end the conspiracy his father had tried so desperately to destroy.

Reaching the set store, he saw that the door to the emergency generator room stood wide open, and so did the hidden door to the staircase inside. He'd hoped, forlornly, that he might find Anya here waiting for him, but no. Sadness turned to weary fear as he saw that Demir had gone, but at least the stick of hexogen explosive still lay in the crate where he'd left it. James decided to take it with him – who knew how many tricks La Velada might have up her black silken sleeve? He would feel better for having one or two himself.

Panting for breath and sweating hard, James pulled off the doorman's jacket and began the long trek down. He ran along the ramp, then took the steps as quickly as he could, ignoring the stitch in his side, the thick, iron tang in his dry mouth, and the cramp creeping into his muscles. He pictured the stockpile down below, looming in the darkness like some sinister pagan totem, waiting to deliver death to thousands ...

Finally he reached the doorway to the tunnels: it stood open ahead of him. Cautiously James approached, legs trembling from his exertions, pulse thumping.

Lamps had been lit in the tunnel outside, and as James ventured out of the passage he could see La Velada, crouched on the floor at the very beginning of the glazed gunpowder trail, ready to strike the match that would light the fuse and unleash fire and flood on the capital. A dark figure sat beside her: it was Mimic, and – James noted with a savage satisfaction – he appeared to be crying. La Velada was stroking his back, murmuring to him as if he was some beloved pet. Then she tenderly took his hand, raised him up and sent him away along the narrow passage.

Sending him off to the transmitter tower, James supposed, *ready to deliver whatever lies and propaganda are to come.* The King wasn't safe yet. He could still die, one more life lost among tens of thousands. The unholy trinity of Elmhirst, Mimic and La Velada were still ready to terrify and intimidate the shattered population of Britain in the wake of the flood and firestorm.

James waited until Mimic was some way along the tunnel before he pulled his father's Beretta from his pocket. He could shoot La Velada now, end this here. She wouldn't even know.

For a second, to his disgust, he found himself sorely tempted. But how much information would die with her? How many of her contacts and co-conspirators would go unpunished, free to continue with their sabotage, if she went unquestioned?

'Drop it,' came a thick male voice in James's ear as a gun barrel jammed up against his temple. Cursing under his breath and letting the Beretta slip from his grasp, James turned to find Demir leering in his face. Where had he come from? Either he'd freed himself or La Velada had found him on her way through.

'Bond. You are here, of course.' La Velada turned and moved towards him, ghostlike and sinister, through the honeyed shadows thrown by the lamps. 'Once again, the spectre at my feast.'

'The King has gone,' James told her. 'He's been taken to safety, and the other VIPs evacuated along with the audience.'

'Even if they knew the true danger, Bond, they couldn't escape London before detonation. The fuse will still be lit, London will still die and Great Britain will be left grievously weakened. How the mourning masses will hang on the words of the "King" in their terror.'

James nodded. 'Mimic broadcasts as planned from your transmitter tower.'

She inclined her head, as if impressed. 'It stands behind Denmark Street, not so very far away. Specially reinforced, it will stand while all around it crumbles – so that the only voice reporting from London will be ours.'

'Whatever you try to do to us,' James spat, 'in the end, we'll only come back stronger.'

'Brave words. But the time for words is past. Now, let there be screaming.' La Velada held up a silver dagger that flashed in the lamplight, and her eyes were just as bright. 'Do you think I can tolerate a child interfering with plans that have been years in the making?'

'Wait.' James pulled out Karachan's loose playing cards from his pocket, holding them up to show Demir they posed no threat. 'No time for a final game?'

'But this *is* the final game, Bond.' With her free hand, La Velada pulled the black veil down over her face, like a judge donning the black cap to pass a sentence of death.

James watched her as he bent the pack between his thumb and fingers – and then, like a conjurer, let them spring in a stream into Demir's face. As the man recoiled, James batted away La Velada's knife arm with an upward strike to the wrist while lashing out with his leg to smash the heel of his boot into Demir's knee. The man went down shouting, scrabbling for his gun. James lunged for it too and suddenly the two of them were caught up in a free-for-all, grappling over the cold concrete floor, splashing through the shallow pools of water. *The hexogen*, James thought desperately, terrified that the high explosive would detonate. *And La Velada – what is she doing?* Butting Demir in the face, his forehead stinging, James finally knocked the last of the fight out of him and scrambled up. He felt for the stick of hexogen and realized with a sick lurch that it had broken in two.

And that La Velada had Demir's gun. She brought it up to aim at James's head.

At the same time James pulled a lump of hexogen out of his pocket, flipped open Karachan's lighter and sparked a trembling flame.

'Drop that,' James hissed. 'There's still enough here to blow you to bits.'

He saw the smile form beneath the veil. 'And you with me?'

'We're far enough from the trigger. And the blast ought to bring people down to investigate.'

'Before Elmhirst can light the fuse himself?'

'What else can I do?' James's voice cracked. 'It's either my life or the lives of thousands . . . this whole city.' He swallowed hard, edged the flame closer to the oily stick of explosive. 'I . . . I have to do it.'

'Very well, Bond. Go ahead.' La Velada stepped back, still covering him with the gun. 'Set light to your stub of hexogen.'

James was breathing fast, trying to build up his resolve. *I have to do it.* Gritting his teeth, closing his eyes, he put the flame to the stick.

The hexogen caught light . . . but there was no blast. It burned slowly, with an oily flame, like an oversized candle.

'Hexogen is not like dynamite, you foolish child!' La Velada thrust out her chin, sneering in triumph as she trained the gun on him once more. 'It takes a percussive impact to ignite this explosive, or a more aggressive source of heat . . .'

Red faced and helpless, looking down the barrel of her gun, James realized that he had finally lost. With a surge of anger, he hurled the stub away – but from where it struck he heard a hungry, raucous sizzle, like a firework catching on bonfire night.

The wide stripe of the gunpowder fuse had sparked into life.

'No!' La Velada swung round to find flames and sparks hopping fiercely from the tunnel floor. She ran towards it. 'You've lit the fuse before Elmhirst is here, you little idiot—'

Swearing, James had already dived for cover behind Demir's prone body as the stub of hexogen ignited and a shockwave of heat and flame rocked the cavern. Eyes dazzled by the explosion, James glimpsed La Velada being thrown through the air. She struck the wall like a fly hitting a windscreen. For a moment she was pinned there, skinny limbs broken and smeared against the rock. Then she slid down to land with a wet thud in a large puddle beside him. The charred nightmare of her face stared up at James through the remains of her veil, her toothless mouth gaping in one final, hideous grin.

James turned away from her, ears ringing and senses shocked. He stared at the burning, sparking fuse as it went on sizzling down the sloping floor of the tunnel, devouring the gunpowder trail on its deadly way to the mountain of explosives. If a greasy stub had caused a blast like that, then when that massive stockpile went up . . .

Suddenly James was no longer dealing with an abstract image of horror. He had glimpsed hell – and he himself had set the gates opening. *When London goes up in flame and flood, it will be* your *fault now. Do something!* But the fuse was perhaps three feet wide and, ingrained in the floor, impossible to interrupt.

Wasn't it?

In desperation, James scooped up the stinking, half-burned corpse of La Velada, dripping with wet clay and water from the pool in which she'd fallen. He ran with it, slipping and staggering like a drunk across the tunnel, following the incandescent display like a rat after Hamelin's piper. La Velada's ruined head lolled in his grip; her twisted, blackened legs looked ready to snap away from her torso. Who was she really, this nameless monster? How many identities had she taken; how many lives? The huge monument of crates and boxes loomed just yards ahead now, ready to go up. But

James kept running, and finally overtook the sputtering firework show, dumping the woman's body over the fuse trail. The sparks seemed to fall upon her: hungry, cracking, eager to consume. But she was wet and bloody, smeared with clay. What was left of her hair went up in foul-smelling smoke, but the rest of her had already burned. Her body made a barrier the entire width of the fuse, and finally, with a last flurry, the sparks burned out.

James stared, haunted and horrified by what he'd seen, and what he had been forced to do. He keeled over and was sick, bile burning the back of his throat. The sparks seemed to burn onwards in his sight, in his imagination, and the air was dirty with smoke. He was certain the fuse trail would start up again, that the menace wasn't over—

'What . . . have you . . . done?'

James jumped at the quiet, menacing words, and through the smoke he saw Elmhirst in the Opera House doorway. He was taking in everything. He knew *just* what James had done.

'*BOND!*' Elmhirst screamed, and pulled out his gun.

32

Last Breath, Last Bullet

Already exhausted, James took flight. Two gunshots and their echoes chased him from the cavern as he pelted along the tunnel to the central stockpile.

Elmhirst will relight the fuse, James thought, terrified. *He'll blow us all to kingdom come.*

But at the moment he seemed determined merely to run down his prey. 'This isn't about ideology, right now!' he shouted. 'And I'm no martyr. This is about me and you, Bond! Me killing you, like I killed your parents! And once you're dead I'm gonna take my time and kill everyone you ever cared about . . . *Anyone you so much as looked at!*'

James kept on running, frantic, as the darkness and echoes hurled the nightmare voice all around him. His foot turned on a loose rock and he fell, sore palms taking the impact. He scrambled to his knees, pain biting through his twisted ankle. Still he dragged himself up and set off once more, his breath ragged in his throat, ribs tight. Plans, half formed and fleeting, passed through his fevered mind: *Wait in the dark, shoot him before he kills me . . . Let him run past, try to double back – perhaps he won't notice—?*

Another gunshot thundered through the stone sky above him and ricocheted off the tunnel wall. Elmhirst couldn't be far behind. James pulled the Beretta from his pocket and fired behind him, a warning shot. But there was surely no warning Elmhirst would heed right now.

Just keep running, he thought doggedly. *Don't stop . . .*

As James rounded the corner, he collided with something, and gasped as he fell, clutching at the darkness. Then a weak yellow glare lit the air between him and—

'Anya?' James couldn't believe his eyes: but he was looking at long dark hair in sweaty disarray, ivory cheeks flushed with effort, eyes wide and terrified.

'James.' She gripped him in a fierce embrace that he returned as they both scrambled to their feet. 'The King – is he . . . ?'

'Safe, thanks to your performance,' James panted. 'But we can't stop here. Elmhirst is after me.' He peered into the darkness but could hear nothing. Could his reckless shot have found its mark? More likely he'd pushed Elmhirst into stealth and caution, made him more dangerous still. He turned and led Anya quickly but quietly back the way she had come, almost tripping over the last crate of hexogen they'd shifted that afternoon and abandoned here.

'I got away from the security men,' Anya said. 'They are slow.'

'And you are fast,' James said. 'Your limp's all but vanished. I'm sorry I missed your dance.'

'It goes on,' she said simply, splashing on through puddles. 'Demir got free, and when I ran through the set store he went after me—'

'And then he came back and got *me* – and I nearly blew us all to bits.' He looked at her. 'La Velada is dead . . .'

'Dead?' Anya stopped walking, breathing hard. 'Good.'

'But Elmhirst's out for more blood than ever. We're not clear of the woods yet . . .'

They pressed on, the water deepening, until Anya stopped again. 'There is no easy way forward here, remember?' She shone the fading torch beam ahead of them, over the familiar spiked jumble of rubble, stone and earthmoving machinery rising up from the dark water. 'This is where we dumped the other explosives.'

'And beyond that . . .' James took a sharp and sudden breath. 'Junction six between tunnels fourteen and fifteen. The weak point in the tunnel system.'

'Where you almost drowned,' Anya agreed.

'Never mind that!' James hissed, his pulse beating faster. 'That last crate of explosives we left back in the tunnel, the thirteenth . . .'

'We use it to threaten Elmhirst?'

'No.' James gripped her hands. 'We set it off. Right here.'

'What?' Anya stared back at him as though he were mad. 'But this could start the chain reaction—!'

'Not here at the weak point. If the blast is strong enough, it could bring down all this with one blow, just as your father told my father!' He looked into her eyes. 'It was what they both believed.'

'But, James—'

'If we don't risk it, Elmhirst will pull the Project's trigger for sure.' James looked back the way they'd come, gooseflesh prickling his arms. 'I don't think he can be following me any more now he knows I'm armed. He must've doubled back to the stockpile. Any minute now he could relight that fuse. We have to fetch those explosives and find a place to put them.'

'You are mad,' she protested, but she hurried after him. 'How do we know there is enough here to affect this "weak point"?'

'We don't,' James snapped. 'So try praying. Try hoping.'

'Or more than this.' Anya caught up with him, took hold of his arm. 'Try believing.'

'What?'

'In the graveyard, in Moscow, I told you of Dido's sister, of a loved one's last breath.' Anya wiped tears from her eyes but her voice was firm. 'The knowledge of this terrible place was the last breath of both our fathers. Now we must breathe it ourselves. Let them live on through our actions.'

James smiled slowly. 'And finish their work.'

They ran now, the two of them, almost falling upon the crate. They heaved it away through the darkness with renewed strength, splashing into the icy water, holding it up in the air with aching arms.

'Tread carefully,' James hissed. 'If we drop this now . . .'

'How can we ignite it?' asked Anya.

'I know now that a percussive impact can ignite the hexogen.'

'You mean, we shoot it?'

'We shoot it,' he confirmed.

Moving as fast as they dared through the stagnant water, James and Anya perched the open crate on the rusting blade of an old bulldozer, knifing out from the dark pool. Then they retreated, holding hands as they splashed back the way they had come, towards the turn in the tunnel.

With his sore and sweaty hands James opened the Beretta to check the ammunition, and closed his weary eyes. 'What do you know? Last breath, last bullet.'

'One shot left?' Anya showed him the ghost of a smile. 'You will make it count.'

James nodded, knelt down in the water. 'When I count to three, put your head under. This muck might just be enough to shield us from the blast.' Anya lowered herself into the water, and he lay down too, all but overcome with a sense of terrible dread. This was it, then: all or nothing! Self-doubt plagued him. What if he was firing from too far away? What if he missed the damn crate altogether, wasted their only bullet?

He imagined his father's hand resting on his tired, aching shoulder. *Don't make such a meal of things, James.* The voice was warmer, more real in his head than any mimic could make it. *You'll do what you must . . . and your mother and I know you'll do it well enough.*

James raised his arm, took aim at the crate.

He fired.

The recoil bucked through his wrist, his signal to dive forward into the silty water – just as the tunnel flashed incandescent. He closed his eyes tight as an enormous explosion boomed, the blast like a roiling wall of air knocking him from the water, drumming him deaf and blind.

Consciousness fled, but Anya's scream brought James back to the horror he'd created. He glimpsed water flooding towards them in a dark, foaming wave. Next moment it had engulfed them, sweeping them back along the tunnel.

Tumbling and spiralling through wet, freezing darkness, breath locked inside his body, James felt shock just as keenly as pain. Now the Fleet's ancient bed had been blown open, dark waters would flood the tunnel network and smother all those obscene stockpiles of explosives . . .

Finally James's head broke the surface of the surging water, the current sweeping him along at frightening speed. But he was too elated to be scared now. 'We did it!' he shouted, the Beretta still held tight. 'Anya . . . Father, Mother . . . we did—'

His foot caught on something and his travel through the water came to a dead stop. James gasped, swallowed rank, freezing water, retched and choked, flapping his arms to stay afloat. Then, tucking the spent gun into his waistband, he felt in the darkness for what he'd hit. Rope mesh . . . cabling . . .

The safeguards to secure the trigger, James realized, clinging on in the current as he fought to untangle his throbbing ankle. *No, I'm not dying now!* he wanted to scream. *Not after this.*

Tearing himself free, James broke the surface of the water in time to hear Anya cry his name, the single syllable cutting through the roaring darkness. 'James! I . . . I think I saw Elmhirst.'

'Where are you?' James bellowed, but she couldn't hear him. He let the freezing tide carry him further, sweeping him towards the passage to the Opera House. The water was shallower here as the tunnel sloped upwards. In the stubborn glow of the lanterns up ahead he caught sight of a dark figure. James ducked beneath the water. His toes touched the ground and he bobbed cautiously back up.

Anya was wading towards him, choking and bedraggled, a livid cut running from left temple to cheek. 'I saw him,' she muttered. 'James – I saw him run.'

'Which way?' She pointed away from the Opera House, to the smaller passage he'd noted on the map earlier. The getaway tunnel that would lead to the tower.

No, he thought. *The man who murdered my parents, who almost destroyed this city, is* not *escaping now.* James turned back to Anya, put his hands on her shoulders, looked into her unfocused eyes. 'I know you're hurt, know you're tired, but you have *got* to get back inside the Opera House. The place should be crawling with police by now. Say you were put up to doing what you did and can lead them to the man responsible. Elmhirst will be making for the transmitter tower, Anya. It's behind Denmark Street. Mimic should be there too, by now. We won't be safe – no one will be safe – until Elmhirst is caught.'

'Or until he's *dead.*' Anya met his gaze. 'He deserves it.' She turned and waded unsteadily through the water to the door.

'Will you be all right?' James called after her.

'Only if you kill him.'

James turned away, shivering with cold and sudden fear, as he faced the darkness of the narrow passage. 'I know where you are, Elmhirst,' he murmured, 'and I'm coming for you.'

33

The Rise and Fall

By the time he emerged from the underground passageway into a sewer tunnel James was a sweating, aching mess. Mechanically he climbed an inspection ladder and put his shoulder to a loosened manhole cover.

Climbing out into the blustering, rainswept darkness, he collapsed on the paved yard of the transmitter tower and lay there, panting for breath. He'd half imagined voices chasing after him through the darkened tunnel; whether ghosts or ballerinas or police drawn by the explosion and its aftershocks, he couldn't say, or care.

The steel latticework of the tall transmitter loomed over him, like an electricity pylon only tapering to a thin spire. Dark clouds swept across the segments of sky bisected by its hard, geometric edges. It was surrounded by an array of smaller radio masts; beside it stood a small brickwork bunker; all was surrounded by a high chainlink fence. The noise of the traumatized crowds carried easily here from the Opera House.

Panting for breath, James noted the heavy wooden door in the windowless bunker. He hauled himself to his feet and drew the empty Beretta from his pocket in the hope that it might intimidate and, without letting himself think of the dangers, ran up to the entrance. He jerked down the handle and pulled.

There was a moment's resistance, as if the door had snagged on something. Some sixth sense warned James that this meant danger, and as the door opened wide, he dived aside onto the paving. A wire attached to the door had pulled taut and triggered a booby trap, firing off a machine gun. James kept stock still; the rattle of the carbine hammered at his senses, but he forced himself to keep watching the door.

Mimic peered out. 'Goodbye, James,' came the voice of Andrew Bond through bared teeth. 'Goodbye.'

'This time it is,' James vowed. He scrambled up and ran at Mimic. The boy turned and saw James coming, dropped down and knocked James's legs out from under him. James channelled his momentum, rolled over backwards and got back to his feet – but Mimic quickly had him around the waist, and attempted a head-butt. James grunted, seized Mimic's little finger with his right hand and bent it backwards. The boy gasped and let go – but, for once, James mimicked *him*. He threw his arms around Mimic's ribs and squeezed with all his strength, determined to crush the life from him.

'*Where is Elmhirst?*' James hissed in Mimic's ear, tightening his grip.

The wiry boy giggled between gasps. 'Where . . . is Elmhirst?' he echoed back in a strangled version of James's voice.

A screech of brakes from outside the yard broke through James's fury, and Mimic wrenched himself free. James turned to see that a police car had smashed up against the chainlink fence. Hobbling out from the back came the man from the Opera House who'd shot himself in the foot; a plain-clothes officer, no doubt. 'Bloody hell, looks like she was right.' Another policeman got out of the back – and through the windscreen James saw—

'Anya!' He waved to her.

'I warned them, James,' she called weakly. 'Said they had to find the tower . . .'

'Now get back, both of you!' the officer told James and Mimic, jamming his gun through the wire fence. 'Get down on the ground!'

'Me?' James protested. 'You don't understand—'

Mimic scooped up some mud and gravel and hurled it through the fence. The officer was struck in the face and jerked back onto his injured foot. With an angry shout, he collapsed and dropped the gun; it fell just inside the yard.

While the other policeman ran to help his colleague, Mimic turned and sprinted back inside the bunker. James made to follow, but as he did so, he caught movement behind him: a stocky figure had slipped out of the bunker and was now scaling the enormous transmitter tower.

'Elmhirst.' James felt a rising fury. Clearly the traitor thought he could escape in the confusion. But what did he expect to gain by heading upwards?

Just then, Mimic ducked back out, perhaps hoping to catch James off-guard. Not a hope: James feinted away, then punched him in the face, a blow as hard as it was precise, breaking the boy's nose. Mimic was propelled straight back into the bunker and James followed him – to find a state-of-the-art broadcasting studio, such as the BBC might use to transmit wireless programmes. James hooked his foot around Mimic's ankle and sent him flying into a microphone. Face covered in blood, Mimic nevertheless parried James's next blow with one of his own, lifting the heavy microphone to bring it down on James's skull. But he hadn't realized that it was still plugged in – and, apparently, switched on. As Mimic waved it near the speakers, an almighty booming squeal of feedback tore through the studio.

The effect on Mimic was extraordinary. He clutched his head and shrieked, quivering in agony. *Your* own *screams this time*, James thought with a savage satisfaction, *no one else's*. Perhaps it was his sensitive hearing that allowed him to mimic others so uncannily? James no longer cared. He clapped his hands brutally hard over Mimic's ears, rupturing the boy's eardrums. Mimic gasped and flailed, a pitiful figure as he fell among the cables as if writhing in a snake pit. James stared at him in disgust, then brought down his fist in a blow so hard that it dislocated Mimic's jaw – and brought silence.

James turned away, staring down at his skinned knuckles, shocked dimly by his own violence. He heard a warning shout from Anya, and saw that the uninjured policeman was scaling the chainlink fence. Meanwhile Elmhirst was still climbing the transmitter tower.

James snatched up the officer's dropped gun, ran over to the tower and began to climb.

'Stop!' the officer called. 'Wait!'

I can't, James thought. Elmhirst was already some way above him. The wind was blowing hard now, and a squall of rain was soon soaking his clothes, making the metal difficult to hold.

Elmhirst shouted down, 'You should know when to stop, Bond!' He fired his gun, and sparks jumped from the metal a foot above James's head.

James kept climbing regardless. 'Everything finishes tonight!' he yelled, the wind driving tears from his eyes. From this height he could see out across London in all directions: St Paul's and the Houses of Parliament, Charing Cross Road stretching like a scar towards the Strand, Shell-Mex House and the OXO tower, the wide, stolid stripe of the Thames. 'You might've killed thousands of people, Elmhirst, and betrayed millions more.'

'You think I give a damn what a jumped-up schoolboy thinks?' Elmhirst yelled back. 'A boy who represents a privileged elite – a symbol of everything I detest in this country?' He fired again, and this time sparks burned from the metal beside James's right hand.

As James recoiled, he slipped; for a sickening moment he thought he was going to fall. He scrabbled at the lattice, just managing to regain his grip, dangling high over the desolate yard below.

'Why are you climbing?' James yelled. 'There's nowhere to go!'

'Then you'll catch up with me, won't you? The same way I caught up with your mum and dad.'

James started climbing faster – straight towards another bullet, which struck the tower just inches from his face. *He wants you mad*, James realized. *He wants you angry and making mistakes.*

But if you're within range of his bullets, he's within range of yours.

As the wind blew, James saw a cable angling down from the tower's summit, stretching over a high wall and out of sight. He understood Elmhirst's plan at last. From a metal box mounted within the trellis, the man was pulling two loops of wire rope that would fit over the cable and allow him to glide down – to make a swift and final escape.

'Stop there!' James pulled out the officer's gun as the chimes of Big Ben struck their funereal rhythm. 'I swear I'll kill you!'

'In cold blood?' Elmhirst laughed. 'You don't have the bottle, Bond.'

'Do it!' Anya's cry rose from the car beyond the chainlink fence, perhaps sixty feet below, as the policeman began the long climb up the tower. 'Do it, for all he's done to us . . .'

James wiped his eyes, tears and rainwater mixing together. 'Elmhirst, I can't let you get away!'

'And you can't stop me, either!' Elmhirst gripped hold of the wire rope, bracing himself to jump.

Bond stared up, aiming the long barrel at Elmhirst's ribs. He thought of all the deaths he'd witnessed these last days, the horror. One more now . . . one more spurt of blood and an agonized scream . . .

The gun shook in his hand as he willed himself to pull the trigger. He was squeezing it . . . tighter . . .

Elmhirst launched himself into space, sliding down the cable.

James fired.

The bullet hit Elmhirst in the shoulder, threw blood against the clouds as he released the wire rope and dropped like a stone for a good twenty feet.

With a sound like a gravedigger's spade into frozen soil, Elmhirst's body was impaled on the smaller radio mast beside the tower. Its aerial, now broken and bloody, had speared through Elmhirst's chest and back. The agent screamed, thrashing like a fish on a hook, a sound more terrible than anything James had heard before.

Then the struggles stopped.

'Ambulance!' James hollered down at the policemen. 'He . . . he might not be dead. Not yet . . .' He closed his eyes, which were hot with tears despite the numbness he felt.

The chimes of Big Ben fell silent, but the city thrummed and the river glided on regardless. James lowered his gun hand. The weapon slipped, but didn't fall. It hung from his index finger, the tip caught between the curve of the trigger and its guard, and the metal bit into his cold, wet skin, and James couldn't let it go.

Epilogue

The sharp red peaks of the Aiguilles Rouges loomed like mourners at a funeral, and so they were, in a way: the only witnesses to an unusual burial.

The only witnesses besides James Bond.

He had left Charmian at their cabin in the French Prealps contemplating the next day's skiing, and walked the high pastures and the wide, virgin spaces for hours in search of a fitting spot. The space and solitude were a great relief after the last days in London, which he'd found a little too noisy just now. Too full of memories and connections and well-meaning acquaintances.

He thought back to his visit to Anya in Queen Alexandra's Military Hospital, with its view – a very welcome one – of the Thames, large in its windows. The cut across her face would scar, but she'd live.

'What will you do now?' he'd asked her. 'Now you've taken your father's last breath.'

'And Madame Radek's too. The *real* Gaiana Radek, that is.' Anya smiled weakly, her hair a jet-black tangle against the crisp white pillow. 'I do not wish my last performance on a stage to be one of violence. I wish it to be beautiful. And so I think I shall teach others, as best I can.'

'Well,' James said, 'you've certainly taught me a few things.'

'And you me.' She looked up at him, bearing so many more scars inside her, James knew. 'There is much we could share.'

The keening rasp of a bearded vulture brought him back to his present, gazing out over the Chamonix valley. *Yes, we could share a lot*, thought James. *We could try to push away the cold and the dark together for a time. But you showed me well enough: nothing lasts.*

He forced the tip of his spade into the frigid earth and began to dig.

It only changes: for better or for worse.

James had given Anya a parting gift – or a souvenir, at least – before leaving the hospital: a copy of *The Trumpeter of Krakow*.

'I read this book when I was younger,' Anya said with a smile. 'I found it far-fetched, but still exciting.'

'I'm afraid I never finished it,' James admitted.

'Of course you didn't.' Anya's blue eyes excelled at their pointed stare. 'I am thinking that you always leave the best stories unfinished ... don't you?'

I'm finishing this one, Anya, James thought.

Memories presented themselves with each turn of the shovel: the ambulance men removing the sobbing Mimic and Elmhirst's corpse from the tower ... The police taskforce swooping on the Mechta Academy to seize intelligence on Karachan's communist network and La Velada's sleeper agents ... Watching soldiers and trained navy divers descend into the secret tunnels to secure and remove the hexogen stockpiles ... and his 'debrief' with the Head of SIS — more of a lecture, really — while his old tutor from Eton with clandestine links to the service, Mr Merriot, looked on with some other men, conferring in private ...

Judging his hole in the ground to be deep enough, James put down the spade and regarded his father's battered backpack — retrieved from Elmhirst's office at the Academy — and the relics it still contained. It had travelled with him so far, and at times he'd clutched onto it as tightly as to life itself. But now his father's work had been completed. It was time to let go of the past and to consider the future.

Carefully James returned the backpack to the snow and earth, planting it inside the hole. There was one thing, though, that he could not bury. He reached his right hand into his coat pocket and pulled out his father's Beretta, snug in its holster.

He heard Elmhirst's voice in his head, words spoken in the safe house the night before they flew to Moscow; words intended to win James's trust: *When you find something that stirs your soul the way that danger stirs yours ... something out of the ordinary that gives you purpose ... keep hold.*

'I don't have to,' James said out loud. 'That purpose has its hold on me.'

In the quiet and the stillness, James buried the backpack under heavy spadefuls of earth and snow. He looked up only when he was finished, sweating with effort despite the cold, and saw a thin line of smoke in the distance, rising from a line of firs. Charmian must have lit them a fire. The cabin would be warm by the time he returned.

James Bond placed the Beretta in his pocket. Then he turned his back on the little unmarked grave, and walked away.

Acknowledgements

My grateful thanks to Caroline Hamilton, Dance and Costume Historian, for her research and advice on Anya's early dancing life, and also to Julia Creed, Head of Collections at the Royal Opera House, for backstage detail.

Further thanks to Elizaveta Karmannaya, Moscow Correspondent, and to Craig Marshall and Gemma Gray at Fettes College, Edinburgh, for their kind support.

Couldn't-do-it-without-you editorial thanks to Sophie Wilson, Ruth 'Prima Ballerina Assoluta' Knowles, Mainga Bhima, Philippa Milnes-Smith, Corinne Turner and Josephine Lane.

A shout out too to Annie Eaton, Harriet Venn, Jasmine Joynson and all the team at Penguin Random House, to Jonny Davidson and all at Ian Fleming Publications Ltd, to Jonny Geller, Alice Dill and Catherine Cho at Curtis Brown and to Georgie Gillings and company at TBS.

To Fergus Fleming, Diggory Laycock, Jessie Grimond and Marek Pruszewicz of the IFPL board for empowering me to take Young James Bond on this run of adventures.

And, of course, to Ian Fleming and Charlie Higson, without whom ...

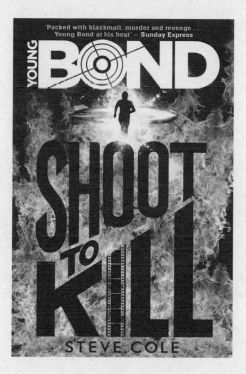

**LIGHTS.
CAMERA.
MURDER.**

**James is caught up in a sinister plot that
goes way beyond any Hollywood movie.
And now he must find a way out.**

Or die trying.

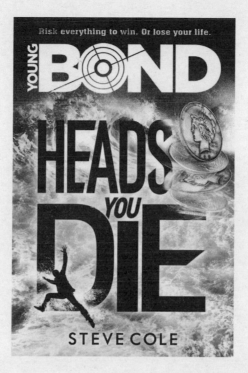

Risk everything to win. Or lose your life.

YOUNG BOND

HEADS YOU DIE

STEVE COLE

James's Cuban holiday has become a nightmare mission to save an old friend from a villain who has perfected 1,000 ways to kill.

With corrupt cops and hired assassins hot on his heels, James must travel through Havana and brave Caribbean waters to stop a countdown to mass murder.

Fates will be decided with the flip of a coin.
HEADS OR TAILS. LIVE OR DIE.

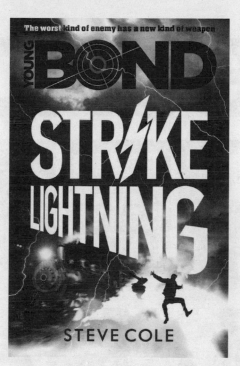

The worst kind of enemy has a new kind of weapon

YOUNG BOND

STRIKE LIGHTNING

STEVE COLE

A flash of lightning illuminates a horrific sight.
What his school claims was a tragic accident
James Bond suspects was murder.

In search of the truth – and revenge – Bond risks
his life to learn of a new secret weapon that could
change the course of history. The trail leads across
Europe to a ruthless warmonger who stands ready
to unleash hell upon the world.

To survive, James must brave traps, trials and
terrifying experiments – and triumph over his
most powerful opponent yet.